Wallflowers to Wives

Out of the shadows, into the marriage bed!

In Regency England young women were defined by their prospects in the marriage market. But what of the girls who were presented to Society…and *not* snapped up?

Bronwyn Scott invites you to

The Left Behind Girls' Club

Three years after their debut, and still without rings on their fingers, Claire Welton, Evie Milham, May Worth and Beatrice Penrose are ready to leave the shadows and step into the light. Now London will have to prepare itself… because these overlooked girls are about to take the *ton* by storm!

Read Claire's story in

Unbuttoning the Innocent Miss

Available now!

And watch for more

Wallflowers to Wives stories—coming soon!

Author Note

Nothing will change until we do! This is the motto of The Left Behind Girls' Club.

Claire's story is the first in Wallflowers to Wives—a series of four books featuring four women who decide to change their circumstances. This is no small feat for a woman in Regency England. The higher born a lady is, the harder it is to challenge Society and families who have had expectations for you since the day you were born. Yet these four young women find the courage to be themselves without living outside polite Society—which, they discover, is a very fine line to walk!

More importantly, Claire finds a way to be herself. She doesn't have to change who she is—just her situation.

This was a fun book to write because it takes advantage of some lesser known destinations in London. I especially loved the parts where Claire and Jonathon sneak off to the French neighbourhood of Soho. There really was one! There was a French market too, but Claire and Jonathon never quite get there—you'll see why.

Happy reading!

Remember, the best way to help an author is, if you read a book you like, to stop by a review site and post your thoughts! I'd also love to see you on my web page, blog and Facebook, so don't be a stranger.

bronwynswriting.blogspot.com

bronwynnscott.com

UNBUTTONING THE INNOCENT MISS

Bronwyn Scott

First published in Great Britain 2016
By Mills & Boon, an imprint of HarperCollins*Publishers*
1 London Bridge Street, London, SE1 9GF

Large Print edition 2016

© 2016 Nikki Poppen

ISBN: 978-0-263-26326-8

Our policy is to use papers that are natural, renewable and recyclable
products and made from wood grown in sustainable forests.
The logging and manufacturing processes conform to the legal
environmental regulations of the country of origin.

Printed and bound in Great Britain
by CPI Antony Rowe, Chippenham, Wiltshire

Bronwyn Scott is a communications instructor at Pierce College in the United States, and is the proud mother of three wonderful children (one boy and two girls). When she's not teaching or writing she enjoys playing the piano, travelling—especially to Florence, Italy—and studying history and foreign languages. Readers can stay in touch on Bronwyn's website, bronwynnscott.com, or at her blog, bronwynswriting.blogspot.com. She loves to hear from readers.

For all my PEO sisters!
This is a series about women
who decide to make their own destinies.
Their ambition to remake themselves is
not all that different from the ambition held
by our seven founders. With special love, of
course, to my chapter of outstanding women.
Thanks for all your support.

Chapter One

London—May 1821

It all started with two words. 'I'm pregnant.' The phrase jerked Claire rudely out of her own admittedly rather self-centred thoughts and thrust her into the horrifying present of someone else's reality. Had Beatrice truly said she was *pregnant*? Claire stared at her friend in abject confusion as the words settled. Pregnant, as in going to have a baby. *Enceinte.* Her brain switched to its fail-safe coping mechanism, French. In a crisis, everything always sounded better in French.

Then the shock came, waves of it. Having a baby implied certain other things had taken place prior unless one was the Virgin Mary. Beatrice, one of her best friends since childhood, whom she had played with as a girl, whom she'd come out with, whom she'd not thought kept any secrets from her, had taken a lover and hadn't told her. Hadn't told any of them if the looks on the faces of Evie and May were anything to go on. They looked much like she suspected her face did—all pale emotion and bewilderment, while their brains picked through all responses possible for such a situation.

All the while Bea sat still, equally pale, waiting for an answer, watching each of them expectantly and patiently while their emotions rolled. This was not at all what Claire had been anticipating today. Today's meeting in the tiny attic garret of Evie Milham's town house was supposed to be like all the other meetings: secret and commiserative. They would bemoan the lack of male attention and/or intelligence, eat some cake and go home, only to meet the following week and do it all over again. It was a comforting ritual they'd sustained over the last three years since they'd come out, when hopes had been, if not high, certainly higher than they'd become after three years on the marriage mart and no takers.

Someone had to say something. Even May

with her ever-ready comments couldn't seem to mount an adequate response. For the first time, Claire noticed how tightly Beatrice's hands were clenched in her lap, two hard, pale fists while she waited for their...verdict.

Suddenly Claire understood. Beatrice was waiting for them to pass judgement on her, against her, no doubt wondering right now which of her friends would move away first. They wouldn't be the first to know. Beatrice had already been through this with her family. Apparently, she thought she knew what to expect: rejection of the very worst sort. Exile. The social death of anonymity. It certainly made Claire's own problems pale by comparison. She'd been selfishly absorbed in her own concerns while Beatrice grappled with something much larger. Beatrice shouldn't have to do it alone.

She would help, if only she knew how. She needed information and that gave her a voice again. The questions came out in a rush. 'How? When? More importantly, who?'

Beatrice swallowed hard, the questions no doubt discomforting, but it was too late to take them back. Quiet Evie shot her a quelling look in scolding and leaned forward to take Beatrice's hand. 'Bea, you don't have to tell us.'

Bea shook her dark head. 'Yes, I do. You have a right to know. I owe you all this much. You will have decisions to make.' She looked at each of them in turn and drew a fortifying breath. Claire's heart broke for her friend. She wanted to tell Bea it would be all right, but she couldn't. Things might never be 'all right' for Beatrice Penrose again.

Beatrice began to speak. 'Over the winter, I became acquainted with the friend of a neighbour who had come for an extended visit. In hindsight, the term "repairing lease" might be more appropriate. There were likely "reasons" he was in the countryside of Sussex instead of London or somewhere far more interesting.

'I did not look past his handsome face, his manners and the acceptance he'd been afforded by local gentry because of those attributes. Others easily accepted him without question and I did, too.' Beatrice's fingers pleated her skirt absently. 'The country in winter is as dull as the weather and he was exciting, new. No one had ever been interested in me the way he was.'

Claire nodded in sympathy. She felt guilty for being absent. Her family had spent the holidays in the Lake District. She'd not been there to steer Beatrice away from danger. Neither had May, whose family had stayed in town, nor Evie, who had gone to one of her sisters'. Beatrice had been entirely on her own. Alone and lonely.

Claire had plenty of experience, they all did, when it came to being overlooked by gentlemen of society for one reason or another; She was too smart with her acumen for languages when most gentlemen could barely master one; Evie was too discreet as to become anonymous and May was just too well informed, too sharp tongued. May had a talent for eavesdropping. She knew everything about everyone and that made her positively frightening to men who preferred to hide their secrets.

'He and I would take long walks and discuss everything: plant life, wildlife, the latest findings from the Royal Academy of Sciences. He *listened* to my opinions.' Beatrice's gaze grew misty with remembrance. Claire heard the wistfulness there even now with ruin facing Beatrice and it surprised her, knowing the perfidy this lover was capable of. Then she saw the dilemma in Beatrice's eyes. Bea wanted to hate him but she couldn't, *didn't*. It was not a dilemma Claire could understand. The cad had left her pregnant. Ruined her. Destroyed her, in fact, and Beatrice could not bring herself to hate him, not quite, not yet.

'Listening turned out to be far more seductive than I could ever have imagined, especially when that listening was accompanied by a pair of grey eyes the colour of a winter storm. I was convinced he valued me in the most important of ways.'

Claire put a hand over her mouth and suppressed a sad sigh. In return for that false respect, Beatrice had given him the most important thing she possessed: she'd trusted him with her reputation. To her detriment, it turned out.

Beatrice looked down at her lap, a wry half-smile on her mouth, her tone part self-reassurance, part self-deprecation. 'The awful thing is, I tell myself surely it wasn't all illusion. Surely he found me interesting to some extent. Even now, with disaster staring me hard in the face, I'm not convinced he'd felt *nothing* for me. Surely one can't fake that depth of emotion. I guess I'll never know.' Instinctively, her hand moved to the flat of her stomach.

Claire's eyes caught the motion. 'How far gone are you, Bea?'

'Eight weeks.' Two months. Long enough to be sure. Long enough for the announcement not to be a mistake. Then again, Claire had never known Bea to make mistakes. Unlike her, Bea was always certain, always sure of her direction.

'And the father? How far gone is he?' May asked, characteristically honing in on the heart of the issue. Clare exchanged a nervous look with Evie. May might have gone too far. But May would not be deterred. 'Well, we have to know,' she said resolutely. 'Will you be marrying him?'

Bea gave a pretty shrug. 'The question is hypothetical only. Perhaps I would, if he was here, if our *affaire* hadn't been a pretence to him.'

Claire's heart swelled with admiration for her brave friend. Even with a baby on the way, Beatrice would not stoop to marry a man if it had all been a game and nothing more. As always, Beatrice's ethical compass faced true north and would not be compromised. It was an enviable commodity, one that Claire had once possessed herself: to be herself even in the face of great social odds, but somewhere in the last three years she'd lost it, ironically perhaps in an attempt to protect it. It was hard to say when it had started to slide. Maybe it had begun with Rufus Sheriden and refusing his proposal on the principle that she was a unique individual and as such deserved his unique regard, or perhaps it had been the Cecilia Northam incident. It had certainly been a slippery slope since then. She was no longer sure who she was, or what she was capable of.

May's cheeks were in high colour, her quick temper rising on behalf of their friend. 'The gall of the man to leave you pregnant and alone, unwilling to do right by you!'

Beatrice shook her head, her tone a soft contrast to May's outrage. 'He doesn't know, May. He left before…well, before I knew. Please do not despise him out of hand.' She took in the whole group with her gaze, perhaps guessing the direction of their thoughts. It was easy to vilify the absent father. 'It was the most delicious, exquisite week of my life. He brought me flowers, he smiled at me in a way that wiped away all reason. He did not seduce me, I went willingly into this folly. We had a winter of long walks in the cold and a week of illicit loving in abandoned cottages and warm haylofts. He told me he had business in a town a day's ride away. He didn't come back.' But he would always be among them. With a baby on the way, he'd never truly leave them. Ever.

'We have some time. That is good,' Evie said encouragingly, still holding Bea's hand. Thank goodness for Evie, always willing to put a cheerful outlook on things. 'It will be a Christmas baby. You shouldn't be showing until the very end of the Season. Fashions are fuller this year. I can start altering gowns right away.' Evie was at her best when she had a needle in her hand and fabric to transform. But her words spoke for them all. They would not desert their friend. Claire glanced around the circle. They were all smiling at Beatrice now; smiling their support, their approval.

Tears prickled obviously in Beatrice's eyes. She swiped helplessly at them. 'Dash it all! I wasn't going to cry. All I've done this past week is sob. Thank you, thank you, all of you. I didn't expect this.'

'What did you expect?' Claire couldn't keep the sense of betrayal out of her voice. 'Did you think we'd desert you at the first sign of trouble? After all we've been through, certainly you know we're made of sterner stuff.'

May took Claire's lead and leaned forward, her hand joining Evie's. 'You were there for me when my family forgot my birthday. You made me a cake and stole a whole bottle of brandy out of your father's liquor cabinet.' Claire remembered that. May's brother had got a prime government appointment and her parents had gone to London to celebrate with him, leaving May home. Alone. For her seventeenth birthday, the last birthday of her childhood.

'We got rather drunk that evening, I recall.' Beatrice managed a small smile.

'You were there for me through both of my sisters' weddings,' Evie added quietly. 'I had so much work sewing lace and pearls on to their gowns I hadn't time to see to my own gown. But you stayed up all night to help me finish my own dress for the wedding.'

'I think my fingers are still reluctant to pick up a needle again to this day!' Beatrice laughed.

Claire added her hand on top of the pile. 'And you were there when I refused Sheriden. And other times, too.' Her voice broke a little. Claire cleared her throat. 'Bea, you've always been there, for all of us, our glue holding us together in our time of need. We wouldn't dream of losing you now.'

It wasn't just a rescued birthday, or a stitch in time on a dress. They'd been there for each other when no one else had. They understood how much it hurt to be left behind by their families, no matter how unintentional, and how much it hurt to face the reality that this was a foreshadowing of their future. They'd been left behind by the dashing gentlemen of the *ton.*

There would be no gallant matches. Those gentlemen had looked right through them for years in London's ballrooms either purposely or accidentally choosing not to see them in lieu of seeing some other dewy-eyed, innocent miss. The world they knew had moved on, leaving them behind because they were too smart or too mousy, too anonymous or too outspoken for the *ton*'s tastes.

May pulled her hand out of the pile and broke the silence that had descended on the room. 'Beatrice is going to have a baby! We should be celebrating. This is a joyous occasion.' May reached beneath her chair and pulled out the basket she'd brought. 'I know just what to celebrate with. Cider and Cook's chocolate cake squares.'

Claire felt a smile of gratitude for May overtake her face. Leave it to May to know exactly what they needed, what *Beatrice* needed; not the chocolate, although chocolate helped quite a lot—the *celebration*. This baby might be a bit unorthodox in its beginnings but it was clear Beatrice was prepared to love the baby, that she already loved it. May passed around chipped cups and the cider jug. She passed around the cake squares, too, until there was only one coveted square left on the plate.

'Hmm.' May tapped a long finger on her chin. 'How shall we decide who gets the last square? How about a game of misery?'

Beatrice laughed, already reaching for the

cake. 'That's easy. I'm the most miserable. I'm pregnant and the father has disappeared.'

'Not good enough.' May lifted the plate out of reach, acting as judge. 'You may not have a father for the baby, but you have three aunties ajust waiting to spoil the little dear. Now, on the other hand, I think *I* should get the square because my parents have threatened to marry me to squint-eyed Vicar Ely this time next year if I don't succeed in the interim.' May pressed the back of her hand to her forehead and sighed in exaggerated distress but Claire knew it was no laughing matter. She'd seen the vicar. Vicar Ely was forty-five, squinty, stooped and forever preaching chastisement for sin from the Sunday pulpit. A more inappropriate mate for the outspoken May was not imaginable. Nor was it imaginable that May would actually succumb to such a fate. May would find a way out. May always did.

Evie jumped in, apparently not willing to lose the cake square or to let May feel sorry for herself. All of them were admirable that way, Claire thought; each of them unwilling to let any one of them suffer. 'May, that's a year off. Anything could happen. A duke could come on the market and you could snatch him up—' Evie snapped her fingers '—just like that. You have time and I don't. Andrew is home and declaring to everyone he means to marry. *Immediately.*'

'But that's good news,' Claire placated Evie with a kind smile, taking her turn. 'He *is* home, after two years away, and he's ready to settle down.'

'He has to notice me. He hasn't noticed me in years. Why would now be any different?' Evie said forlornly. They were all aware of her long-held and unrequited secret crush on her childhood friend, Andrew Adair. 'At least when he was gone, I knew he wasn't unavailable. I don't think I can bear it once he marries and there's *no* hope.' Evie shuddered and Claire could imagine all too well what her friend was envisioning: a lifetime of encountering Andrew and his bride at social functions in Little Westbury and watching Andrew's children grow up in his ancestral home. That particular horror too closely mirrored the fear she had grappled with lately.

It was the bane of living in a tight-knit community. It was impossible to get away from it unless Evie married and moved. Which wasn't a bad option. In Claire's opinion, Andrew Adair was a little less worthy of Evie's regard than Evie realised. He would only disappoint her in the end.

'He's just starting to look for a bride. Men say they want to marry and then they look for ever,' May put in cheerfully. 'Remember Viscount Banning? He looked for over three years before deciding on a wife. Sorry, no cake for you. You, like me, have time, too.' She cast a sly glance in Claire's direction and Claire froze. No. Not here. Not today. This was her private hell. She wasn't ready to air it to the others. She regretted even telling May. She tried to signal May with her eyes. Either May didn't take the hint or chose to ignore it. 'Tell them, dear. At the very least, you could win the cake square.'

That had all of Beatrice's attention. 'What is it, Claire?' She was not going to tell them, but she was very likely going to kill May. They should be focused on Beatrice now. 'It's *nothing*.' Claire shot a quelling look at May. 'There are *far* bigger concerns for us to deal with. We should focus our attentions on Beatrice.'

'No, we shouldn't,' Beatrice put in firmly. 'We have seven more months to worry about me. Besides, I could do with a little less self-focus these days. Tell us, May.'

May obliged. 'It's Lashley. I have it on excellent rumour from the Foreign Office that he's to go abroad in a plum diplomatic post in Vienna and Cecilia Northam is angling to go with him as his wife.'

Claire wanted to groan. 'Excellent rumour' meant May had heard it from her brother, Preston, who was friends with Sir Owen Danvers, head of the Central European Diplomatic Corps. If Preston said it, it was infallibly true. She wished it wasn't. She wished there was a margin of error that allowed her to dismiss the news as heresy. Aside from Beatrice's news, this was the single worse thing that could happen in her world: Jonathon Lashley, set to marry without having even laid eyes on her, without her even having had a chance to win him.

She supposed it was no less than she deserved. What had she ever done to draw Jonathon's regard? Unlike Evie, who was naturally retiring, Claire had deliberately chosen to retreat from society after a disastrous first Season. She was being served her just desserts for that choice.

'It was never anything more than a fool's dream.' Claire shrugged, valiantly acting as if it were indeed nothing of import. Compared to an unwed pregnancy, it wasn't of any significance, but from the pitying expressions on their faces, she was not succeeding. They all knew she'd longed after the dashing Jonathon Lashley for years. As open secrets went, it didn't get any more open. She'd been sweet on Jonathon since the summers they'd all run together in Sussex, four nine-year-old girls relentlessly chasing after May's older brother and his visiting friend. Back then, Jonathon had gone out of his way to be kind to four nine-year-old girls. She'd fallen hard for those kindnesses. She was falling still and about to hit bottom. 'Lashley hasn't even looked twice at me in all the years I've been out.' And now he never would. According to Preston's rumour, any day, Jonathon would choose Cecilia Northam.

'Maybe he should. Look twice, that is,' Beatrice said staunchly. 'You don't give yourself a chance, Claire. You are lovely. Women would die for your hair, all those soft brown waves like a rich cup of coffee. You should let me do your hair one evening and Evie could fix up a dress or two for you.'

Claire shook her head at the compliment. 'Yes, lovely *brown* hair. Too bad current fashion prefers blondes to brunettes and blue eyes to amber.' But it was a preference that ran to more than just looks.

She was a pragmatist at heart. English society preferred not only a certain physical ideal, but a particular mental ideal as well—a blank-slated miss to one who could converse with a gentleman in four languages. Statistically speaking, four languages should have increased Claire's odds. Socially speaking, it had not enhanced them. Her one failed attempt at making a match had proven that. Sir Rufus Sheriden, baronet, had made that quite clear. There would be no tolerance for female intelligence in their marriage. His clarity had been her point of retreat, the point at which her defences had gone up. She refused to yield her intelligence for any man. After a while, London had given up the siege. There were others more willing.

'Why would Lashley look twice when he has Cecilia Northam to hand?' It hurt to admit defeat, but that didn't make it less true. What man would look at a wallflower when faced with a veritable garden of perfection: Cecilia of the pale-blonde locks, the bright blue eyes and the porcelain skin. Cecilia was everything an English gentleman wanted in a bride.

'Because you're so much better than she,' Beatrice offered encouragingly, but that didn't change facts. Cecilia was like salt in a wound. She was a darling of the *ton*. She'd debuted with them and become instantly popular where they had not. She might also have been out for three Seasons, but Cecilia's experience was vastly different than theirs. She was looking to make a match this Season and finish her debut where they did not have such prospects.

Claire had long thought it was too bad men couldn't see Cecilia Northam for what she really was. Or maybe it was just that Jonathon could not see her for what she was. Cecilia was beautiful, but beneath that beauty, she was conniving and she'd managed to draw about her a coterie of the *ton*'s loveliest, most devious young women—women just like her, all of them desiring to snare the *ton*'s most eligible men. Claire could have ignored that. She didn't much care for those eligible men. Cecilia could have them. But now that Cecilia's sights were set on Jonathon, it was much harder to ignore. Apparently, kindness would not carry the day no matter what fairy tales argued to the contrary.

Once upon a time, she would have fought back, she would have been brave. She wasn't brave any more. There was no point to it. Bravery counted for nothing. Cecilia had seen to that. Rufus Sheriden had seen to that. London society had seen to that. She wasn't sure when that had changed for her, only that it had.

'No.' Beatrice stood up and Claire froze. She recognised the stubborn tilt of Beatrice's chin. Beatrice on a mission was a formidable creature.

'No? What?' Claire was afraid to ask.

'No, as in we shall not stand for it. *I* may be ruined, but there is no reason the rest of you have to settle for futures not of your choosing.'

Claire opened her mouth to protest, but Beatrice overrode her dissent with quick words and plans. 'We've been overlooked and forgotten. It's not entirely our fault. But we have had some hand in the blame. We've *let* the *ton* treat us as if *we* accept we're destined for nothing better than country marriages to dried-up vicars and poor third sons of baronets.'

'It's just how it is. What can we do about it?' Evie ventured hesitantly.

'We can use our special talents for our own betterment instead of detriment.' Something stirred inside Claire. She liked that—*betterment not detriment*. It sounded like something the workers at Peterloo would have chanted. Beatrice began to pace and Claire could feel herself getting caught up in Beatrice's fervour. 'It's so obvious. Why haven't we seen it before? We have to go after what we want. It's a simple principle of nature. A system dies when it has no new stimuli.' Beatrice rounded on the group, gesturing to Evie. 'We'll need your skill with the needle to create eye-catching fashions for those who need to stand out. Claire, you can coach us on French phrases to drop into conversation since it's coming back into vogue. May, you can help us research our quarry: where they'll be, when they'll be there, what they like. You can start with Lashley.'

Claire's passion for Beatrice's crusade came to a crashing halt. Why Lashley? Oh. Beatrice was starting straight at her, delivering her directive. 'Time is of the essence. You shall be first.'

'Me?' Claire choked on her cider.

Beatrice offered her a consoling smile, but she would not relent.

'Yes, you,' Beatrice said sternly. 'And it's certainly time you forgot about that idiot Sheriden. You've let his opinion of you hold you back for far too long. And it's time you forgot about Cecilia's dress prank. I don't think Lashley even noticed. It was years ago.'

Claire groaned. 'That just proves my point. He didn't even notice my most embarrassing moment.'

'That's *not* the point,' Beatrice argued. 'It's time we *all* forget. We've been complacent too long. No more. It has taken this pregnancy for me to realise I don't have to settle for the life society dictated for me. I don't want my friends to endure a similar tragedy in order to realise it, too. Each of us can have the lives we want, but only if we stand up for them and for each other.'

She fixed Claire with her best stare. Claire felt something warm and forgotten start to come to life deep inside her, a flicker perhaps of who she was, who she was meant to be instead of whom she had become.

'It starts with you, Claire. We are not going to let Cecilia Northam take Lashley, not without a fight, by God. She's had her way far too long and for no good reason.' Beatrice lifted her cup of cider in proclamation. 'I hereby officially declare this the "Left-Behind Girls Club", where, through acts of vigorous self-improvement, social courage and the protection of one another, we will change our circumstances by living life on *our* terms, not society's. Because, ladies, nothing will change until we do.'

Chapter Two

They had to be the ones to change. Beatrice's words still echoed three nights later. *They* had to stop accepting and start fighting for the life they wanted. Claire did not take issue with the concept in theory. Beatrice's speech had been rousing, inspiring even in a Henry the Fifth, 'once more into the breach' sort of way. But did she have to be *first*?

Claire pressed nervous hands against the flat of her stomach, repeatedly smoothing the silky material of her Evie-enhanced gown as she mounted the steps of the Worth town house behind her parents for dinner. Her friends should have started with someone they could succeed with. There was nothing like attempting the impossible to doom morale. She knew. She'd attempted it once. That's what this mission was: the impossible, an experiment doomed to failure. Jonathon hadn't noticed her for three years. Why would he suddenly notice her now? Why would anyone? She'd spent three years trying *not* to be noticed, trying to avoid reminding people she was the girl who had worn a gown *identical* to Cecilia Northam's at the largest ball of the Season the year she'd come out.

Inside the high-ceilinged hall of the Worth town house, with its blue-veined marble floor and white-arched niches filled with expensive statuary, Claire's nerves hit a ceiling of their own. Changing one's circumstances was all well and good in the hypothetical, but in practice it was far different, far more *real*. It was some comfort to know that May would be there with her tonight, playing hostess with her mother, but the comfort was outweighed by the knowledge that Jonathon Lashley and his parents would be in attendance, along with Cecilia Northam's family.

There would be others present, too, all of whom most likely outranked the Weltons in terms of social cachet. Her father was an unobtrusive man, a quiet viscount possessed of an old title, the sort of guest who could always be counted on to fill seats. As such, he and her mother were invited everywhere. It was a comfortable but not demanding popularity. Tonight was a case in point. The Worths liked to seat an even twenty for supper when they entertained, hence the need for the Weltons.

The butler led them into the drawing room and May was immediately at her side, slipping an arm through hers. Claire felt some of her nerves ease. May, like Beatrice, had been there when she'd refused her one and only offer of marriage and her family had been livid with her. May had been there when Cecilia had pulled her awful prank. Without May, Claire would have given up society years ago and retreated firmly to the country with her books. She'd probably know six languages by now instead of four.

'You look beautiful,' May whispered, looking lovely herself in a dress of midnight-blue silk.

'Do you think so?' Claire tugged self-consciously at the newly lowered bodice of her gown. Evie had recut the old conservative square one into a more modern style that was off the shoulder and considerably more revealing, before horizontally ruching the fabric to make the expanse of bosom now on display appear fuller.

May slapped her hand. 'Stop fussing with it. The cut is fine, more than fine. Evie has outdone herself.' The dress *was* hugely improved. Claire had hardly recognised it when Evie finished. It was just that Claire wasn't used to it. It wasn't the sort of dress a girl like her wore—a girl with no prospects, a girl who blended into the wallpaper. This was a dress that got a girl noticed. She'd not been oblivious to the second glances cast her way. The realisation made her fidgety. She wasn't used to being looked at, only looked over, or was that overlooked?

Of course, being noticed was part of the plan: no more matching the curtains, no more blending in. Being different meant looking different and there'd been no time in the last two days for an entirely new gown to be made. The girls had crowded into Claire's room and meticulously gone through her wardrobe until every gown had been scrutinised and discarded. Claire had not realised how plain her wardrobe was until it had needed to pass their inspection and failed.

The girls had decided she should wear blue, 'Ethereal', Evie had called it. Evie had taken notes on her little pad and had worked wonders with the gown. After the bodice had been re-made, Evie had added wide chocolate-brown grosgrain ribbon at the hem and thinner silk ribbon of the same colour along the bodice and the tiny puffed sleeves: a striking effect against the sky-blue that brought out the amber colour of her eyes.

Truth be told, Claire *did* feel different in the dress, but it would take some getting used to. Maybe she felt *too* different. A dress could change her on the outside, but it couldn't change her on the inside, could it? She scanned the room bravely, her eyes finding Jonathon; dark haired and tall, at the wide fireplace mantel that domi-nated the far wall. He was smiling, looking en-tirely at ease as he conversed. She didn't think she'd ever seen him without that smile and that air of confidence he carried everywhere with him, trademarks of who he was; a man with the world at his fingertips.

It was no wonder he was picked for an impor-tant diplomatic post. He was witty, charming, informed and there wasn't a talent he didn't possess; he could sing at musical evenings, fence, box, ride and shoot. He was perfect, the Regency's incarnation of Da Vinci's Renaissance man.

He stood with his father and Lord Belvoir, Cecilia's father. Cecilia Northam was at his side dressed in an exquisite rose silk, her hand on his arm, possessive and proud as if he already belonged to her. Cecilia's eyes caught hers, her steely-silver gaze perusing Claire's gown.

Claire could hear the old, hurtful words. *'I wear it better. Far better. You should have known you could not wear my signature colour.'* Claire hadn't worn pink since.

This gown was not that gown, she reasoned with herself. In no way did Evie's blue creation resemble the rose silk Cecilia wore tonight. But Claire still felt her confidence falter. 'I feel as if I've been thrown to the lions,' she murmured to May.

'Then be Daniel,' May whispered. 'Keep your head up and look them all in the eye. Let everyone know this Season you mean business, beginning tonight.'

Claire did her best as they made the rounds of

the room, stopping to talk with the little clusters of guests, May leaning over to announce *sotto voce*, 'Cecilia is not the only one who's noticed. Even Lashley's been looking a time or two. Discreetly, of course.'

Of course. It was how Jonathon did everything. Claire hazarded another look in Jonathon's direction, unable to suppress a little trill of delight at May's words. Everything Jonathon did was tastefully done, from clothes to manners to conversation. When he spoke with someone, they had the impression of being listened to. At least that was her experience in the few, brief interactions she'd had with him over the years. They hardly qualified as conversations, more like extended greetings. Unlike other men who merely went through the polite motions demanded by society before moving on to the women they were truly interested in, Jonathon had always taken time to ask a question and then listen to the answer. She'd understood the attraction of Beatrice's lover too well. Listening was a vastly underrated commodity. It made one feel they had value.

She and May had just left one group and were

moving on to another when she felt it: Jonathon's gaze on her. She looked up, allowing their eyes to meet for the briefest of seconds. A small smile played on his lips, giving her the impression his smile was for her alone and Claire's pulse rocketed as she looked away.

It was a silly, unwarranted reaction. She wanted to stand out to him, the way Cecilia Northam apparently did. She wanted to be the one with her hand resting lightly on his arm as she looked up into that handsome face with its deep-blue eyes and sharp-cut lines.

'Come on.' May tugged at her arm. 'Let's go speak with his group. We haven't visited them yet and later, I have *news*.'

Claire froze, Old Claire getting the better of New Claire with her new dress and hair. Talk to Jonathon *now*? 'No. I couldn't possibly do that. What would I say?'

She wasn't really warmed up. She'd just arrived.

'How about "good evening"? *He* smiled at you. Take the opening.' May laughed. It was easy for May to laugh. She didn't understand. She didn't get tongue tied every time Jonathon was around.

In fact, May was hardly ever tongue tied around anyone. It was her gift and her curse. Where Claire had made herself invisible, May had made herself far too noticeable.

'No,' Claire insisted. 'Not yet. Let's wait until after dinner', when she would have had time to get her conversation up to par with her partner, when she might finally be used to this dress and how it made her feel. May merely smiled, her hidden dimple coming out in the corner of her cheek. *That* worried her. May hardly ever admitted defeat. Claire had the distinct impression she was being flanked.

A moment later, she knew it. Claire had barely settled into her chair when he spoke. 'Miss Welton, it's a pleasure to see you this evening.'

She looked up and met Jonathon's sharp blue eyes, quite possibly the exact shade of her gown. 'The pleasure is all mine.' The words tumbled out without her consent, her mind too busy grappling with the fact that he was sitting across from her, too busy to pay attention to what her mouth was doing. Her mind was focused on another heart-stopping fact: He was all hers to look at for the entire meal.

He smiled broadly at her ridiculous words. What lady said such a thing? It was far too bold for a genteel dinner, but that's what new dresses did—they made one feel as bold their neckline. She looked away, fussing with her napkin to give herself something to do. She would have thought she was used to looking at him by now. She'd been doing it most of her life. The logic of familiarity suggested the sensation should have numbed by now, should have faded from the intense pleasure of seeing him into something more comfortable. But it hadn't. If anything, it was sharper. She was acutely aware of every angle of his face, the strong line of his jaw, the curving planes of his cheeks when he smiled, the firm sensuality of his mouth. That last was a wicked thought indeed to entertain at the table.

Claire turned her thoughts to other, less wanton ideas like revenge. She shot May a knowing glance across the white-clothed expanse. Her instincts were right. Either through fate or finagling—Claire highly suspected the latter—that minx of a friend had engineered the seating arrangement. She gave May a nudge with her foot under the table to acknowledge the ploy. *I am on to you, May Worth.*

But there was nothing she could do about it now. Claire was not going to get her reprieve. There would be no waiting until after dinner to speak with Jonathon. If she knew May, the plan wouldn't stop here. May had something more in mind to get her noticed. The thought was both exhilarating and agitating. She wished May had made her a party to the plan. No, wait, she didn't. If she'd known ahead of time, she would only have worried. All she could do now was stay alert and watch for her chance. She simply had to apply herself.

Right now, all it seemed she could apply herself to was avidly staring as the first course was set in front of her. Jonathon had the most intriguing lock of errant hair that fell to the side, escaping any efforts to pomade it into place. She was doing such a good job of staring, she missed her conversation partner's overture.

But in truth, it wouldn't have mattered how many times her partner repeated himself. Her attention was claimed elsewhere, so it was no surprise during the fish that her ears cringed when she heard the butchered word *'bonjure'* from across the table. Claire responded out of reflex and years of study, 'You mean *bohnzhooh.* The French don't pronounce the "r" strongly at the end of *bonjour.'*

Jonathon's blue gaze landed on her, his handsome mouth smiling politely, easily, as if he was not offended at the correction or the interruption. Claire shut her mouth in horror. She wanted to melt into a pile of blancmange beneath the table. She might have if May hadn't kicked her, a rather painful reminder that she would not shrink from the world any longer, not after Evie had re-made her gown, not after Beatrice had done up her hair, not after May had done whatever it was May had done to make this possible.

Tonight, she was representing all of them. She had to be brave. But, oh, sweet heavens, it was hard to do when she'd just corrected Jonathon Lashley, future diplomat. In public. At a dinner table in front of eighteen other guests. That was certainly one way to get his attention, although probably not the best way. Oh, dear Lord, people were starting to stare.

* * *

'Bohnzhooh,' Jonathon amended, acknowledging the correction. The quickest way to dispel unwanted attention was to persuade onlookers there was nothing to see. There was no show here. 'I appreciate the opportunity for improvement.' But why had she done it? And why here at the table of all places? His eyes remained riveted on the woman across from him.

Miss Welton had *all* of his attention now, whereas before, her dress had held most of it. He'd noticed the dress the moment she'd walked in this evening, but now he was noticing her. A fact that was strange in itself. She'd never been particularly noticeable before. He knew of her, most certainly. She was a friend of Preston's sister and a neighbour to the Worths in the country. She'd been out for several Seasons and their paths crossed sporadically in London at larger catch-all affairs. She'd always struck him as a woman who didn't *want* to be noticed. So he hadn't. Noticed. Not really. Not until tonight.

She was different tonight. She'd made a rather subtle but grand entrance in her blue dress. He was sure the ladies had a sophisticated word for the colour, something more descriptive than simply blue. But to him it was blue—the colour of an English summer sky and on her it was positively stunning, although not precisely the shade or cut worn by a woman who didn't want to be noticed. Perhaps this was Miss Welton's way of announcing she was seriously hunting a husband this Season? Or perhaps she already had one? In his experience, women dressed well when there was a man to impress.

What a woman *didn't* do was correct a man at dinner and yet Miss Welton had, drawing an uncharacteristic amount of attention to herself in the process. Part of him wanted to applaud her boldness. Miss Welton was certainly coming out of her shell. Well done her. Although he wished she hadn't chosen to do it with a remark about his French. Still, she wasn't to be blamed. She couldn't know it was a touchy subject with him at the moment. The French didn't pronounce all the letters in their words, but apparently that didn't stop him from doing it and doing it wrong. Wrong was something he wasn't use to being.

Beside him, Cecilia was not quite as forgiving behind her frosty smile. She leaned slightly towards him as if what she had to say was between the two of them, but it was an illusion only. She *meant* for the table to hear. 'I did not realise we had a Francophile at the table, Lashley.'

Jonathon stiffened, feeling his senses go on alert. Stares returned. This was not a friendly remark. He did not need or want Cecilia defending him, nor did he see the need to attack Miss Welton. Francophile was the most insulting name Cecilia could have decently called her and Miss Welton knew it. *Everyone* at the table knew it. Her hand halted just for a fraction of a second as she reached for her wine glass. Jonathon willed that hand to keep going, to give no sign of Cecilia's comment having any effect.

But the damage was done. The fish was nowhere near as exciting as Cecilia Northam verbally calling someone out. People near them stopped eating and cast interested glances their way. The war might have been over for seven years, but to be a lover of anything French was still not a popular pastime.

Jonathon locked eyes with Miss Welton as if he could lend her some strength, some encouragement with his gaze. He could see how she fought the urge to retreat in the way her hand tensed around the stem of her wine glass.

Don't you dare apologise, Miss Welton. I was incorrect and you called me on it. You've done nothing wrong.

If there was any apologising to be done, it should be Cecilia. Her comment had bordered on the pale and he had no wish to see anyone put down whether it be on his behalf or not, especially not a woman who had chosen tonight to step into the light.

To his everlasting delight, Miss Welton straightened her shoulders and met Cecilia's gaze. 'French is the language of diplomacy on the Continent, Miss Northam. One need not be a Francophile to appreciate the importance of being conversant in the language.' She managed a sophisticated smile as if to say she would not be embarrassed over her knowledge or made to feel lesser for her education. Jonathon wanted to applaud.

'You are lucky to be so well schooled in the language.' He smiled, lending her support with his words, well aware that Cecilia bristled beside him, fully understanding his support of Miss

Welton was a subtle but resounding denouncement of her accusation. Cecilia would not be pleased.

On his other side, a more pleasant May Worth picked up the lagging conversation. 'Miss Welton is fluent in French and three other languages as well.'

Jonathon raised a dark brow in genuine interest over Miss Welton's accomplishments, trying hard not to stare at those cognac eyes or lower at the expanse of bosom on display. Her bodice was no lower than anyone else's, but it had become unexplainably more alluring. 'Is that true, Miss Welton? I had no idea you were so accomplished.'

He envied her that accomplishment. It would come as a surprise to everyone at the table if they knew how much he wished to be her—the quiet, heretofore unobtrusive Miss Welton—in those moments. It would solve a lot of his problems. Oral fluency in French was all that kept him from finalising the Vienna appointment, a post he very much wanted for personal reasons. But it was a skill that had eluded him since he'd come home from Waterloo. Even after countless tutors and in spite of his ability to write and read the language with perfect comfort, he couldn't speak a word of it.

A footman set down a beautifully arranged plate of beef bourguignon in front of him. Great. A French dish. Now even the food was mocking him and there was still Cecilia to contend with as the table turned; pretty, petulant Cecilia who was supposed to make him the ideal bride— her beauty and wit a representation of English womanhood to those abroad. He was expected to offer for her by the end of the Season, one more venue for securing the Vienna post was official. He would do it if that was what it took, just as he would master oral fluency in French. They were merely the last two hurdles to be overcome, he told himself. It was the least he could do in the name of his brother's memory. He would be part of establishing peace in his time, so that no one else would have to die.

Jonathon shot one last look across the table at Miss Welton, catching her eye before she turned away to give her attention to the man beside her. What other languages did she speak and why? Did she ever intend to use them or need them?

Cecilia tugged at his arm when he was too slow to give her his attention, but before he turned, Miss Welton mouthed a single word: *'Merci.'* Thank you. Suffice it to say, his curiosity was piqued even if it shouldn't be.

Chapter Three

'Spill! What is your news?' Claire's curiosity was more than piqued by the time she and May set out for Lady Stamford's ball in the Worth carriage, her parents having taken May's folks up with them in their town coach. Waiting for whatever May's news was had been a herculean task, especially since Claire was sure it involved Jonathon and May always knew the most delicious things.

May's eyes twinkled confidentially. 'Lashley's French tutor has left him. No one knows why, but it doesn't matter. It only matters that he's gone and there's no one to teach him.'

Claire grimaced, disappointed. She'd thought the news would be more significant than that. 'Isn't he a bit old for a tutor?' What could Jonathon Lashley possibly be studying for? At twenty-eight, he was years out of university, years past the age of being a student, and he was perfect at everything he did. She furrowed her brow and examined the flaw in her conclusion. He hadn't been perfect at dinner. His French had been deplorable. Whoever his tutor had been, the man hadn't been any good even if he had been from Paris.

May leaned back against the leather squabs, looking irritatingly smug. 'There's more to it. While Evie was busy altering your dress, I was busy, too. Jonathon Lashley can't *speak* French to save his life and I mean that quite literally. Preston says Lashley's been given an ultimatum: learn to speak passable French by August or he'll lose his diplomatic post.'

'What am I supposed to do about that?' Claire said, still trying to wrap her head around the fact that Jonathon Lashley had an imperfection, a weakness in his formidable social arsenal of skills *and* she'd accidentally called him on it. This was getting worse by the minute. She had not meant to embarrass him. If the correction hadn't been bad enough, she'd also managed to highlight a rather sensitive incompetency. This was more than alerting someone to a spot on their shirt. He must thoroughly despise her. And yet he hadn't shunned her, hadn't cut her down with a cruel remark when he had the chance and Cecilia had certainly given him one. Instead, he'd championed her with his words and with his eyes. Maybe she'd dream about that tonight. She hoped so. She wanted to remember how he'd looked across the table at her, how he'd smiled at her, each word he'd spoken to her. It had almost been a real conversation. There had been that moment when he'd turned away and she'd had the impression he'd like to have said more, *asked* her more. Was it possible to fake that impression? Surely not. Claire gave a wistful sigh. She'd like to believe just for a moment, she'd entranced Jonathon Lashley…

May snapped her fingers in impatience and Claire snapped to attention. Apparently she'd let her thoughts wander too far afield. 'Do I need to spell it out? Step into the breach, Claire! Be *his* hero in his hour of need. Teach him French. Secure his post.' Her eyes danced with a naughty light. 'Who knows, he might just be eternally grateful.'

She could do that. At least the girl in the ethereal blue dress could do that. Claire sat up straighter, her mind alert as possibilities began to spark. She started to see the brilliance of May's suggestion: long hours of working together, alone, the subject itself rather invigorating to the mind. French wasn't called the language of love without reason.

She worried her lip in thought. 'There's only one flaw. How do I get him to come to me?' He didn't need her specifically. He needed anyone who spoke French. 'There is no guarantee he will seek me out.' Or that she'd succeed, but she kept that to herself. Doubt started to seep in. Why would she succeed where a Paris-born tutor had clearly failed? But she kept that doubt to herself.

May was undeterred. 'After tonight? We planted the seeds at dinner. We may not need to do any more. Did you see the way he looked at you when I mentioned you spoke four languages? It was as though he saw you with new eyes. His clock is ticking. He needs someone close at hand. He's desperate, Claire.' *Like her.*

Desperate? Claire winced. It wasn't exactly the best recommendation. She'd prefer he come to her out of respect for her intellect rather than desperation. But she was desperate, too, and she understood the emotion. She knew better than anyone that beggars couldn't be choosers. 'We're wagering rather a lot on him connecting the pieces that lead to me,' Claire warned.

May shrugged, starting to lose patience with her. 'Then send him a letter. Connect the pieces for him. What do you have to lose? Tell him you heard about his situation and would be glad to help. He won't expose you. It would be too embarrassing for him. A scandal is the last thing he would want at this point before the position is officially his. At best, he takes the offer and at worst he politely declines. You're no worse off either way.'

Which really translated as: she was already so bad off, she had nothing to lose. That wasn't true for Lashley, though. It occurred to Claire as the carriage rocked to a halt outside the Stamford rout that Jonathon was only better off *if* he took the offer. If not, he stood to lose a great deal that mattered to him.

Of all the things she'd dreamed of having in common with Jonathon Lashley, desperation wasn't one of them.

'Jonathon, I am desperate, positively desperate. The last time you spoke French at a state reception, you nearly started a war!' Sir Owen Danvers, head of the diplomatic corps assigned to central Europe, gave Jonathon an exasperated look from behind his desk in the Whitehall offices.

'I mispronounced an adjective,' Jonathon clarified. That had been two weeks ago. He was tired of talking about it, tired of thinking about it. It was one more reminder of all the things that were different now.

'And nearly started a war!' Danvers repeated forcefully. 'You seem to be missing that piece.' He lowered his voice. 'I need you in Vienna, you are my man and yet you insulted the visiting French Ambassador.'

It wasn't so much misusing as it had been mispronouncing. The word in question was *beau-*

coup, meaning 'a lot'. It had come out *beau cul*. He had inadvertently referred to a particular visiting ambassador as having a nice ass. Really, too much was being made out of a single instance. No war had *actually* occurred. It seemed petty to dwell on what had *not* happened.

Jonathon pushed a hand through his hair and blew out a breath. He preferred to think of it as a potential war *averted* instead of potentially started. Then again, he'd always been a glass-half-full man himself. Apparently, Danvers wasn't. But no matter how Jonathon dressed it up, or tried to laugh it away, he couldn't dismiss the fact that it was *not* a mistake he would have made seven years ago.

'You must appreciate my position,' Danvers went on. 'You're smart as a whip when it comes to understanding the nuances of the Ottomans and the Austro-Hungarian Empire. You grasp those delicate balances like no other. You read French with ease, which makes you ideal for translating documents and reading correspondence. You write it well, too, in a pinch which is the least of my worries. But you can't *speak* it worth a damn, not any more. The time was, you were fluent as hell.'

There was the rub. He had been fluent before the accident, before his brother Thomas had disappeared. Between those two incidents, his brain had been wrecked somehow. Jonathon rose from his chair and strode to the long windows overlooking the Thames. This was no dark office buried in the bowels of Whitehall. This was the office of a man who controlled great power in England and beyond. He could imagine the secrets Owen Danvers knew, the secrets the man *kept*.

Today, Jonathon only cared about one thing: Owen Danvers had the ability to break him, old chum from school or not. His appointment to Vienna hung on Danvers's recommendation. Jonathon helped himself to the brandy in a crystal decanter on a sideboard placed along the window. 'You know what that post means to me, Owen,' Jonathon said quietly, calling on their old friendship as he looked out the windows. He idly sipped his drink. The post meant everything: He could avenge the loss of his brother with peace, he could make his brother's sacrifice at Waterloo worth something. He could prove to the world that he was more than a viscount's heir, that he was more than a man who was worth something only because he'd had the good fortune to be born first to another man of wealth and title.

'Dammit, I *know*, Jonathon. I would have sent you on your way long before now if I didn't know how hard you've worked for this and how much you want it.' Owen Danvers relented with a sigh. Owen had been two years ahead of him, but back then, Jonathon was on top as a peer's son and Owen merely the scrapping son of a baronet eager to make his way. Owen had done just that and now he was the one on top, the one who had what Jonathon wanted.

Wanting seemed such an inadequate word. He wanted this so much he was willing to bend his whole life to it, even marry for it. Cecilia Northam's father, Lord Belvoir, was a powerful man in Parliament. Belvoir had made it clear he'd champion him for the post in exchange for marriage to his daughter. He'd also made it clear the opposite was true. If Jonathon failed to marry Cecilia, that support would be withdrawn.

What Cecilia wanted, Cecilia got. She'd set her sights on becoming the future Lady Oakdale last Season. She'd sunk her teeth in since then and hadn't let go. He had to marry someone some time. It might as well be her, yet he wondered if there should be something more between them than a trading of skills that, while not symmetrical skills, were certainly complements.

Owen put a hand on his shoulder, his voice quiet. 'We all miss him. Thomas was a brave man. He died in the service of his country, nobly and honestly. It's been a long time, but sometimes I still think I can hear him laughing. I'll turn around at the club and expect to see him, but he isn't there.'

'I know. Me, too.' Jonathon paused to gather himself. 'Do you really think he's dead?' he said quietly. It was a thought he only voiced aloud to a few select people. After all this time, too many people felt he was ridiculous to hold on to what was becoming a ludicrous hope. There'd been no body. Thomas was just simply gone.

Owen didn't laugh, didn't try to argue with him. 'It's been a long time, Jonathon.'

A long time indeed. He'd had seven years to

get used to Thomas being gone and yet somehow he hadn't mastered it any more than he'd mastered the return of his French. Maybe he never would. 'He was just so damn young.' Jonathon breathed, unable to hold back the emotion that flooded his voice. 'He was barely past his twentieth birthday. He'd hardly had time to grow up.'

'He honoured us with his life.' Owen cleared his throat. 'We can honour him with ours. Jonathon, I need *you* in Vienna. What will it take?' Owen paused, taking a moment to cleanse the intensity from his tone. 'Has there been any progress?' he asked carefully, kindly.

'I need time.' Never mind that seven years hadn't been time enough. He tried not to think about last night's debacle. 'I need to find another tutor and continue my lessons.' Jonathon said it as confidently as he could, as if he truly believed more study would fix what plagued him. It had been unfortunate his last tutor had a family emergency in Paris and been called away at a most critical juncture, but perhaps it didn't matter. A pair of sharp brown eyes swam to the fore of his memory, accompanied by a polite voice: *The French don't pronounce the final 'r' in* bonjour. Perhaps his problem wasn't something that could be fixed by study. Still, he had to try. For Thomas.

'We need the post settled before the Season ends, Jonathon. Elliot Wisefield is champing at the bit should you fail and we need a replacement for Lord Wareborne in Vienna by the New Year. I have good men there—Viscount St Just, Matheson and Truesdale—but Central Europe is on the brink of exploding.'

Or imploding, depending on how one looked at it, but sending Wisefield? The name made Jonathon cringe. They'd been rivals since school as much as he and Owen had been friends. How fitting that they'd now be vying for the same diplomatic post. How could Danvers, how could any of them, be considering Wisefield? He might be smart, might have an encyclopaedic head of knowledge when it came to history, but he hadn't an ounce of finesse to his name.

Jonathon couldn't protest, though, it would be bad form to malign a competitor. Instead, he had to be confident. He didn't want Owen Danvers to think he was begging. Weakness persuaded no one, not even friends.

Jonathon turned from the window, a strong smile pasted on his face, the one he used to charm overprotective mothers. 'The end of the Season will be fine. Thank you, Owen.'

Owen Danvers rose from behind his desk. His face was etched in concern and for the first time, Jonathon saw the worry his friend carried as the man clasped his hand in a firm handshake. 'Let me tell you again, I want you there, Jonathon. The Phanariots are rising, the Greeks are making their bid for an independent state. These next few years will be volatile times. The Treaty of Vienna will be tested. Whether or not the treaty holds will depend on the men who stand behind it.'

'The treaty *must* hold. It has to.' Jonathon's mind was already racing with moves and countermoves. The Phanariots thought Russia would be their saviour from the Ottomans, but Russia dared not move without France and Britain, Metternich's concert of Europe demanded it. The Ottoman Empire was weak, but was now the time to crush it? A hundred questions surged. None of them would matter if he couldn't overcome this last hurdle.

'Do you have someone in mind for tutoring?' Danvers asked.

'Yes, I do.' Jonathon answered with a confidence he didn't feel. He thought once more of amber eyes and a pretty blue dress showing a nice bosom. It was madness. He hardly knew her beyond his association with May's brother and suddenly he was pinning his future on her, Miss Welton, Viscount Stanhope's daughter, May Worth's friend from Sussex—what was her name? Clarice, Clara, Clarinda, Catherine? None of those seemed quite right. *Claire*. That was it. Would she even do it? *Could* she do it? Was her French as good as her very brief demonstration at the table and May's endorsement indicated? He was in no position to accept mediocrity. He needed excellence and he needed it fast.

A hasty plan began to form and it started with flowers. Jonathon hurried out of Whitehall, headed towards the nearest florist. There was a spring his step even as he reminded himself this whole gambit smacked of desperation. He was hoping for quite a lot from a woman whose first name he barely recalled.

* * *

'Mr Jonathon Lashley to see you, Miss Welton.'

The butler's announcement sent a thrill of excitement down Claire's spine. How many times had she imagined hearing those words? How many times had she dreamed of this moment—Jonathon Lashley calling on her? Then she forced herself to remember why he was calling. Not once in those imaginings had he called on her for French lessons. It seemed May's plan had worked thus far. She should be ecstatic, so why did she feel a bit fraudulent, dangling her French out there like so much cheese in a mousetrap?

'Send him in, Marsden,' her mother shot, her eyebrow raised as she spoke a single crisp word. 'Interesting.'

It wasn't all that interesting from where Claire sat. She knew exactly why Jonathon was here. He'd arranged his call perfectly to ensure privacy. The time for afternoon calls was nearly over, the sitting room at Stanhope house empty. The last callers had left ten minutes ago. There was no chance of anyone noticing his arrival. Was he that embarrassed to be seen calling on her? The nuance stung.

She and her mother rose as Jonathon stepped into the room and made his bow. 'Good afternoon, Lady Stanhope, Miss Welton. I trust I am not too late?' He presented her with a bouquet of flowers, fresh white-petalled snowdrops and deep butter-yellow roses.

'Thank you, they're lovely.' She took the bouquet, irrationally touched by the gesture. It meant nothing. It was protocol. But, oh, it was so easy to forget she'd angled for this very moment. She signalled for Marsden to get a vase. 'Will you take tea?' Claire gestured to the tea pot and the trays of cakes beautifully frosted and arranged to appeal to the eye.

'I have come with a request,' Jonathon began once they were settled with cups and cakes. He balanced his plate on his knee, his fingers preternaturally gripping the delicate handle of his teacup. Now, *that* was interesting. Claire watched him carefully. If she didn't know better, she'd think the urbane Jonathon Lashley was nervous. Impossible. Then again, just last night she'd been disabused of the notion that he was perfect. If he squeezed Grandmother Highthorne's Wedgwood any tighter, the slim handle would likely burst under his grip.

She understood the feeling. She thought *she* just might burst under his gaze. He was looking directly at her as he spoke and her pulse was about to go through the ceiling. He'd never directed any conversation to her this long before. If she had something in her hand to grip, she'd be squeezing the life out of it, too. But her teacup remained on the table, perhaps for the better. Claire tried to focus on what he had to say. 'I'm in need of a French tutor to help me brush up on my conversation. I believe you mentioned you had some experience last night with the language, Miss Welton.' His gaze shifted to her mother. 'If it met with approval, I would very much like to engage your daughter's assistance for the duration of the Season.'

He'd just got his request out when it happened. There was a small snapping sound and Jonathon's teacup crumbled, the delicate handle splitting in two as the cup fell, liquid pouring down his fawn breeches. 'Damn! That's hot!' He leapt up, looking around rapidly for a napkin, but Claire was faster.

'Oh, I am so sorry! Allow me!' She wiped frantically at his trousers, thinking only of wicking away the boiling water, of wicking away his distress. 'Are you all right? You're not burned, are you?' She'd got most of it. Claire pressed her napkin high against his thigh, blotting the remainder of the water.

His hand covered hers, insistent in halting her efforts, his tone somewhat stiff as he relieved her of mopping duty. 'I am fine, just a little damp. Thank you, Miss Welton for your, ah, speedy assistance. I can take it from here.'

Claire sat back in her chair, watching him mop up his trousers, mortification setting in at what she'd done. She could feel her cheeks heat, rivalling the tea water. Just an inch or two to the right and…good Lord! She'd nearly felt up the future Viscount Oakdale and in front of her mother no less.

'A thousand pardons, Lady Stanhope, for the language and for the teacup, I hope it wasn't an heirloom.' Lashley remained standing as he apologised, trying valiantly to ignore the obvious dark wet stain on his breeches.

'It is a trifling thing, Mr Lashley, do not worry

yourself over it.' Her mother smiled smoothly as if nothing untoward had just broken out in her drawing room, as if her daughter hadn't nearly manhandled their guest's private parts in an attempt to be helpful. 'I'm only glad you were not harmed unduly.'

Or molested by my daughter. She doesn't get out much, Claire thought as Lashley left the room with considerably more dignity than most men would have managed. Would she ever be able to look him in the eye again? She'd have to though, wouldn't she? Then she remembered, she hadn't answered his question.

Claire raced to the door, never mind that running after a man was hardly appropriate, but decorum had departed the moment she had tried to wipe up his trousers. 'Mr Lashley!' she called, stopping him at the front door.

Jonathon turned. 'Yes? Miss Welton?'

'I never answered your proposal.' She mentally winced. That was entirely the wrong word. 'I would be honoured to help you with your conversation.'

A broad smile took his face, bordering on brilliant. Her decision pleased him. Did she imagine it or was there relief in that smile, too? It had taken strength of character to ask her, strength enough to break a teacup. Not every man was strong enough to admit when he needed help. 'How are mornings at eleven?'

He'd agreed! The realisation swamped her with amazement and disbelief. Beatrice and May's plan was going to work! But then what? She pushed the thought away. She'd worry about that later. For now, she was practically giddy. Jonathon gave her an expectant arch of his brows, as if he was waiting for something. Oh, yes. A response. He was waiting for words. What a looby she was. He would be wondering how she could master French if she couldn't even manage basic English.

'Mornings at eleven are perfect.' She pushed a stray curl behind her ear and tried to sound composed while her insides leapt. Jonathon had said yes! True, it was just for French lessons, but it was a start.

Chapter Four

The lesson was perfectly awful on all levels. They were one hour in and Claire was at her wits' end. Never did she imagine those rather considerable wits would reach their end so quickly or that her patience would have such a short fuse, especially where Jonathon Lashley was concerned. As an opportunity for Lashley to notice her, this was an absolute failure.

Her stays were suffocatingly tight in their attempt to push her breasts up in Evie's latest creation—a low-cut morning gown in pale green—and Lashley couldn't sit still long enough to appreciate the effort. He kept getting up from the long table that ran the length of the Welton library and walking to the window, where there was absolutely nothing of interest to see—she'd checked after his fourth trip just to make sure. Perhaps the gardeners had decided to work naked, after all. But no. Quite thankfully, the gardeners were all clothed. There was nothing to see, just the garden and the wall that separated it from the alley.

Apparently 'point of interest' meant something different to Lashley, though. This was the *eighth* time now he'd made the trip and, while it was something of a treat to watch those broad shoulders in blue superfine and those long legs sporting tan breeches *sans* tea stains walk across the room in a pair of highly polished boots, it wasn't helping her cause or his.

She wanted to push him into his chair and yell, 'Sit down and look at me!' Not only because she'd worn this ridiculous dress just for him, but she couldn't very well use the tips May and Beatrice had given her for attracting a man's attention if he was forever walking away. He had to *sit* in order for her to lean over the table and point out something in the book. He had to *sit* in order for her to stand behind him so that her breasts might brush his shoulder as she pointed something out. The operative word in all of these suggestions was 'sit', of course, an assumption she had felt safe in making an hour ago, not so now. It was all good advice, Claire was certain, if she ever got to use it. None of her friends' tips dealt with a man who acted like a jack in the box.

How did he expect her to uphold her end of the proposition if he wouldn't uphold his? He'd asked for her help and she couldn't give it if he wouldn't sit still. She couldn't very well teach him French if he wouldn't read the sentences from the book and do the lesson she provided.

But a lady did not screech like a fishwife in the presence of a man she wanted to impress. Still, good manners and playing by the rules had got her very little in the way of progress today. Claire shot a frantic glance at the clock. Their time would be up and they would have accomplished nothing. Lashley would think she was incompetent. The realisation spurred on the last of her reserves. Whatever else she was, she *knew* she was an accomplished linguist and she would prove it. Claire drew a deep breath, calling on the final remnants, nay, the last shreds of her patience. 'Let's try again, Mr Lashley.' She crossed the room to the window, book in hand, muttering under her breath. *'Dağ sana gelmezse, sen dağa gideceksin.'*

'What did you say?' Lashley's head jerked away from the window, startled at the words. At last something had caught his interest and it hadn't been French. Of course. That was how her luck had been lately.

'I said, "If the mountain won't come to you, you must go to the mountain". It's from *The Essays of…*'

'Francis Bacon, I know. But Bacon wrote his essays in English,' Lashley finished. 'Turkish would be my guess.'

'Yes, you're correct. Most people don't recognise Turkish.' That he did was pleasantly surprising but it didn't make up for the fact that he couldn't focus on his lesson. He was a grown man, used to long meetings about estates and ledgers, there was nothing drier. Why couldn't he focus on French which was anything but dull?

'And yet you speak it, Miss Welton? Is it one of your four languages?' He was watching her now, his sharp blue eyes on her face. He'd remembered May's carefully placed titbit from dinner. She flushed, pleased that he'd recalled something about her.

'It will hopefully be my fifth. Since the Ottoman Empire appears destined to demand British attention, it seemed prudent to pick up the skill.' Maybe this was the opening she needed. She leaned forward, pointing to the page and hopefully displaying a pleasing expanse of bosom. 'We're not here to learn Turkish, Mr Lashley. Perhaps we might try the French sentences again? Read the first one, *si'l vous plait.*'

Lashley drew a breath. His jaw tightened almost imperceptibly *'Ow est lee salon?'*

There it was, the second reason this lesson was a disaster, in terrible ear-splitting reality; Lashley was horrible. As if his attention deficit wasn't problem enough, Lashley's French sounded awful when he did try. Suffice it to say, she'd taught younger children French with more success than she was having here. Abysmal didn't even begin to cover it. Praise was a good way to encourage success, but what could she say about *this?* 'All right, it sounded like a question, that's good. It was meant to be one.'

Lashley saw right through the comment. 'I'm

not a child, Miss Welton. Lying to me won't help. You make it sound so easy. I look at the words and I see what they mean, but I can't say them, not like you.'

'Not yet anyway,' Claire insisted. She couldn't stand the look of resignation that crept across his face. 'We simply have to practise.'

Lashley moved away from the window and ran a hand through his hair. He shook his head. 'I *have* been practising. For years. I'm sorry, Miss Welton, to have wasted your time. This simply isn't going to work.'

He was leaving? No. Unacceptable. She was not losing him after one lesson. If Beatrice was willing to brazen out having a baby with no father, perfect Jonathon Lashley could learn to speak French and she could teach him. But she had to act fast. He was already halfway to the door. Something fiery and stubborn flared inside Claire. He was *not* leaving this room. Claire strode across the room—no, wait, who was she kidding? She was nearly running to beat him to the door. The rules could go hang.

She fixed herself in the doorway, hands on hips to take up the entire space, blocking the exit. He would not elude her. 'I never figured you for a quitter, Mr Lashley, or perhaps you have simply never met with a challenge you could not immediately overcome?'

'Do you know me so well as to make such a pronouncement?' Lashley folded his arms across his chest, his eyes boring into her. This was a colder, harsher Jonathon Lashley than the one she knew. The laughing golden boy of the *ton* had been transformed into something dangerously exciting. Her pulse raced, but she stood her ground.

What ground it was! She'd never been this close to him before; so close she had to look up to see his face, so close her breasts might actually brush the lapels of his coat without any contrivance on her part, so close she could smell his morning soap, all cedar and sandalwood and entirely masculine, entirely him. She'd waited her whole life to stand this close to Jonathon Lashley and, of course, it was her luck that when it happened it was because of a quarrel—a quarrel *she'd* provoked.

She'd never thought she'd fight with him, the supposed 'man of her dreams'. She'd been thinking 'never' a lot since this all started. Yesterday, she'd *never* thought they would have desperation in common. Today, she'd *never* dreamed his French would be this bad, or that she'd have trouble teaching him or that she'd quarrel with him.

'You are a very bold woman, Miss Welton.' His tone was one of cold caution. 'Yesterday you mopped up my trousers and today you are preventing me from leaving a room. One can only wonder what you might do to my person next. Perhaps tomorrow I will find myself tied to a chair and at your mercies.'

Claire flushed violently. The rather descriptive words conjured hot images of just how that might look and the mercies she might indeed invoke flooded her mind in vivid colour. Jonathon bound, his perfect cravat undone, his shirt open, those long legs wrapped about the chair, his thighs spread wide, his tight breeches unable to disguise what lay between them. Sweet heavens, where was her fan when she needed it? Where was her self-restraint? Those were thoughts for the dark of night when she was alone in her bed. But it was bright day and he was standing right in front of her, present for every one of them.

That was outside of enough. She had to stop. Claire put a tight lid on the images and stuffed them back inside whatever Pandora's box they'd sprung from. This was all his fault, every scrap and speck of it from the disastrous lesson to the heated imaginings of rope tricks involving knots and a gentleman who wasn't necessarily wearing clothes.

'You asked for it!' Claire's temper snapped. Where had *that* come from? She hadn't been this bold in years. She'd thought she'd forgotten how. Apparently not. She could lay her boldness, too, at the altar of his provocation. He was going to damn well be accountable for all of it. Great. He had her swearing now as if erotic fantasies of tying him to a chair in the middle of her father's dusty library wasn't enough. 'You wanted my help and you shall have it. You need me if you have any chance of claiming that post in Vienna!'

She ruthlessly gripped his arm and turned him around, dragging him back to the window, the furthest point from the door. If he was going to run, she'd have plenty of warning, and if he couldn't sit still, then she wouldn't belabour it. Chairs might not be the best idea just now anyway and she had to pick her battles. 'Now, we're going to go through the sentences again. This time, all you have to do is watch my mouth. Do you think you can manage that?'

Probably not. He hadn't managed to do anything right since the lesson started. He'd made an apparently lurid comment about chairs and provoked a lady to an unladylike show of temper and it was all her fault. Watching her mouth was what had caused the problem in the first place. What the hell was wrong with her? This was not the Miss Welton he knew, assuming he knew her at all?

It occurred to him that perhaps he *didn't* know her any more than he'd accused her of knowing him. What did they know of each other beyond face recognition? Before today, their adult life together consisted of encountering each other at various entertainments where politeness required he acknowledge her.

She'd been out for three Seasons. What had she

been doing all that time besides learning Turkish and blending into the wallpaper? Perhaps she *had* been tying men to chairs and having her mad way with them. She'd certainly blushed furiously enough when he'd made the remark. He'd give a guinea to know exactly what nature of thought had passed through her mind. It was always the quiet ones. And yet, he couldn't rid himself of the notion that quietness didn't come naturally to Claire Welton. It was, perhaps, an acquired skill. Interesting to think someone would want to *become* quiet.

'Are you watching me?' she insisted. 'You *have* to concentrate.' She started her French sentence all over again, having divined correctly that he'd missed it entirely.

He *was* concentrating. On her mouth. Just like she'd asked. Did she have any idea how difficult it was to stare at that wide pink mouth with its rather lush lower lip and those straight white teeth as they formed around impossible French syllables and keep his mind on the lesson? The task was nearly Herculean and it shouldn't have been.

Perhaps the question wasn't what the hell was

wrong with her, but what the hell was wrong with him? Not once in three years of polite encounters had he ever felt quite so encouraged to look at her as he did today. Today he noticed everything, not just her mouth: those sherry-amber eyes, the nut brown of her hair, the rather distracting show of firm breasts lifted temptingly high in that bodice. Pale green was an *excellent* colour on her and whoever the modiste was who did the bodices of her gowns—suffice it to say that was a job well done.

'*Répétez. Je m'appelle Claire.*' He watched her mouth form the words and he repeated the phrase, his eyes taking the opportunity to stay riveted on her lips instead of other less seemly places.

'*Juh mapel Claire.*'

'Jonathon,' she prompted softly. The sunlight through the window picked out the hidden auburn hues of her hair.

'Yes?' He lifted his eyes momentarily.

'No, not a question. I meant, you should insert your own name in the sentence. You said "Claire".'

'Right. *Juh mapel Jonathon*,' he corrected, feeling like a stupid schoolboy.

'That was lovely. It was so much better,' she complimented and he felt absurdly pleased at having mastered the simple sentence. She cocked her head to one side, studying him, and this time he couldn't escape to the window. He was already there. That look of hers, as if she was trying to fathom the depths of his soul, had unnerved him and then aroused him since the lesson had started. Certainly, women had looked at him before. Being the object of their attentions wasn't new. He knew they found him attractive: physically, fiscally, socially. His attraction was multi-faceted. But no woman ever looked at him *that* way. She wasn't measuring him, she was searching him. What did she see? That made him a little nervous.

He'd got up to move so many times she must think he had a problem. He couldn't very well explain he was moving to spare her the obvious sight of an erection well in progress. Fawn breeches had not been his friend lately. First tea, now this.

'May I ask you a few questions?' Her tone was

softer now, more ladylike as she searched. It better matched the soft shades of her eyes than the scold she'd given him. 'You can translate the language? You can write it?'

'Yes. Quite well.' A hint of defensiveness crept into his tone. Did she think him an entirely ignorant buffoon? His pride stung. For a moment he thought it might be better if she did see his erection. Better that than to think he was illiterate.

'How did you work with your tutors in the past? Did you read from sheets like the one I had for you this morning?'

'Yes, we'd read passages out of books.' He tried to guess where she was going with this. 'What does that have to do with anything, Miss Welton?' Now he was feeling defensive on behalf of his instructors. He'd had the best.

'We won't be doing that any more. I don't think it will work for you. If it was going to work, it would have worked by now.' She tapped her chin thoughtfully with one long finger. 'I have a hunch, Mr Lashley, that you may suffer from performance anxiety.'

Clearly she had not seen the state of his breeches.

'Whoa, wait a minute, Miss Welton, I assure

you I do *not* have "performance anxiety".' If anything, this morning's debacle proved just the opposite. He was fully functioning, all right, aroused by a woman he barely knew because she wore a pale-green dress and did gorgeous things with her mouth.

She gave a delicate cough. 'There are many types of performance anxiety, Mr Lashley. I am not entirely sure what sort of performance anxiety you are referring to, but I am referring to the idea that when you've spoken French in the past, you've felt as if you were on display or under judgement and it hampered your ability to perform the task.'

Jonathon gave a snort. 'And *you* can solve this problem?' He already feared she couldn't, through no fault of her own. He wasn't telling her everything about his apparent disability.

She nodded without hesitation, never suspecting he was holding out on her. 'Yes, I believe I can. It may require some unorthodox teaching methods.' Ropes and chairs came to mind unbidden. Perhaps he hadn't been wrong after all. 'We won't be sitting at tables and reading from books.' Oh, so no ropes and chairs. 'I believe reading, the presence of visual cues, has been part of the problem. When you read, you see the words, you don't hear them. You pronounce them as we would in English. While the French may have the same letters in the alphabet as the English, they don't always have the same sounds. *You* need to *hear* the language, not see it. We'll work from there.'

Jonathon raised a dark brow, in part impressed with her theory, but also doubtful. He really ought to tell her the rest of it. 'Countless tutors have tried.' It was unfair to hold back the last piece. It wasn't that he couldn't speak French. Only that he couldn't *any more*. At one time, he'd been perfectly fluent on all levels; before he'd gone to war, before he'd lost Thomas. Before his life had been put on hold.

'They haven't tried my method. Are you willing? We'll start with simply having you repeat my phrases and then we'll eventually move on to conversations where you will construct your own responses. We won't be doing any of this sitting at a table in a stuffy old room. Tomorrow, we'll walk in the gardens so you might feel more at ease, more natural.' Ah, the performance anxiety theory again. He had to give her points for trying.

The clock on the mantel chimed. It was one. The lesson was over. '*Au revoir*, Monsieur Lashley. *À la prochaine.*'

'*Alla pro-shane…* Claire.' Such familiarity was bold of him. His voice hovered over her name, drawing it out as if it were a new discovery. In its way it was precisely that. He couldn't think of her as Miss Welton any more. Miss Welton belonged to a wallflower of a woman, but this woman, the woman he'd met in the library, had been anything but retiring. This woman had fought for him. Claire Welton was *tenacious*.

He let his eyes hold hers as if she were a woman he'd met at a ball and found interesting. Something flickered in her eyes and she dropped her gaze first. Apparently tenacity had its limits and while those limits extended to throwing herself in front of doors and saying provocative things like 'performance anxiety' and 'watch my mouth', it drew the line at returning a man's extended gaze. It was an interesting dichotomy to be sure. Claire Welton was not all she seemed. She had layers.

He wouldn't mind peeling them back, not so much like peeling an onion—that just left the onion in a shambles—but like the petals of a rose, where the petals were pulled back not to ruin, but to reveal.

Chapter Five

The garden worked well for him, at least. Jonathon was more settled, more focused the next day. Claire noted immediately that the words came more freely for him now that his mind had other things to occupy his attention and he was less aware of being under scrutiny. Claire wished she could say the same for herself. She might have resolved some of his performance anxiety, but she'd not helped her own.

Garden paths weren't assisting her at all. In her desire to help him relax, she'd overlooked a few potential barriers to her own comfort, namely that the garden held an intimacy the library lacked. There were no dusty books, only the lovely faint scent of her mother's roses. There were no long tables to enforce distance, instead, they were expected to walk side by side, her hand on his arm out of necessity if not propriety, and they'd been strolling for the better part of an hour.

Be careful what you wish for. She was well aware this was the very thing she'd coveted just a few nights ago in May's drawing room: to stand beside Jonathon, to place her hand on his arm. She wouldn't lie. She *did* revel in the opportunity to be so close to him and for such an extended period of time. But it also made it hard to concentrate on anything *not* him. Still, she made a fairly good go of it. The garden—*le jardin*—provided all sorts of conversation starters and vocabulary to practise, from words like *l'arbre* to sentences like *ouvrez la porte.*

'I can imagine what that word looks like on paper.' Jonathon laughed as they practised the last sentence. '*Ouvrez*. What kind of word is that?' Today, he was the Jonathon she knew, all laughter and light and easy perfection. Gone was the cold, dangerously exciting man from the library.

'A French one and don't imagine it. I think that's your whole problem. You see the words with English eyes.' Very attractive eyes, but English none the less.

He smiled, a smile that crinkled those eyes and lit up his face when he looked at her. She felt that smile to her toes. 'Hopefully, I've proved I'm not a complete dolt.'

She heard the search for affirmation in it. How strange to think Jonathon Lashley needed that from her. Everyone adored him. Everyone found him perfect. She returned the smile and gave him the assurance he sought. 'I never thought you were.' Far from it, if only he knew. 'Now that we know we're going the right direction, it will keep getting better.'

'Everything depends on it.' They reached the end of a path, their steps bringing them to the fence on the edge of the property. Jonathon paused as they turned and she sensed the hesitation in him. 'But you know that, apparently. May I ask *how*? Yesterday, you mentioned the Vienna posting.' His dark brows drew together. 'It's not something that is widely known, at least not the part where I have to demonstrate oral competence.'

Claire worried her lip. She didn't have a good

explanation for that. She should have been more careful with what she blurted out in the heat of an argument. 'I did not mean to offend you.' She'd promised herself she would be good today. She'd been given a second chance—no mopping up spills, no blocking entrances. Nothing unladylike.

'No,' he answered quickly. 'I'm not offended, just surprised that you knew.'

'The appointment is important to you?' Claire asked, steering away from directly answering him. She didn't want to get May in trouble. They began to walk again, their steps slow as they moved towards the house. His other hand had moved to cover hers where it lay on his arm. It was a gesture he'd likely done a hundred times with any number of ladies. He was probably unaware he'd even done it. She *knew* it meant nothing and yet her mind was fixated on it, just as it fixated on the sweep of her skirts against his leg as they walked, as if they were a real couple, as if they belonged together. It was an easy fantasy to fall in to.

He nodded. 'It means everything to me. The appointment is a chance to do some good in the world. To stop war, to find peace, to rebuild a continent one decade at a time. It's a chance to make a difference.'

Claire hazarded a glance up into his face, surprised to see his merry blue eyes serious. He meant every word. Here was another brief glimpse into a different Jonathon Lashley than the one she was used to seeing.

She nodded slowly, digesting the import of his words. 'I think that's very noble.' It wasn't the passion behind them that made them noble, it was his motivation. He didn't want this for his glory, but for the good it would do others. 'You have a cause. I didn't know, didn't realise.' She wondered what else she didn't know about him. Yesterday and today had proven there were depths to plumb that went far beyond his smile and good looks.

'You're not expected to know. It's hardly an appropriate topic of discussion during the waltz or a quadrille.' Jonathon smiled, but she recognised the tactic as one of avoidance. He was trying to dismiss the topic.

Claire shot him a sideways look from beneath the brim of her bonnet. 'You've given yourself a difficult task. Empires thrive on wars, it seems. It takes war to build them up and wars inevitably follow when they collapse, leaving uncertainty in their wake.'

Jonathon nodded. 'I fear we may be losing another empire and it's too soon. The Ottomans can't last and they've been the instruments of their own downfall. It's too soon to lose them after Napoleon. There is still so much instability since 1814. I can only imagine the land grabs that would go on. It's been only seven years. If not handled correctly, Central Europe will erupt.'

She listened intently as Jonathon elaborated on Slavic states and nationalism, Phanariots and the Christian Millet. How had she not known this side of him? How *could* she have known? She'd never had any time with him, only seen him from a distance. Did *anyone* know this about him? The jolt of unlooked-for jealousy startled her. Was this a side of himself he kept strictly for those who knew him best? Claire was suddenly envious of any and all of those friends, those close enough to bear witness to his thoughts, his passions. 'And Miss Northam, does she share these opinions?' Perhaps that was the blonde beauty's appeal?

She was staring at him. He feared for a moment he'd talked her into a stupor. Usually he was so very careful not to overwhelm people with his opinions. But Claire had seemed enrapt. She'd been such a good listener. Once he'd got started, he'd felt encouraged to continue. Only when she'd asked her question did he realise how he must have run on. 'Miss Northam? Oh, no. We've never discussed it at length. She prefers to talk about fashion and society.' Jonathon answered easily as if those preferences were entirely natural and expected.

'Of course,' Claire said shortly and Jonathon recognised his mistake. For being a usually skilled diplomat, he'd managed to step on Claire's feelings with regularity. She was certainly interested in goings-on abroad. She'd learned Turkish, after all. He should have anticipated she'd view his response as a veiled reprimand.

'*I* find a well-read woman refreshing, however.

It doesn't have to be all fashion and gossip.' He hurried to cover his unintended slur.

She gave him a wry smile. 'You don't need to say that for my benefit. I am well aware my intellectual appetites are not appealing to many men. I would never ask you to pretend.' He didn't care for the coldness he heard in her voice. Had she learned that lesson the hard way? It was one more thing he didn't know about her. Had there been suitors? Had they been driven away by her inquisitive mind? Neither did he like the implication that he might be capable of duplicity.

'I never pretend,' Jonathon said solemnly. 'Do you? Were you pretending to enjoy my discourse on the Ottoman Empire?'

'Why no, I...' Her protest was drowned out by the warmth of his smile.

'I've made my point, then. We can be honest with one another.' He gave her a considering look. 'It's fair to say, though, that you are different than I expected. You're not at all what you seem.' He was pushing the boundaries of propriety now. He should stop. What he was about to say in order to justify his comment was hardly appropriate either.

Her sherry eyes narrowed in wary speculation. 'Different how?'

'In the past, I've had the distinct impression that you didn't want to be noticed.' *And your dresses have become much more attractive.*

'You can hardly have failed to notice that I am something of a bluestocking, Mr Lashley. Men don't tend to enjoy that sort of female companionship.' Her response was polite, but there was a cold honesty to her words. They'd reached the back terrace, their starting point, and arguably a signal that he should depart. Jonathon chose to ignore the signal.

'Is that why you've set yourself apart until now?' Jonathon ventured, a suspicion taking root. Had she set herself apart out of deference to her intellectualism and her desire to preserve it instead of sacrificing it to society's whim? If so, it was done at great cost to herself. She had to know such a choice would leave her unwed, alone. Her modest dresses, her quiet demeanour would have driven off any man before he got within twenty feet of her. But this Season, things had undoubtedly changed. Those dresses were certainly not designed to repel.

'Until now?' Her brow furrowed.

'May I ask, is there someone you are interested in? Do you have a suitor?' He wasn't quite ready to let go of his hypothesis that a woman dressed to impress. There was a man involved.

She looked down at her hands, suddenly uncomfortable. He should apologise, but Jonathon couldn't restrain his smile. 'So I *am* right. There is a man of interest? May I ask who it is?' Perhaps he could help things along. Maybe he could offer the man some encouragement if he saw the fellow at one of his clubs. She came off a bit aloof with her occasionally sharp tongue and sharper mind. The gentleman in question might not know she was interested. It was the least he could do for her. She was helping him. He'd like to return the favour and he could hardly *pay* her the way he would a tutor.

She shook her head. 'That is not necessary. He is unaware of my interest,' she stammered, taking great care with her words.

He pulled out his pocket watch, surprised to see that it was half past one. He'd overstayed his welcome. 'Perhaps we should make him aware. Will you be at Lady Griffin's tonight? You might save me a dance.' The fastest way to make a man notice you was to dance with another. Arrogant as it might seem to admit, women who danced with him were noticed because *he* was noticed. A flirty widow who wanted more than a waltz from him had once told him matchmaking mamas sat in a corner keeping lists of his partners.

'Oh, no! I couldn't.' She was truly aghast.

He would not let her withdraw. 'Come now, I'm not proposing we drag him out into an alley and beat some sense into him.' Although maybe the fellow needed it if he was oblivious to Claire's charms.

'Well, if you put it that way, *je voudrais rien de plus.*' She gave him a little curtsy. 'Nothing would please me more.'

He could think of a few things that would please *him* better than a dance. Perhaps a kiss. The errant thought struck him hard. He wanted to kiss Claire Welton? It was admittedly a bit more tame than yesterday's chairs and ropes, but *where* had *that* idea come from? She was his French tutor, nothing more.

Perhaps it was mere male curiosity. Now that

there was another man involved, perhaps he wanted to know what he was missing. There was a difference between wondering and wanting. Wondering was objective and wanting was not. There was that dress to consider, too. She'd worn a deep-yellow gown today, the shade of daffodils, and it brought out the glow of her skin and the darkness of her hair. She looked positively radiant, a beam of sunshine that drew the eye. Jonathon drew a breath. He was a healthy young male. It was natural to be drawn to a pretty girl.

A stray curl had come down and tickled her cheek. Jonathon reached out and pushed it back behind her ear without thinking. 'Until tonight, then. I am looking forward to our dance. Whoever the man is, he's a fool not to have noticed you.'

To his surprise, the compliment did not please her. 'Do you know me so well then after a few days' acquaintance?'

'I've known you far longer than that.' His tone was sharper now, sensing an argument coming and warming to it. When it came to discussing herself, she was prickly, defensive. 'We played together as children.'

That brought a flush to her face. 'Please don't remember it. We chased you and Preston. There was very little playing involved. We must have been very annoying little girls. A past acquaintance does not require you to say things you don't mean.'

How do you know I don't mean them? He was tempted to say the words for the sake of the debate, but where the words would please another sort of woman, the response would only insult Claire. She was too smart for such elementary banter. She would not accept empty flattery. Most women would. Cecilia Northam certainly would. She ate up compliments like chocolate. He kept her well supplied with both. It was the simplest way to keep her in good spirits. He had enough experience with women to know he should quit while he was ahead.

Jonathon made his bow, determined to leave before he could lose the argument entirely. 'Think what you like, Miss Welton, I shall look forward to seeing you tonight.'

Chapter Six

Jonathon had asked her to dance! Not even the knowledge that the request had come from some notion he harboured about helping her could diminish Claire's good spirits. She stood on the sidelines of the Griffin ball with her friends, fairly bristling with energy at the prospect and feeling pretty in the most recent of Evie's re-made creations: delicate cream lace discreetly highlighting the elegance of her olive silk—a gown that had not lived up to its potential with its old black trimmings and higher neckline.

Around them, gentlemen flocked to ladies, filling in the tiny dance cards that hung from delicate wrists while their own cards remained woefully unpopulated except for the usual. Preston had scrawled his name on an obligatory country set. May's brother always did his duty as did a distant cousin or two of Evie's, but it was nothing like the traffic of gentlemen gathered around Cecilia and her coterie of young ladies, all of them deemed the *ton*'s finest flowers. She'd gathered them all to her and Claire felt a brief stab of envy. What would it be like to be sought after? Adored by the masses? Ladies eager to see what you wore? Gentlemen hanging on every word? She knew it wasn't well done of her to be selfish *and* covetous, especially when she had chosen this path. After her less-than-successful debut, she'd chosen not to engage society. If society now chose not to engage with her, it was merely following her lead.

A horrid thought took her. What if Jonathon followed that lead? What if he'd changed his mind and thought better of dancing with her? The old insecurities, born of a miserable proposal, and a cruel girl's prank, flooded back. What if he'd taken one look at Cecilia Northam this evening and decided he had better things to do and better people to spend the evening with? That was the problem with re-engaging, she had to face those old demons.

'Miss Welton, you look particularly lovely this evening.' Suddenly Jonathon was there, standing before her, bending over her hand, elegant in his dark evening clothes, his smile warm as his errant lock of hair fell forward, the imperfection serving to make him look more handsome.

'Mr Lashley, good evening.' Her smile was so wide she could feel it at the far corners of her face. He had not forgotten her.

'I would like to request the honour of a dance. That is, if you have any left?' His eyes glanced expectantly to where her card hung from her wrist.

'Of course. It would be my pleasure.' *There's plenty to pick from.* She watched as he wrote his name next to the fifth dance of the night, a waltz, and tried to stay cool while her insides were a crazy mess of excitement. Jonathon was going to waltz with her! Surely that alone was worth the cost of actively rejoining polite society.

'Is your young man here?' Jonathon leaned in conspiratorially, the sandalwood of his *toilette* captivating her. For a moment the reference confused her. Then she remembered.

'Um, yes.' *Standing right in front of me, actually.*

'Then perhaps we should take a stroll about the ballroom before our dance.' Jonathon smiled and offered her his arm. He gave her a friendly wink. 'We can practise our French.'

'This was actually a very good idea, Mr Lashley,' Claire said as they concluded their rotation of the room. She'd relaxed, falling easily into the role of instructor as they strolled.

Jonathon laughed. 'I am known to have good ideas on occasion.'

'I got to see you in your native habitat. You did well. Your French is coming along nicely,' Claire complimented. He had done so well, in fact, that it had given her other ideas for improving their instruction.

'My native habitat? You make me sound like a zoo exhibit.' His eyes twinkled as he teased her.

'I don't mean to. Truly, I don't think I've ever seen you uncomfortable in any setting.' The words were out before she could take them back for being too bold. He seemed to bring the boldness out in her without even trying. Maybe he even brought out the crazy.

He acknowledged the words with a nod, his eyes losing some of their shine. 'You are too kind. I suppose a ballroom is my native habitat these days. I spend enough time in them.' She wondered if he would have said more if the orchestra hadn't chosen that moment to strike up for the fifth dance. 'I believe that's our cue, Miss Welton.' His smile was back in place, his eyes bright again as he led her out on to the floor, taking up a spot in the centre.

Claire felt her throat tighten. 'Everyone can see us.'

'That's the point, isn't it?' His grin was infectious as his hand slid to her back, firm and confident as he guided her into position.

Claire felt a moment of panic creep up. 'It's been ages since I've waltzed.' Not since her debut ball, in fact. What if she tripped? What if she stepped on his toes? What if she didn't remember the steps?

'You think too much.' Jonathon laughed, reading her every thought. 'I won't let you fall.'

'Easy for you to say!' Claire whispered frantically. 'You waltz every night.'

'You could, too.' Jonathon arched a meaningful eyebrow as the music began. He moved them into the dance, his hand signalling her to move with him. Hesitantly, her feet followed, her body followed, picking up the rhythm. Jonathon made it easy to remember. He waltzed as well as he did everything else, effortlessly making adjustments.

'You're doing splendidly! You're a wonderful dancer.' Jonathon took them through the first turn. 'Why don't you dance more often?'

It was a good question. It was hard to remember why when she was whirling away in Jonathon's arms. Dancing was liberating. The first time she'd waltzed, she'd felt as if she were flying. She felt that way tonight, only better. This wasn't flying, it was soaring. 'I don't know. I just stopped.'

His eyes held hers, bright and merry. 'Maybe it's time to "just start" again.'

Maybe it was. But dancing required partners and partners required calling attention to oneself. She'd given up drawing attention years ago.

It was too risky. It would have to be enough to enjoy this moment for the singular event it was, something she didn't expect would ever happen again.

Jonathon was an exquisite partner in all ways. Never once did his eyes stray from her, never did his conversation falter, or his grip slacken. His interest stayed entirely fixed on her. Even in a room crowded with people, there was an intimacy to his attentions.

It was over all too soon. The dance ended and she could think of no way to keep him with her. He'd already walked with her, danced with her. He returned her to the sidelines and took his leave with a promise to see her the next day. He gave her another flash of that dazzling smile and was gone. It was all very proper. What had she expected? Did she think he'd claim a second dance? Take her in for supper? Spend the rest of the evening practising French as they strolled among the guests?

They were silly notions when he had Cecilia waiting for him and other obligations requiring his attention. For a man like him, a man with ambitions, these evenings were for work as well as pleasure. There were people to meet and to impress, networks to be established. Europe to be saved. Claire smiled to herself. How many others knew what dreams he harboured? It felt good to think that for a little while, maybe she knew a piece of Jonathon no one else did. It could be her secret.

Where did that leave her? Considering the weighty matters that occupied his mind, she wasn't sure where she stood on his list of priorities. How had he viewed tonight's dance? Was she another piece of work he had to conduct or was she part of the pleasure? Something he *chose* to do or *had* to do? She didn't want to think about it for fear the answer would tarnish the perfection of the moment. She wanted to be part of the pleasure for him, as he'd been for her.

May tugged at her hand. 'You're practically glowing so it must have been as good as it looked. Come to the retiring rooms and tell us all about it.'

The girls were excited, talking over each over on the trip down the hall. 'You looked beautiful, Claire. No one could take their eyes off the pair of you!' Evie exclaimed.

'Even Cecilia,' May offered pointedly. 'She left the ballroom halfway through.'

'Even Lashley. His eyes were on you the whole time.' Beatrice's voice was wistful.

'He has that way about him. He knows how to make everyone feel special, not just me.' Claire tried to establish some perspective. As much as she'd like to believe in the romance her friends were intent on seeing, she had to be practical or she'd get hurt by her own fantasy. 'It was only a dance.'

'She's right, you know.' Crisp tones sounded from the doorway of the retiring rooms. Cecilia floated in, her entourage of debutantes filing in behind her. She sat down in front of a vanity and studied her hair. 'Good evening, Claire. It's good to see at least one of you has any sense.' She smiled in the mirror and Claire felt her neck prickle in warning. Claire fought the urge to leave the room before she found out what the warning was for, but Beatrice gripped her hand, a clear message that they would not be chased away.

'My dear Lashley is terribly good with people. He can charm anyone.' Cecilia reached in to her reticule for a small comb, everything about her suggesting this was merely a casual conversation. She used the gesture to study Claire. 'Olive is a much better colour on you than pink. Much quieter. I do think your style is improving.'

Claire flushed. With just a few words, Cecilia brought it all rushing back: the humiliation, the cut, the laughter, as if it had happened yesterday and not three years ago.

'Make no mistake, you looked lovely with Lashley tonight, but he can make anyone look good.' Cecilia glanced around at the group of girls with her, making sure she had all their attention. 'I just love wearing Lashley. He's my new favourite colour.' She paused to let the girls giggle in adoration of her wit. She tilted her head to one side, catching Claire in the crosshairs of a considering glance. Claire stiffened at the attention, wishing she didn't feel such a thread of fear, that she was somehow finer, braver, than Cecilia's threats. 'Well done, Claire. If I was only going to dance once in an evening, I'd choose him, too.'

Cecilia laughed, a half-hearted attempt at sounding self-deprecating. 'What am I saying?

I get to dance all the dances I want and I *still* choose him.'

Claire felt her face burn. She heard Cecilia's implication. *Once again, we've chosen the same thing and once again I have triumphed over you, a bluestocking from the country. I looked better in pink and I look better on Jonathon's arm.*

The girls with Cecilia tittered. Cecilia leaned towards them, feigning confidentiality. 'We'd dance all the dances if society allowed it. As it is, I have to settle for just two until it's official.' Cecilia sighed dramatically. Her entourage sighed with her.

Claire wanted to gag. The false sweetness was sickening. Did no one else see through Cecilia's façade? Worse than the saccharine sweetness was the way she objectified Jonathon, as if he were a prize to be won, a handsome ornament and nothing more.

The girl next to her giggled. 'You're so lucky to be marrying him. I wish my father would find me a man just like him instead of gouty old barons.' Marry him? Was it as final as all that? The words hovered in the air, arrows looking for the target of her heart.

Cecilia tapped the girl lightly on the arm. 'But that's impossible, Lizzie,' she teased. 'There's no one quite like Lashley.' Cecilia gave Claire a sly smile. 'Isn't that right, Claire?'

Claire had no answer. She was still reeling from the news. It was one thing to suspect Cecilia was meant for Jonathon. It was another, entirely different and awful thing to hear those speculations voiced so casually out loud from the source itself. It became real, no longer just the purvey of gossips. A punch to the stomach would have been just as effective in knocking the wind from her, the news was that devastating.

'Why don't you just shut up?' Beatrice stepped forward, arms crossed over her chest, her dark eyes hot, looking every inch an avenging Fury. There was a collective intake of breath throughout the room. No one spoke to Cecilia Northam that way. One word from Cecilia and she could ruin your Season. Claire was living proof of it and she hadn't even been the one to copy the dress, Cecilia had.

'*What* did you say to me?' Cecilia rose slowly

from the stool in front of the vanity, eyes narrowed for combat.

'I said, "shut up".' Beatrice was unwavering and why not? Claire stifled a little smile. Cecilia's threats wouldn't work here. Cecilia had no idea she couldn't possibly ruin Beatrice's Season any more than it already was.

'May I ask why?' Cecilia looked down her nose, a supercilious stare designed to intimidate after hours of practice in the mirror. Everything about Cecilia was designed, from the hair to the stare, everything calculated to gain maximum results. 'Does the truth offend you?'

'Oh? Then he has asked for your hand? I must have missed the announcement in *The Times*,' Beatrice retorted with false sweetness. 'Which issue was that in?'

Claire felt a little thrill of victory flicker through her at Cecilia's hesitation. She felt envy, too—she wanted to be brave like Beatrice, brave enough to back Cecilia to the proverbial wall. Beatrice had her there. Cecilia didn't dare lie. She would look foolish if she claimed such a thing.

'Everyone knows it's just a matter of time.'

'*Everyone* knows? Not me. I don't think Lashley will offer for you at all. I can imagine what you see in him, but I *can't* imagine what he sees in you.' Beatrice took another step closer to Cecilia, they were nearly toe to toe now.

'Everyone who *counts* knows,' Cecilia snarled, her lip turning up, wrecking the pretty features of her face. It was an ugly expression. Claire had never seen Cecilia appear less then perfectly beautiful but there was no beauty now. However, she had seen Beatrice angry before, once, when the former village butcher had cheated a poor woman out of a good cut of meat. Beatrice had railed at him for his unfair treatment and when that had failed, Beatrice had put a butcher knife to his privates. Needless to say, the butcher had relented and the woman had gone home with an excellent ham for free.

'Who would that be? Your father? Is he going to buy you a husband like he bought you a pony? You are nothing without his money, his title.' Beatrice hurled her insult. Claire saw something flash in Cecilia's eyes. For a moment Claire almost felt sorry for her, but then Cecilia's gaze turned in her direction. Cecilia stepped back from Beatrice and smoothed her lavender skirts.

'I don't care what you believe, Beatrice Penrose. Claire knows the truth. She knows what tonight was: a charity dance. Lashley was doing his duty, nothing more, although what he thinks he owes you for is beyond me.' She flicked open her fan with a snap and headed for the door. 'Come, ladies. I believe *our* dance cards are full and the gentlemen are waiting.'

'What a bitch!' May exhaled, flopping into a chair in relief. 'Good Lord, Beatrice, I thought she was going to hit you.' May snickered. 'You made her leave the room, Bea. She might pretend it was all her doing, but she had to retreat. It just proves there's a first time for everything.'

'You shouldn't have,' Claire gently scolded her friend. 'She'll make life difficult for you.'

Beatrice snorted. 'I'm pregnant and unmarried—how much more difficult can life get? I have precisely two more months before I'm packed off to the wilds of some place where my family can forget I'm giving birth to a bastard.'

'Oh, Bea, is it that bad?' Claire knelt beside

her, clasping Bea's hands. 'We won't let them send you away.'

'We'll go with you, if they do,' Evie chimed in.

Beatrice smiled, over-bright. 'Let's not talk about me. Let's talk about Lashley and Claire and what comes next.'

Claire stood up, suddenly feeling tired. 'Maybe we could talk later. I think I'd like to go home.' She had danced with Jonathon, shared a stroll with him, Beatrice had bested Cecilia. They were all reasons for celebration, but that didn't mean some of her joy hadn't gone out of the evening anyway.

Chapter Seven

The carriage was waiting for her at the head of queue at the kerb. The Welton family driver knew her habits. She never stayed long at these affairs and he parked close so she could make a quick getaway.

Claire leaned back against the squabs, drawing a lap robe over her legs more for comfort than for warmth in the spring evening. It was always a getaway. The last three years had been one getaway after another. At first getaways had been her solution. But now, they were fast becoming her problem. In hindsight, she could see the pattern. She was always retreating. At first, retreating had been a defence mechanism, a means of protecting herself, but then that very means of protection had become the means by which she'd started to lose herself.

What had Jonathon said? *You are different than I thought.* He thought she was quiet, submissive, unobtrusive. She was not naturally any of those things. But she'd become them until she wasn't entirely sure who she was any more. Was she quiet Claire, who stood on the sidelines watching others dance, or was she bold Claire, who wore new dresses and scolded handsome men who wouldn't do their French lessons?

She simply didn't know. She knew who she wanted to be, though. She wanted to be the latter; a woman who could fight for what she wanted, a woman who wouldn't back down to Cecilia because of a moment's embarrassment years ago. That was the woman Jonathon would notice. That was a woman Claire could respect.

But how to be someone she'd hadn't been for years? Someone she might never have been? The road back would be difficult and scary. There would be fits and starts. There would be successes and failures, and those would, by necessity, be public. There would be witnesses and there would be Cecilia, ready to remind her at every turn.

Claire closed her eyes as the coach bounced over the dark London streets. She forced the painful memory to materialise. It had started nicely enough; the happy laughter of a party, girls exclaiming over one another's gowns, the Season still new and fresh, the ballroom sparkling with light, young men lining up for dance cards, for *her* dance card. Her hair was done in an elegant sweeping up-do, her grandmother's pearls proudly at her neck, an understated complement to the pale-pink gown that had arrived from the dressmaker's that afternoon in a white box.

She was beside herself with excitement: Her first ball gown that wasn't white. She'd loved it on sight in the pattern books, had patiently stood for hours of fittings until the gown was just right. She felt magical in it, as if she could command a room. She laughed at something Jerome Kerr had said and the room about her suddenly went silent. The crowd parted, forming a phalanx, and at the other end stood Cecilia

Northam, blonde and regal in a gown identical in colour and cut to hers—her dream gown, worn by another. Not just *any* other, but a girl poised to be a Diamond of the First Water. Now that girl stood ten paces away, facing her not unlike a duellist.

'Very pretty, Claire, but even so, I wear it better. Pink is more my colour than yours.'

Cecilia fired first and the words were deadly. Everyone had laughed. People had backed off, leaving her alone to face Cecilia. Only Claire hadn't faced it. Young and unprepared, Claire had fled.

Claire opened her eyes, regretting for the thousandth time her choice that night. She'd fled and let the incident become her legacy. Now she was stuck with it. It would have to be overcome, only there was so much more of it to overcome. That moment had defined her. She'd made choices and those choices had changed her.

She'd withdrawn from society and now she wanted to re-engage. In order to do that, she would have to face her fears, have to face Cecilia. The road back, the road to Jonathon, was through Cecilia Northam. Claire might have been brave enough once, but now? She didn't know. She should have gone back in, faced whatever scrutiny was thrown her way and got it over with.

Nothing will change until we do. Could she change again? She wished with all her heart she'd never left the ballroom that night.

Claire hadn't returned to the ballroom. He'd been watching long enough to conclude she wasn't coming back. The realisation stole some of the excitement from the evening. Jonathon excused himself from the group he was with and sought the relative quiet of the hall. Anyone out there was too busy with their own concerns to pay him much mind and that was fine with him. He was poor company at the moment; restless and suddenly dissatisfied with the evening. He gave a short nod to an acquaintance just arriving and kept moving before the man could engage him. He didn't feel particularly social at the moment.

Why did it matter if Claire hadn't returned?

He'd danced with her. His self-imposed duty was done. Perhaps, even now, she was dancing with her suitor. He could devote his evening to Cecilia without interruption. But was it really a duty if it was self-imposed? No one had made him dance with her. He'd *wanted* to. He'd offered. And he'd *enjoyed* it. More than enjoyed it. She'd actually looked at him when they danced instead of peering over his shoulder to see who was watching them.

Cecilia constantly looked around the room and whispered a social commentary in his ear. *'Amelia Parks is wearing yellow—why does she persist? It's such an awful colour for her...makes her look sallow, and she needs all the help she can get or she'll lose Robert Farley. Bertie Bagnold is dancing with Miss Jellison again. I think he'll offer for her soon. She can't expect to do better...'*

The comparison was poorly done of him and not for the first time. He'd held Cecilia up to Claire Welton earlier in the garden. Cecilia Northam was all he'd been raised to desire in a mate; lovely—there was none more beautiful if a man preferred the idea that beauty was de-

fined as blonde and blue eyed; socially astute—
she was perhaps the most well-informed young
woman in any ballroom. She knew who was
courting whom, who would be successful and
who would fail, she knew what to wear, how and
when to wear it. She would never embarrass him
at any occasion, never contradict him in public,
unlike a certain sherry-eyed miss.

But in private, she could be petulant. He'd
been raised to understand that was the nature
of women, too. His father had suggested as much
with a weary sigh. It was the price men paid for
a hostess, someone to grace their table, make
guests feel at ease, run their homes, raise their
children and ensure the continuance of their
line. In exchange, a man offered that woman
his home, his title, his money, his name, his patience, for the rest of his life. It was difficult to
imagine Claire fitting that image. She would be
empathetic, listening carefully and contributing
a thoughtful opinion. He laughed at himself. His
father would be quick to disabuse him of such
a fantasy.

Marriage in the echelons of the *ton* simply
wasn't meant to be that way. It was meant to

be a compromise, a trading of tasks and goods. It was interesting to note what was left off that list; neither offered the other loyalty, fidelity, affection, devotion, care. The old question that had plagued him raised itself again—shouldn't marriage be more? He'd been thinking about that often lately. It was probably due to the social pressure he was under.

Lord Belvoir had stopped by at the club yesterday to subtly talk about Cecilia and his posting to Vienna. It had all appeared very casual, but Jonathon knew better. There were expectations in that direction. A wife was essential to a diplomat abroad, especially in a city like Vienna where navigating the social whirl was the key to political success.

He needed a wife by August, just as he needed oral fluency in French, one more thing to check off his packing list. Thinking of it that way seemed so impersonal. While his valet was busy acquiring trunks and clothing, he was supposed to be busy acquiring French and a wife, *sa femme*. Claire would be proud of him for thinking in French.

'Lashley, there you are!' Cecilia crossed the

hall with purpose and latched on to his arm, a bright smile on her face. 'The supper dance is coming up and I didn't want to miss it.' She dropped her voice to a conspiratorial low tone. 'It's my favourite time of night, because I get you all to myself.' He remembered how it had once felt to hear her utter those words and look up at him with those eyes—like he'd won a prize. This evening, there was the faintest hint of dread in hearing them, his restlessness raising its head.

When had the thought of Cecilia become tarnished instead of tolerable? Probably when he'd started attaching words like 'for ever' and 'marriage' to her. Jonathon forced a smile. 'Do you suppose they'll have lobster patties?'

She laughed uncertainly at the remark, unsure how to interpret it. Taken literally, it was the question of an idiot. Taken with the slight undertone of sarcasm as he'd intended, it might pass as a dry joke, a commentary on the sameness of every evening. 'They always have lobster patties.' Cecilia covered her uncertainty with a bright smile.

His point exactly. There wasn't a party all Season that didn't have the required delicacy. Everything was the same: every night, every day, the same routine of clubs and activities until now. This week there'd finally been a crack in the routine: Vienna and Claire. He was in a sour mood. It was unfair to take it out on Cecilia.

He had to stop the negativity. He had to remember Cecilia was part of that dream, too. He needed her on his arm to succeed in Vienna; a pretty hostess who could organise parties and make guests feel welcome; a wife who could run a flawless house and command the servants while still looking like perfection at the head of his table; a wife with strong connections to policy makers in England. He would need all that and more. Going to Vienna was about peace in his time certainly. But it was more than that. It was a chance to know at last what had happened to his brother. For the first time, he'd have the authority and resources to retrace his brother's last steps.

Jonathon clasped Cecilia's hand and gave her his best smile to soften the blow. He just needed a night to himself, a night to settle his thoughts. 'Will you pardon me? I am terrible company this evening. I could not do your sparkling presence justice. I have papers I need to go over for the morning. I'm going to call it an early night.' He let go and walked away without looking back. His native habitat could do without him for a while.

Chapter Eight

'*You* left the ball. Early. Not long after we danced.' The words brought Claire to an abrupt halt in the garden, forcing Jonathon to stop beside her. After speaking French for the past hour, the English words sounded markedly out of place, almost jarringly so. But perhaps more jarring was the subject matter. They'd been practising a conversation about flowers to give Jonathon a chance to use his vocabulary of colours and adjectives. This conversational topic was definitely a non sequitur.

'I'm surprised you noticed.' She played with the soft petals of a rose, idly stroking its velvety surface and trying not to look at Jonathon. It was difficult looking at him today, remembering their dance, the heavenly feel of his hand at her back guiding her through the patterns, and then Cecilia's cruel words ruining the most delightful waltz she'd ever experienced. The girl who was meant to wear Evie's new dresses would not be bothered by any of it. But the girl she was out of those dresses couldn't ignore the words.

'No worries. I left early, too. Shh… Don't tell anyone.' Jonathon's voice was a conspirator's whisper, friendly laughter humming beneath the surface of his words. 'Your friends came back in from wherever you had all gone, but you weren't with them.' There was a spark in his eye. This time she heard the teasing in his voice. 'Might I hope our dance bore fruit?'

If you count sour lemons. Your soon-to-be fiancée reminded me our dance was a charity project. But that clearly was not what he was referring to. It took her a moment to understand his meaning. Ah, he meant the 'suitor' she was trying to impress.

When she hesitated, he became concerned. 'I hope your gentleman wasn't upset?'

'No, he wasn't upset.' Definitely true. Jonathon hadn't appeared fazed by their dance one way or another, and why would he be?

Jonathon seemed perplexed by her answer, however. It was clearly not the outcome he'd expected. 'Did he see us dancing? And he didn't whisk you off to the terrace to politely stake his claim on your attentions before he lost you to another?'

The image was so ridiculous the laughter slipped out before she could stop it. 'Good heavens, what sort of life do you imagine I lead? I hardly have a dance card full of jealous suitors vying for my attentions.'

'You are sure he saw us dancing?'

'Yes.' Not a lie, but just barely the truth. She knew full well he would misconstrue the answer. She kept her attentions fixed on the rose.

'Well, good.' Jonathon sounded staunchly positive beside her. 'Maybe that's something your oblivious suitor should see again, say tonight at Lady Rosedale's.'

Another dance, another chance at heaven. Only this time, she knew the price for it. She was leading him on, letting him believe there was a gentleman of interest. She was leading herself, too. But this time she couldn't pretend it was a fantasy come to life. She ought to put a stop to it. No good could come of stealing more dances with Jonathon Lashley. She was supposed to win his heart by teaching him French, not by dancing with him. 'I don't want charity, Mr Lashley. I can manage my affairs on my own.' A poor choice of words perhaps.

She felt him stiffen beside her. 'Charity, is it?' Now she'd offended him. There probably wasn't a woman in the *ton* who viewed a dance with him as charity. 'Are these French lessons charity? Perhaps I have misunderstood the nature of our association.'

'They're not charity, you came to me asking for assistance,' Claire stammered. She could see where this was going and she had no grounds for argument. She could speak four languages and yet she couldn't carry on a decent, logical conversation with one attractive man in English.

He gave a 'my point exactly' smile. 'Neither is dancing with you. Dancing, like French lessons, is merely two friends helping one another achieve their goals.' He gave another considering pause. 'We are friends, are we not?'

Claire tried to ignore twin sensations that thought evoked—one of them warm and lovely over the thought of being considered Jonathon Lashley's friend, the other one slightly more practical. 'I am your French tutor for the time being. Nothing more.'

That gave Jonathon pause. She had him there, but there was no triumph in it. She wasn't sure she wanted to be right. Being right certainly didn't help her cause. She wasn't supposed to be driving him away, but drawing him in. Beatrice would kick her if she was here.

'Is that what you do? Push people away by telling them how inconsequential you are?' Jonathon drawled slowly. 'No doubt, it's a very effective strategy. I feel obliged, however, to tell you it won't work on me.' He gave her a devilish wink. 'In fact, the effect is quite the opposite. You intrigue me. What are you hiding that must be so vociferously protected?' He grinned. 'Claire Welton, do you have secrets?'

I've been crazy about you since I was nine. 'I hate to disappoint you, but I'm pretty much an open book.' Her throat was dry and the words stuck.

Jonathon laughed. 'You're a terrible liar, Claire. Don't ever try out for espionage work.' He waggled his dark eyebrows in dramatic humour. 'Everyone has secrets.'

'Even you?' She couldn't resist. It was so much fun to play with him like this. He was alarmingly easy to be with. But she'd known that, she'd always known that. It had been a large part of his appeal from the start. More than being good-looking, Jonathon was good company, a rather subtle trait others took for granted.

He put a hand over his heart in mock shock. '*Moi?* Why, Miss Welton, what a leading question! Are you implying my reputation as a gentleman isn't pristine?'

She shot him a coy look, daring a bit of flirtation. 'Well, is it? Pristine?' She had a sudden urge to know his secrets, to know a piece of him that no one else knew. She'd had a taste of that unknown and she was hungry for another.

There'd been years when he'd been gone, war years. A thought occurred. 'What do *you* know of espionage, Mr Lashley?' she joked.

'If I knew anything at all I certainly couldn't tell you. It would defeat the purpose.' His tone was light, but some of the twinkle had gone out of his eye. Perhaps she'd dared too much. She hadn't thought.

'I forget sometimes that you've been to war,' Claire offered, hoping he'd hear the apology in her words. She'd been miserable when he'd gone away. 'It is difficult to picture you as a soldier.' That smile, the tailored clothes, the immaculate *toilette*, all bespoke the well-kept heir, not the soldier.

'Good.' His grin was back in full force. 'Then I have succeeded.' He bent to pluck a rose from a bush. 'War is not something anyone should be constantly reminded of. Will you permit me?' He tucked the blossom in her hair, his fingers brushing the top of her ear. The delicate contact made her shiver. What a dichotomy he was: the warrior, the gentleman, one with perfect manners, the other for whom manners would be a negligible thing. One was safe. The other was dangerous, a man who had seen and done worldly things, who could do those worldly things to her. Another shiver took her. If only the gentleman in him would allow it.

'Now you know one of my secrets, Claire. You

must let me guess one of yours.' Jonathon tapped
a finger against his chin and studied her.

'But I don't have any,' she protested, suddenly flustered. *Would* he guess? How morti-
fying would that be? She would have to deny it.
He had not moved away after tucking the flower
behind her ear. He stood close, his dark head
cocked. She scarcely dared to breathe.

'I know,' he said after a while. 'Have you ever
been kissed, Claire?'

That was even more embarrassing. Maybe he
should have asked if he was her secret crush
instead. 'I cannot possibly answer that. A lady
never tells.' Claire took refuge in the high moral
ground.

'Correction.' Jonathon leaned an arm against a
low-hanging branch, his posture lazy and close.
'A lady never tells just anyone. A lady might en-
deavour to tell a friend.'

Back to that, were they? It seemed this conversation had started out with such a discussion
before it had meandered in this very dangerous
direction. How had they gone from French lessons, to a game of twenty private questions?
'I had a marriage proposal once.' There was

no good answer. If she said no, he would think her prudish, a dried-up stick. If she said yes, he might think she was loose.

He wagged a scolding finger. 'Tut-tut, Claire. That's not what I'm asking. Have. You. Ever. Been. Kissed?' There were dangerous glints of mischief in his blue eyes now.

She wanted to take a step back, but there was nowhere to go. She dropped her eyes. If she said no, would he kiss her now to remedy it? She hoped not. She didn't want a charity kiss any more than she'd wanted a charity waltz. And yet, she did want him to kiss her. Just not like that.

'Ah,' Jonathon said softly. 'I have my answer. Never fear, Claire. It will happen when it should.' He dropped his voice low. 'Now, we know each other's secrets. We are really truly friends.'

She should let it be. But the statement provoked Claire. Couldn't he see how impossible it truly was? 'Men and women being friends? Is such a thing realisic, Mr Lashley?' She moved the discussion back to the intellectual high ground where she was more comfortable. *This* was a debate she could win, although at the moment she wasn't sure why it was so important *to* win it.

They began walking again and she was glad to give her body something to do besides look at him, besides imagining a kiss that couldn't happen. 'Society doesn't think so. It has numerous rules in place to keep men and women apart aside from the purpose of marriage.' She made her case. 'For instance, does Miss Northam know you visit me daily for French lessons?' There. That would be a bucket of cold water on a conversation that had gone astray. She already knew the answer. Cecilia had no idea how Jonathon spent his mornings. Most didn't. It was a source of embarrassment for him. To have those lessons from her, a wallflower out for three years and a noted bluestocking, would further that humiliation no matter how neat the bloodlines of her birth. 'How would Miss Northam feel if she did know?' Another rhetorical question. She already knew the answer. 'Miss Northam would see me as competition.'

'But that's ludicrous!' Jonathon began his rebuttal and she tried not to be hurt by the truth. It *was* ludicrous. The old doubts surfaced. How could she possibly compete with Cecilia Northam? Why would a man like Jonathon, who had everything, have an illicit interest in some-one like her when he had Cecilia draped on his arm.

And yet, it was what she'd hoped for, wasn't it? Had waited years for: a moment when Jona-thon would see her for herself and love her for it.

'I think we should prove them wrong,' Jona-thon said. 'We should declare ourselves friends and we can start by dispensing with the "Mr Lashley" bit. Let us be Jonathon and Claire,' he declared with an elaborate expansiveness that made her smile as he stuck out his hand.

She took Jonathon's hand and shook it, meet-ing his warm eyes. Oh, foolish, foolish hope. She was too late. Cecilia had all but claimed him. She was setting herself up for failure and heartbreak and she couldn't seem to stop herself from doing it. Just for a moment, she let herself believe in the impossible: He'd missed her. He had noticed she'd left the ball and then he'd left early, too. *He found her intriguing.* Those were words she could live on for the rest of her life.

What the hell was he doing, asking for friend-ship from the likes of Claire Welton when he knew better the impossibility of such a thing? Jonathon was still asking himself the question as he walked down Bond Street that afternoon.

It wasn't just the social impossibility of such a friendship. Claire had made good points there and he felt compelled to agree with her. Men simply weren't friends with young, unmarried women of good breeding, especially when the man in question was committed to another.

Well, that was arguable. He wasn't *technically* committed to Cecilia. Even as his mind made the debate he felt guilty. He was playing with semantics now. But who could blame him? Claire had caught him entirely unprepared: the feel of her in his arms as they danced, the look in those sherry eyes, all of that intelligence, all of that innocence turned on him. It had been a heady combination on the dance floor. Hell, after a week of lessons, it was becoming a heady sensation wherever she was: the garden, the ballroom, the library. He wouldn't for a moment suggest Claire Welton was naïve. Naiveté implied the person in question was unworldly and she was far too intelligent to ever be that. She was merely untried, her desires and dreams untested beyond the confines of her quiet life.

And she was ready to test them. The answer came to him so suddenly he nearly tripped over a crack in the pavement. The new clothes, the desire to actively pursue her erstwhile suitor. It was all there. She was ready to break out of her self-imposed exile, a butterfly emerging from the cocoon, still somewhat fragile, still learning the powerful of its wings, its beauty. After all, she'd left early for whatever reason. She had not told him why she'd left, but since it hadn't been to sneak off to the terrace with her beau, he could only conclude that the lack of success in that regard had encouraged her flight.

Jonathon stopped outside the window of his usual florist's on Bond Street, studying the blooms on display. He could help her with the metamorphosis and not only with dances. The bell over the door jingled as he entered the exclusive Bond Street florist. The man behind the counter looked up from where he stood arranging a bouquet of yellow and white daisies, one of a hundred he did daily for the aspiring debutantes of the *ton* and their hopeful suitors.

'Ah, Mr Lashley!' He wiped his hands on his wide apron and hustled forward with a smile. 'Have you come for something for your lovely girl?'

'Yes, the usual for Miss Northam, if you please.' He always sent a bouquet of pale pink roses, her signature colour, to Cecilia on the days she and her mother hosted their at home. 'And the irises in the window, I'd like to send them to a second address.' He pulled out his card case from the pocket of his coat. 'Perhaps, you could mix in something yellow to go with them?' He wrote a short sentence carefully in French on the back of his card. 'Send this with it.'

Phipps nodded. If he thought anything above the ordinary about two separate orders to two separate women, he gave nothing away. 'I have some daffodils that have just arrived.'

'I leave it to your discretion, Phipps.' It would be a vibrant but sophisticated arrangement, not a mere debutante's bouquet. 'I would like them delivered this afternoon.'

Jonathon signed the bill, feeling very smug imagining Claire's surprise when the flowers arrived, and then the surprise of her suitor when the man realised he couldn't take her affections for granted, that there was, perhaps, another hound at the hunt. He had expected the action to leave him with a feeling of accomplishment. He'd done something to help a friend. But the feeling eluded him. Why did he feel more like a dog in a manger than that hound at the hunt?

Chapter Nine

He was prepared for her that night at the Rosedale ball. He signed not one, but two dances on the little card dangling from her wrist, making sure that the second one was late into the evening to ensure that she stayed.

The first dance was early, a lively country romp that left them breathless and laughing. 'I haven't danced like that in ages!' Claire exclaimed between gasps, reclaiming her breath afterwards. It had been exhilarating. If he'd thought, or hoped, that the waltz had been an anomaly, that he couldn't possibly feel after a country dance as he had after that waltz, he was wrong. Incredibly so. If anything, he felt even more alive. When he was with her, some of the suffocation of his life receded.

'I need some air, would you come out with me?' Jonathon asked, struggling to get his own breath back. The floor hadn't been as crowded as it would be later. There'd been plenty of room to whirl and turn, and they had with his hand firm at her waist, holding her tight, her face turned up to his, laughing, and for a few minutes he stopped worrying about everything—about French, about Vienna, about Cecilia—and it seemed she had, too.

He noticed, because he missed that sense of relaxation as soon as they stepped outside. She was tense again. *'Tu es nerveuse?'* he asked in low tones, moving them down the shallow stone steps into the Rosedale garden.

'Perhaps. I've never been out on the terrace or the garden during a ball.' She gave a little laugh, making the statement sound like a joke.

Then her suitor was either a prude or a dolt. 'No stolen kisses?' Jonathon teased, 'Your suitor must be the epitome of manners.' And her last one as well. Not a single purloined kiss between them.

'No.'

'He's not the epitome of manners?' He was

completely unprepared for the shadow that crossed her face.

'No.' Claire laughed, a musical, magical sound when her guard was down. 'I can claim no stolen kisses, as you've already divined. My life isn't very exciting, Mr Lashley, despite your persistence in believing the contrary.'

'Jonathon,' he corrected. 'I thought we'd decided to be Jonathon and Claire this afternoon.' According to social protocol it was a bold decision. First names were definitely reserved for those of privileged standings with one another, as was this discussion. He knew it was beyond the pale to discuss kisses, but he had very little toleration for the rules these days. It suddenly mattered greatly to him that he be Jonathon to her, not mere Mr Lashley who stopped in for an hour or two a day for French lessons. What would happen when those lessons ended? They *would* end, whether he failed or succeeded in them. August loomed like a big red X on his mental calendar. If they were not friends, what happened then? Would 'they', Jonathon and Claire, simply end? The thought sat ill with him.

She turned to face him, her jaw set. 'Listen,

Jonathon. My life is hardly adventurous, as embarrassing as it is to admit.'

'Why is that, Claire?' he asked in soft challenge, sensing he was on to something important. It was the question he'd wanted to ask since that first day in the library. If he knew the answer, he might have the key to unlocking all the mysteries of her. What *had* she spent the last three years doing and why?

'What's the most exciting thing you've done in the recent past?' he prompted when she said nothing more.

'The truth? You're the most exciting thing that has happened in ages.' Giving French lessons to a desperate man was the highlight of her day. The thought made him cringe.

'Perhaps we should change that.' Jonathon gave her one his charming smiles, trying hard to keep his eyes from drifting to the vee of her bodice, but the dress had been designed by a witch. She'd worn peach chiffon tonight and it looked stunningly feminine and softly appealing where it curved over the swells of her breasts. 'We should make your life exciting.' It saddened him to think that 'exciting' might very well be limited to bringing the as-of-yet anonymous suitor to heel who hadn't even tried to kiss her. Surely a girl who knew four languages was entitled to more excitement than that.

'I know how you feel,' he found himself saying to fill the silence. 'Sometimes I think nothing will change, that this is my whole life, that every day will be the same, every spring in London, every fall at the hunting box, every winter in the country.' He paused, casting around for the right word. 'I feel like I'm waiting for something to happen and nothing does. The sameness is suffocating and I can't shake it. I can't do anything about it.' No variety, no spice, just going through the motions and yet he should be grateful. 'I'm being buried alive.'

Had he said that out loud? There was pain in Claire's eyes for him confirming that he had indeed. 'I'm sorry, I don't know what possessed me.'

'You don't have to apologise.' Her eyes held his, searching for something. 'If that's how you feel. We might all be better off if we told each other how we really felt, what really haunted us, instead of always pretending everything is fine when it's not.'

A strange kind of relief poured through him. She hadn't mitigated his impotence with false, bolstering phrases like, '*You have Vienna to look forward to, a marriage to look forward to.*'

'I'm a cad to complain about my life.' He tried for a winning smile. 'I have so much more than many.' So much more than the woman standing before him. There would be changes for him, small as they were. For Claire? There would be nothing, not even a husband and family to share the sameness of her days with if her suitor didn't come up to scratch. He wondered if she equated sameness with helplessness like he did. He'd come home from war without Thomas and the guilt had become paralysing.

'Claire, I'm tired of prowling ballrooms, waiting for the future to happen. I need Vienna. I need my life to start.' He'd never dared to tell another person any of this and yet tonight it was pouring out of him. He'd like to blame it on the night, the pretty decorations, the scent of early summer flowers in the air, but he couldn't. He could only blame it on the woman. This was the second time he'd taken such liberties in conversation with her.

'Then it will happen because you've chosen it.' Her eyes were solemn as she held his gaze and it seemed to him that the world fell away in those moments, narrowing itself down to just the two of them in this empty garden as she spoke her soft words. 'But this is what I believe, Jonathon. We are the authors of our own destinies intentionally or otherwise. Need, want, it's all up to us. Nothing will change until *we* do.'

She could have no idea how seductive those words were. He wanted to believe her, wanted to be a man who wrote his own destiny, intentionally, not a man to whom destiny happened by accident. It was just that the future he was intent on seizing had a cost. Looking at Claire, here in the garden with her back against the bark of a tree, the light of party lanterns shining on her hair, he was struck by the enormity of that cost.

She was a cross between the wisdom of Athena and the beauty of Aphrodite in those moments. He wondered if it was her words, or the realisation of her loveliness that had him under her spell. But it didn't change what he wanted to do in those moments. He wanted to kiss her.

He gave her no warning, leaning in and taking her lips, slowly but firmly at first, letting her mouth accustom itself to the press of his, letting her open to him and she did. Beneath the hesitancy was a curiosity, a slow blooming eagerness as she moved into the kiss, into him, their bodies coming together effortlessly as the kiss deepened. He had not been wrong. She was ready to be awakened.

He held them there together with his hands at her hips, his thumbs pressing gently through the delicate fabric of her gown. He ran his tongue along her lip, delighting in her soft sigh. He took her mouth again, this time with more insistence. She was ready for him, willing for him, her arms about his neck, her body pressed so close to his he could feel the heat of her. God, he wanted to devour her, to lose himself in her. A moan escaped her as his mouth moved to her throat, part pleasure, part…regret? Dismay?

'Jonathon, don't. You don't have to.' She broke the kiss, her eyes wide. 'It's too much.'

'What's too much?' He nuzzled her neck, determined not to let this moment slip away, wanting her mouth back.

'The dancing, the flowers, which were beautiful by the way, *too* beautiful. You don't have to be my excitement. It would be easy for a girl to misunderstand.'

She meant Cecilia, of course. Cecilia had no claims on him. But under the grounds of Claire's argument earlier today that men and women couldn't be friends, Cecilia and her self-made claims would be jealous. She shouldn't be envious of flowers and a dance. Still, he knew the kiss was not well done of him, even if it was one kiss to weigh against a lifetime spent doing his duty.

'Claire, I…' He should apologise but he didn't want to. He wasn't sorry and wasn't that what apologies were for? He wanted to kiss her again.

'I should go.' She stepped around him and he let her by, knowing he wouldn't get that second dance. If he let her go now, she would be gone from the ballroom when he returned inside.

He had no right to have taken such a liberty. He couldn't even justify it as an act to inspire her suitor. He'd asked far too much of her today:

friendship, a kiss in the Rosedale garden that had inflamed him far more than a simple kiss should have. She knew nothing of him other than what she saw at parties, that polite social mask he kept carefully fixed in place. Cecilia would never look beyond that mask; would never feel the need to or the want. She was perfectly happy with the smiling, charming Jonathon Lashley. But Claire would not settle for such a façade.

Claire *had* glimpsed beneath that mask. He'd let the façade slip for just a moment tonight and she had filled that moment with prophetic words: *this is what I believe...nothing will change until we do.* Cecilia would be an easy wife in that regard, never pushing him to expose himself. He could spend his life walking around pretending he was happy, like he had been before the war, before Thomas.

He pulled a leaf off the tree and twirled the stem between his fingers idly. He'd once believed he could masquerade himself back into happiness. If he pretended he was happy, eventually he would be. So far, the façade had fooled everyone except himself. Well, if he couldn't be happy, he could at least make Claire happy. He would help her with her reluctant suitor whether she wanted him to or not. It would be easier if she'd just tell him the man's name. But everyone was entitled to their secrets. Secrets were secrets no matter how big or small, his being larger than most.

He drew a breath. He needed to return to the ballroom. Just in case. But he knew when he stepped inside that Claire was gone. He scanned the perimeter any way for good measure. There was no sign of her. He might as well leave. There was no reason to stay. He made his excuses to the hostess and left, pretending urgent business had come up.

The strains of music and merrymaking followed him out from the ballroom into the hall. What would all those people inside think of him if they knew the truth? What would Claire say if she knew he'd been the one who'd made the decision to leave Thomas behind?

That night he dreamt of Thomas...

Cannon fire sounded down the road, the rumble still in the distance, but nearer than it had been before. His horse moved uneasily beneath him as he argued with his brother. 'You cannot deliver the dispatch, it's too dangerous.'

'Someone has to and it sure as hell can't be you. You're the heir. Everyone is counting on you to come back.' Thomas was being obstinate while the rest of his men cast nervous eyes down the road and with good reason.

'The entire French corps could be out there,' he insisted, urging Thomas to see the impossibility of the task.

'All the more reason for me to go.' His brother's jaw was set and Jonathon recognised intractability when he saw it. 'There are officers waiting for what's in that bag.'

'Headquarters didn't know the road would be blocked when they sent us out. Those officers are capable of making their own decisions.' Another cannon fired and Jonathon struggled with his horse. 'We will not make it through, Thomas, don't you understand? We have to retreat.' He was angry now. He was not risking the lives of his men for a dispatch bag. But this was classic Thomas, the stubborn hero, and Jonathon worried that war was still very much a game to his younger brother.

Thomas wheeled his horse around, a big, strong bay gelding, and peered down the road. 'A single man could do it. A good rider could make it through. Of the two of us, I'm the better rider.' That was debatable, depending on one's definition of 'good', Jonathon thought. If one defined it as reckless, then Thomas had the right of it.

'Let me go, Jonathon.' Steely grey eyes met his, reminding him that while his brother was younger than he by two years, his brother was no longer a child. 'Dithering with me any longer puts the lot of you at risk and it diminishes my chances.'

'We can't wait here.' Jonathon prevaricated one last time. The ride might take only an hour, but an hour was an eternity in battle.

'I know.'

'You know the meeting point? We'll stay there as long as we can.' He reached over and gripped his brother's arm. 'No heroics. You come straight back and meet us there.'

Thomas laughed. 'I'll probably beat you there, slowcoach.' He wheeled his horse around one last time in a brave circle and was gone.

'Thomas, no!'

Jonathon woke up in a sweat, heart pounding. Even in his own dream, he couldn't change the outcome, couldn't stop Thomas from riding off into the unknown.

Thomas hadn't met them at the checkpoint even though Jonathon had held it far longer than anyone required. It had been bloody work, too. How would Thomas find them if they left that last point of contact? Even when they were forced to move out, he hadn't been ready to give up. There were so many reasons Thomas was late. The most harmless reasons were delays— the roads were full of fighting, he couldn't get through, someone else had needed a rider and Thomas had volunteered. Or perhaps the big bay had thrown a shoe, or taken lame on the road and couldn't ride. Thomas loved that horse. He'd never leave him behind.

But there were darker explanations, too. The longer Thomas was gone, the more seriously Jonathon had to contemplate them: the big bay had been shot down, Thomas thrown, as absurd as that seemed. It was impossible to throw Thomas. Knowing how improbable that was only made the other scenarios worse: Thomas shot from the saddle, wounded in a ditch without help. Thomas dead.

Jonathon got out of bed and poured himself a brandy. He poked up the fire in the grate, any activity to keep the black thoughts at bay. His body was starting to recover from the dream; his pulse slowing, but his mind was still racing. To this day he couldn't bring himself to believe Thomas was dead.

He took a seat in the chair closest to the fire. There was no point in going back to bed. He wouldn't sleep now for a while. Even if he did, he'd only dream again. He knew this routine well. The farewell dream was always accompanied by the searching dream—the one where he wandered the battlefield looking for Thomas. He'd done it, too, in real life. The dream was no fantasy.

He'd combed the fields afterwards, looking at body after body, hoping each one he turned over wouldn't be Thomas. He hauled wounded men to the surgeries, asking them if they'd seen a tall brown-haired man who looked like him. When those efforts had failed, he turned his attentions further out to the woods and roads near the fighting, to places where a rider on a long-distance mission might have met with trouble. There was carnage there, too, in the ditches and in the trees, but none of it was Thomas.

There was danger in those places still and that danger gave him hope. Perhaps Thomas had been captured and was being held for ransom. He took his searches further and into more treacherous places. He'd been warned not to stray from English protection for fear of French renegades or deserters. He'd been warned to wait. But he had no patience for waiting when his brother might be out there hurt and minutes, let alone a day, could make a difference.

He should have listened to cooler heads. If his first mistake had been letting Thomas go, this was his second. A single man absorbed in a task made an easy target and that was what he became. Jonathon took a long swallow of his brandy, remembering. He'd gone back to the road where he'd last seen Thomas and walked every inch of it again and been shot for his troubles—a nasty wound in the shoulder courtesy of a bullet with enough rust on it to give him an infection and a fever that got him shipped home in the midst of his delirium.

He remembered nothing of the trip home or even that the trip was being made. His men told him he raved two days straight in fluent French. It was the last time he'd been able to speak French with the same acumen with which he wrote it—yet another secret he kept. It was too embarrassing to admit to.

He'd woken up, lucid and aware, back home in England, and he'd been furious. How dare someone send him home, send him *away* from Thomas? How dare he be safe when Thomas wasn't? But he knew the answer. He was the heir. Perhaps Thomas had known the answer, too, when he'd yanked that dispatch bag out of his hands on the road. His parents would survive losing Thomas, but not him.

Jonathon pushed a hand through his hair and blew out a breath. Seven years gone and he wasn't sure he would survive losing Thomas. He couldn't even accept Thomas *was* lost to begin with, a thought he only voiced to Owen and to Preston these days.

He finished his drink, thought about pouring another and decided against it. Brandy this late would only make the morning worse. It was going to be hard enough as it was. He checked the mantel clock, squinting in the half-light. On top of a sleepless night, in just six hours, he'd have to find a way to casually speak French with a woman who'd run from a ball after he'd kissed her. Having no past experience with such a thing, he had no plan for how he'd deal with that.

He toyed with the idea of skipping the lesson off and on for the next three hours until he dozed in his chair. It would be easy to send a note with his excuse, but it would also be cowardly and Claire would know it. He didn't want her thinking it was because he regretted the kiss. No woman wanted to think a man would rather not have kissed them.

When he woke shortly before nine o'clock with a crick in his neck and sore muscles, he knew there was no getting around it. He'd go and face the awkward consequences. Besides, he'd eventually have to go back. For whatever reason, whether it was the unique teaching methods, he *was* making progress. He could hear his fluency and pronunciation growing stronger each day. He couldn't quit now that he was finding success after all these years.

Fate had other ideas. Jonathon had just made his decision and rung for his valet when the urgent note arrived from Owen Danvers, giving him his reprieve.

Chapter Ten

Owen Danvers stood before his long windows, hands clasped behind his back in classic military stance. Jonathon recognised the posture, a sure sign there was trouble or, if not trouble, at the very least, a situation. 'I trust I didn't disrupt your morning?' Owen enquired without turning from the window.

'No, I was already up,' Jonathon answered just as tersely. He didn't need small talk any more than Owen needed to give it. 'If something's happened, just get to it. You needn't dress it up for me,' Jonathon encouraged.

Owen finally turned to face him. 'How are your French lessons progressing? Is your fluency coming back?' His face was haggard as if he, too, had been up all night plagued with worries. There was desperation in Owen's face, too, as if he could will the right answer from him.

'Yes, I believe it is.' Jonathon fought his own nerves. Was this about Vienna? Had the post already been decided?

'Good.' Some of the desperation seemed to ebb from Owen's pale features. 'Will you tell me who the instructor is? I would like to congratulate them.'

'No.' Jonathon moved his attention to a paperweight on the desk. 'My instructor would prefer to remain anonymous.' He hadn't told anyone he was seeing Claire Welton for lessons. At first, he'd done it to protect his pride. He'd been too embarrassed. But now, he wanted to protect her. Perhaps she wouldn't like it to be known. Claire might have certain qualms about drawing attention to herself, especially if there was a suitor to impress.

Owen nodded and took the chair next to Jonathon, his expression serious as he dropped his voice. 'There's been news.'

Jonathon's body went rigid. 'News', when said that way, could only mean one thing. 'Thomas?' It was almost too much to hope for.

'Perhaps. I've prevaricated about saying anything too soon. But if it was me, if it was my brother, I'd want word, any sort of word as soon as possible. But I can't take this to your father, not yet.'

'Thank you.' Jonathon understood. Nothing was confirmed. Whatever Owen was about to share was unverified. It wasn't proof, he reminded himself. It would destroy his father to get his hopes up and it was likely of a confidential nature. Owen was sharing this out of respect for their longstanding friendship.

'There's word that a man meeting Thomas's description has been located in a farming village near the River Leie.'

Also called the River Lys in French. Leie was the Dutch name. The river formed part of the north-eastern border between the two countries. Jonathon knew it and hope surged. Waterloo wasn't far from the location. It was probable that if Thomas had been lost and wounded he could have ended up there either under his own power looking for shelter, or taken there to recover by a farmer in a cart.

'Is that all we know?' Jonathon tried to keep

his voice calm, after all, it was hardly enough to go on. 'What do you mean by description?' Thomas looked like him, but that wasn't saying much. Thomas shared general features with a lot of people: brown hair, grey eyes instead of brown, tall with broad shoulders. His height might stand out to some. He and Thomas were usually the taller men in any given room, just a little over six foot. But surely there were tallish men everywhere. It wasn't necessarily extraordinary to be a taller man.

'An Englishman,' Owen said quietly. 'The man in the report has your brother's features and he's English, or should I say he's not native, neither French nor Dutch. That's the part that isn't quite verified. All anyone knows is that he showed up in the village seven years ago. The timing is right.'

Jonathon rose. 'I want to go and see him. I can leave this afternoon.' He would travel to the ends of the earth if there was the slightest of chances. Maybe his French would hold. Maybe Claire had taught him enough to break through his barriers so he could communicate. Maybe.

Owen put a hand on his arm. 'The informant is coming here. He wants to arrange a meeting. There should be word within the next week.' It would be the longest week of his life and it might be for naught. There'd been sightings before, some quickly smashed, others lingered with potent hope.

'Jonathon, it's been a long time,' Owen began cautiously. 'Perhaps I was wrong to tell you. So much time has passed.'

He didn't have to say more. So much time. Either Thomas was dead, had always been dead, or he hadn't come home. 'Why wouldn't he come back if he could?' Jonathon voiced the question. Why would his brother stay away for years with no word when he knew how worried they'd all be, how devastated they'd all be?

'We all wear masks, Jonathon. I do, you do. You put on that handsome smile of yours and no one guesses there might even be an ounce of darkness in you. Why should Thomas be any different?'

'I just can't imagine what reasons he'd have,'

Jonathon admitted. Thomas had everything: a family, money, social status. He was well liked.

Owen rose, signalling the conversation was over. 'We're getting ahead of ourselves. It might not be him.' In fact, it was unlikely that it was after seven years. What it *could* be was dangerous. This could be a trap, an attempt at extortion that played on a family's desperate hopes. It wouldn't be the first time. There'd been earlier attempts right after the war to claim money in exchange for 'information' about Thomas. Those attempts had devastated his parents.

'The best thing you can do is go brush up on your French.' Because Vienna loomed, because if there was a chance this fellow was Thomas, Jonathon would have to be ready to go at a moment's notice.

Jonathon stood, too. He knew what he needed to do. He needed to find Claire and step up the lessons. He needed to forget about kisses in the Rosedale garden, or lowered bodices, or sherry eyes that sparkled when she looked at him, or the feel of her dancing in his arms. He needed to concentrate all of his attention on the lessons as if his life depended on it, because it did—his and quite possibly Thomas's.

Of course, he had to *find* her first. For a person who claimed her life was uneventful, she was proving difficult to track down. She wasn't home and neither was Lady Stanhope, which meant no one precisely knew her direction, only that she was out making calls. The butler did, however, know where Lady Stanhope had gone: Lady Morrison's, the *ton*'s most notorious gossip. For a man to show up there was nothing short of walking into the lion's den.

Jonathon tried there, but it only earned him a tepid cup of tea and crumbly cakes. Once he'd been announced, he had no choice but to put in his fifteen minutes before he could leave again. In exchange, though, he got a rather shockingly long list of possible locations from Lady Stanhope. He might try the Worths or the Penroses or the Milhams, she told him, eyeing him speculatively as she gave the advice. 'The flowers you've been sending are positively gorgeous, Mr Lashley,' she added with sly calculation. He didn't imagine it. Every ear in the room perked up at that.

He left the moment those fifteen required minutes were up, but fate was determined to play with him a little. He called at the Worths, the Penroses to more tea but to no avail, the calls eating up more of his time before he arrived at the Milhams, only to be told the ladies were indisposed at the moment by a butler who was a stickler for propriety, even though they both knew very well the lady he was after was inside somewhere.

After a sleepless night and dubious news over Thomas, Jonathon was in no mood for mannerly games. He stepped around the butler and into the hall. He was a man who believed in never leaving a place until he got what he came for and, right now, what he needed most was Claire Welton. He spied a sitting room off the corridor. 'I'll wait.'

Claire couldn't wait. She blurted out the words, 'We have to stop. It has gone too far', as soon as the foursome was seated in the Milham's garret the next day. She'd been up all night thinking it through and she knew her decision was the right one. Apparently, fate agreed with her. Jonathon hadn't shown up for the lesson that morning and she knew why; things had got out of hand in the Rosedale garden.

'It sounds to me like it's gone just far enough,' Beatrice argued with a twinkle in her eye. 'He's sending you flowers and dancing with you every night.'

Claire gave an exasperated sigh. How many times did she have to explain it? 'Only because he thinks I have a gentleman whose attentions I would like to attract.'

'You do.' May laughed over the rim of her teacup. 'His.'

'But he thinks it's someone else and I've let him,' Claire insisted. 'He thinks he's helping me in exchange for the French lessons.' While that line of reasoning explained everything up to a point, that point had run out fourteen hours and eleven minutes ago.

The words came out in a rush. 'Last night, he kissed me.' Everyone began to talk at once, but she raised her voice to be heard. 'This morning he didn't show up for the lesson.' She didn't want him to quit the lessons over a kiss. He needed them too badly, more than he needed to feel remorse over a kiss. Had it been such a poor kiss that he didn't want to see her again, not even for lessons? She had thought it was rather nice. More than nice...extraordinary.

'He kissed you?' Evie's eyes were dreamy, but May's eyes were sharp.

'Well, this is certainly a development,' May drawled. 'He didn't *need* to kiss you in order to help you. I'd call that progress in the right direction.' May fixed her with a hard stare and Claire braced herself. 'You wanted Lashley, Claire, and now it seems you can have him. You can't stop now. You do want him, don't you?'

'Yes.' More than before if that was possible. After spending hours with him in lessons, walking and talking with him, she was discovering a whole new Jonathon Lashley. When she'd started this, it had been with the intention of showing him a different side of her. She'd not bargained on also seeing a different side of him. Now, there were consequences she'd not planned on. 'But not like this—' Claire insisted.

'Like what?' Beatrice interrupted. 'We're doing

what every woman since Eve has done to get a man and that's use our assets to attract a man's notice. The last time I checked, that wasn't a sin.'

'But if I hadn't forced my way into his life, he would still be on a trajectory headed for Cecilia. I don't want to steal another girl's beau.' Even if that girl was Cecilia and there was definitely some settling to do between the two of them.

'I think your definition of stealing is a bit too liberal, Claire. There's been no formal an-nouncement, except for Cecilia clinging to his arm for the past year.' May shook her head. 'If that was all it took to claim a man, we'd all have the husbands of our dreams by now. If he wants to marry her, he will. It's simple.'

'It's not simple at all, May.' Because Jonathon was not simple. He had layers beneath that easy smile, layers she was just beginning to discover. 'He can't sell himself to her. She will never un-derstand him. You heard her, he's nothing but the "colour" of the month.'

She had to tell them. 'You've all worked so hard for me and I appreciate everything you've done, I truly do. Evie, your gowns are lovely and I feel beautiful in them. Bea, you gave me the courage to seize my moment and I did. May, you made everything happen by setting up seats at the dinner and dropping the right hints at the right time. It all worked wonderfully, but I don't want to stoop to Cecilia's level,' Claire said firmly.

She hoped they wouldn't notice how hard it was to say such a thing calmly. It had been a difficult decision to make. She wasn't as sure as May and Beatrice that the kiss signified progress, but if there was even a flicker of 'progress' it was even harder to give up knowing she might have success. But at what price? She did not want to 'lure' Lashley away. After last night, she felt that might be the case. 'I think it's gone too far.'

He'd kissed her out of desperation over his own circumstances or over hers. And that was the 'good' explanation. Perhaps he'd kissed her because he felt sorry for her, the poor blue-stocking girl who had never been out in a garden with a beau before. She looked her friends in the eye. 'I have to give him up.' It was the right thing to do. *Il n'y a pas d'oreiller si doux comme une conscience claire*—there is no pillow softer than that of a clear conscience, as the French would say.

Beatrice was staring at her, dark eyes hard. 'I would say it hasn't gone far enough. I thought you wanted more than a few stolen moments and a couple waltzes. I thought you wanted *Jonathon.*'

She did. 'I do, it's just...'

'What? Hard?' Beatrice was relentless. 'Of course it's hard. You are going to have to fight for him. You're going to have to fight Cecilia and you're going to have to fight yourself. In fact, you're probably your worst enemy.'

Claire bristled, Bea's comments stoking her anger. 'What do you mean?'

'Bea, be careful,' May warned, looking between the two of them.

Beatrice flicked stern eyes in May's direction. 'No, she has to hear this. We've coddled her too long.'

'What are you talking about? Coddling me?' Claire was angry now. Had her friends been keeping secrets? About her?

'We let you retreat, Claire, when we should

have pushed you forward. You are not a wall-flower, but we let you play at it until you became one. You've changed and not for the better. You've created far more doubt for yourself than Cecilia Northam ever could.'

This was stunning. It was definitely not what one expected to hear from one's friends. But that didn't mean it wasn't true. Just uncomfortable. She'd come here anticipating that they would all nod their heads and gather around her in support of her decision to give up Jonathon. They'd fought the good fight, gave it a good run and all that, but in the end it was probably best to stop here. Claire stared at her friends, each of them in agreement with Beatrice. '*Et tu*, Evie?'

Evie nodded. They were disappointed. In her. Why shouldn't they be? Hadn't she thought much the same thing lately, although not quite in Beatrice's succinct terms? She was different when she was with Jonathon, bolder, braver, stronger. And it scared her. She liked that girl. She didn't want to lose that girl again. It was a big risk to take. Maybe too big.

'Excuse me, Miss Evie.' The butler coughed discreetly to announce his presence. 'Pardon my interruption, but there's a gentleman downstairs who is asking to see Miss Welton. He's quite insistent. He says he'll wait. I think he means it. He's been here a half-hour already. What shall I tell him?'

Claire stiffened. Everyone looked at her, even the butler. No one actually expected Evie to answer. Beside her, May murmured in *I told you so* undertones, 'He's come for you. It seems he doesn't want to be dismissed. Perhaps he didn't mind that kiss so much after all.'

Bea gave her a challenging stare. 'Begin as you mean to go on, Claire.' Apparently she wasn't giving him up after all.

Chapter Eleven

Jonathon rose the instant she entered the room and came to her, his hands gripping hers, his face tight, devoid of his usual smile. She searched his face for a clue. Something had happened if he'd made the effort to follow her here.

'Claire, I apologise for the intrusion, but I must speak with you right away.' She felt the hard pressure of his hands where they covered hers. Her mind slowed down over that one thought, repeating the idea once more: *Something had happened and when it had, he'd come to her.* Another sort of woman might have taken a vindictive sort of pleasure in knowing that he'd rushed to her and not to Cecilia. But Claire was far more concerned about Jonathon to spare thought for a petty girlish rivalry.

He glanced towards the door, indicating he'd rather not talk here. She understood at once. He wanted privacy. 'We can walk in the key garden just across the square.'

Claire was all efficiency, calling for her maid and her pelisse. Within moments she and Jonathon were out of the house. The key garden was quiet, frequented only by nannies and prams and a few small children who were too busy to notice them. 'Now, tell me what's happened.'

'We have to step up the French lessons. I have to get my fluency back faster.' Get it back? That was an odd word. She'd been unaware he had any fluency to 'get back'.

'All right.' Claire hoped she sounded patient, sounded calm. Her mind was reeling with questions. What had sparked such urgency? She assumed it must be the Vienna position. 'We can meet twice a day or for a longer period of time.' The idea that the Vienna position had been moved up would also mean her time with Jonathon had been shortened as well.

'No, that's not enough,' Jonathon said hastily, his own impatience showing in the roughness of his tone. 'I think I need a more immersive experience,' Jonathon argued.

She knew what he meant, but it would be more difficult to arrange. Claire nodded. 'I've been thinking about that, too, only I had thought to wait just a bit longer. But you're right. You need to be able to speak French without the safety net of English in order to truly test how much you can do. There are eating houses in Soho that are French and other small businesses that cater to the expatriates. We should go there.' There was an entire French *émigré* society living in London. They could make use of that, but he still hadn't told her why.

'Yes, we could go to a restaurant or two, a bookshop perhaps.' Jonathon paused, perhaps realising the implications. A man could go anywhere he liked any day of the week, but a woman had limitations. Gently bred girls seldom left Mayfair. 'Would you be able to get away?'

She ought to say no. It wasn't just the getting away part that created difficulties. What he proposed was more than slightly scandalous, especially if she did it without her maid in tow. Unmarried women weren't allowed alone in a room at home with an unmarried man without a door wide open or chaperon present. To go out in public was, well, frankly unheard of, but she found herself saying, 'I can manage something.'

Already, plans started to form in her head. It would be easy enough to tell her parents she was going to one of her friends.

'Good. We can go tomorrow. I'll come for lessons as usual and we can plan then.' Jonathon smiled, looking relieved. 'Thank you, Claire.'

They had made a complete circuit of the garden and had reached the gate. He opened the gate for her and gestured she should go through, but Claire held back. If she left the garden she might not get the answers she wanted. 'You still haven't told me why. Where has all the sudden urgency come from?'

He hesitated just a fraction. 'I may have need of it sooner than expected.'

'Has the Vienna post been decided then?' She pushed forward her earlier hypothesis. There were people behind them now, waiting to exit.

'Something like that,' Jonathon muttered. It wasn't an answer, but it was the best she was going to get, a reminder perhaps that while he'd been willing to run to her in his time of need, he wasn't ready yet to fully confide in her. A reminder, too, that the man she saw in London's ballrooms was far more than the sum of his smile. Jonathon Lashley was a man with secrets.

They walked the short distance to Evie's in silence, their time taken up with the effort to cross the street, avoiding mud from last night's rain and late-afternoon carriages. Too soon, it was time to let him go. It wasn't until he'd driven away that she realised his tactic of omission had worked in another sense as well, although perhaps unintentionally so. Her mind had been so focused on what he wasn't telling her, she'd not realised the one thing she thought they would talk about hadn't been addressed at all. He hadn't mentioned the kiss once. Claire supposed she ought to be glad. After all, what was there to discuss? But it was still lowering to realise it had been so inconsequential as to not merit comment. Surely, if the kiss had meant something, if it had been intended to alter the nature of their relationship, he would have addressed it? By not mentioning it, they were politely, tacitly, admitting it was a mistake that ought to be put behind them. At least it seemed that Jonathon certainly had. She might have to settle for being Jonathon's friend, as hard as that might be.

No one would ever mistake Cecilia Northam for a soft woman. She made sure of it. She was beautiful the way a diamond was beautiful: multi-faceted, sparkling, a dazzling treat to the eyes that came with sharp edges. She was not afraid to cut with words or actions. A lady had to know how to defend herself among the *ton*. It was an important skill to hone as a debutante as much as the art of flirting or dancing. Some day, the successful flirt would have a husband to defend against the cats of the *ton* and later children to launch. The fight to protect and to establish would be a successful lady's lifelong career. Every other woman posed a threat to that success unless they were taken down.

The bloodthirstiness of Cecilia Northam's outlook would definitely have surprised the girls seated around her as she tried on her new ball gown for a final fitting at the dressmaker. Cecilia took a twirl, liking the feel of the skirt against her ankles. 'What do you think?'

'I think it will be just the thing to bring Lashley back to your side.' One of the girls, Anne, fanned herself languidly as if she hadn't let drop a juicy piece of news. A few others held their breaths and shot Anne a warning look. Cecilia looked at the girls' responses and knew she had to address the issue immediately. This was touchy ground indeed if they were trying to censor Anne.

She stepped down from the dressmaker's dais and faced the offender. 'I was unaware Lashley had to be brought back,' she said coolly. Of course that was a lie. Lashley's behaviour *had* been somewhat troublesome this past week. In a Season comprised of three months, where matches were made in a matter of weeks, a week of erratic behaviour was worrisome indeed. It was hardly something she talked about though. However, hearing the words made the concern real. She was on the verge of reeling Lashley in. She didn't need anyone smelling blood here at the last.

'He's dancing with Claire Welton out of the blue.' Anne didn't back down. 'It seems odd to me that he's had years to dance with her and hasn't. But now…' Her voice trailed off in implication.

Cecilia narrowed her eyes. Was that all? She would enjoy taking Anne down. 'Claire Welton is nothing. He danced with her out of pity. He's friends with the brother of one of her friends. It was probably arranged.' She paused. 'I forgot you weren't with us that night, Anne.'

'Perhaps dancing with her once might be explained as friendly charity, but twice?' Anne tossed her dark hair with a competitive smirk. 'They did more than dance at the Rosedale ball last night. He took her out to the garden.' She paused. 'Oh, I forgot, *you* weren't there,' she mimicked.

'Fresh air is not a marriage proposal,' Cecilia replied in her most unconcerned tone. 'Heavens, Anne, you're such a prude. A gentleman and a lady can walk in a garden without it meaning something. Didn't Viscount Downing take you out to the garden last week?' The others laughed nervously. Good. She was putting the rebellion down.

'And kissing?' Anne shot back with feigned

innocence. 'I suppose that's of no consequence either?'

Cecilia shot her a thunderous look, but Anne was unrepentant.

'Don't kill the messenger, Cece. I'm just telling you what I saw.'

Cecilia relented. She was smart enough to know she couldn't fight a war on two fronts. Maybe Anne meant well and maybe she meant something more predatory with her remarks, but that would have to wait. The immediate concern was Claire Welton. Anne posed no threat to Lashley, but apparently Claire did— that blue-stocking mouse who'd come out of nowhere this Season with her new dresses. She'd guessed there was a man involved when she'd first seen the gowns. But she'd never guessed those attentions were for Lashley. Claire Welton overstepped herself when she knew Lashley belonged to her. Nor had Cecilia guessed Lashley might be so easily swayed from her side.

She stepped back on to the dais, taking a final spin in the pale ice-pink silk. Anne was right about one thing. This was the perfect gown for getting Lashley back. It was time to defend what was hers. Better yet, it was time to claim it. 'I think,' she said out loud to the girls. 'It is time for Lashley to come up to scratch.' She would compromise him to the altar if she had to. She was going to be the future Countess Oakdale. Claire Welton and her four languages were not going to stand in her way.

Chapter Twelve

The little issue of propriety and a chaperon wasn't going to stand in the way of a grand adventure. It had taken some planning on her part and a slight almost-lie to her mother, but Claire had done it. She *was* going to Evie's. She just wasn't going to stay there. Going to Evie's covered a number of problems, the foremost being the need for her maid to accompany her. Evie only lived a street away and she'd been going to the Milhams for years on her own.

'Are you sure you don't mind covering for me?' Claire asked for the tenth time as they waited for Jonathon in the key garden. She'd lost the fight an hour ago to contain her excitement and she was fairly bristling with unbridled anticipation.

'It's only for a few hours,' Evie insisted, almost as excited as Claire was over the prospect of an illicit adventure. 'I can manage until you get back. Besides, my mother thinks we're going to May's.'

Claire worried her lip. 'It's just that I don't want you to get into trouble if anything should go wrong.' Nothing would though. She'd thought this through and it was only a trip to a little French bookshop in Soho. Bookstores were harmless venues. More was the pity.

'Do you think he'll kiss you again?' Evie asked in a whisper, her cheeks turning pink.

'No, I doubt a musty old bookshop would do much to spark a man's ardour.' Claire gave a small smile and a laugh, but deep down she rather regretted that the bookshop wasn't a more inspiring venue. It seemed unlikely Jonathon would be encouraged to kiss her again amid the tall aisles of bookcases. 'He didn't even mention the first kiss.' On those grounds, it would take far more than a bookshop to inspire a second one.

'In that case, maybe *you* should kiss him?' Evie suggested quietly. Coming from Evie, the idea was positively shocking. It was the kind of thought Claire expected Beatrice or May to have. But Evie? 'Bookstores inspire you, Claire. Perhaps you could read to him from a French romance, an old troubadour ballad or some such, and then lean over and just kiss him, nice and soft on the lips, and see what he does. If it's a little kiss, there's no harm in it. Now, if it were a big one, all open-mouthed with a little tongue, that might be a bit more difficult to come back from if he's not up for it.'

'Evie!' Claire smiled in shocked surprise at her quiet friend. She'd never guessed thoughts of that nature filtered through Evie's brain. Apparently they did and in great detail. 'How do you know about such things?'

Evie smiled back. 'I read books, too, Claire. I've picked up a few pieces of knowledge on the way.'

'I'll take your idea under consideration.' Claire hugged her friend. 'Hmm. There are hidden layers to you, Miss Evie Milham.'

'Everyone has them, Claire. We just need to know where to look. Just look at you.' Evie's eyes shone with admiration. 'You've always been pretty, but it hasn't always been obvious.

These past weeks, you've been livelier, more out-going. Jonathon has been good for you. I think you've inspired us all with your quest.'

The gate to the key garden swung open and Jonathon stepped through, promptly on time as if he, too, understood the importance of every second. They only had the afternoon. They couldn't waste it. He bowed to Evie. 'Miss Milham, good afternoon.' He offered Claire his arm. She didn't think she'd ever get tired of taking it, of feeling the flex of his muscles beneath his coat as she lay her hand on his sleeve. 'Claire, are you ready? My carriage is outside.'

The adventure moved from theory to practice the moment she took her seat beside him on the curricle. Anyone seeing them here in Mayfair would see that Jonathon had his tiger with them, riding on the shelf in the back. There was nothing odd about a gentleman taking a lady for a drive this time of day, she told herself. Unless, of course, the oddness lay in who was driving whom.

If there was any real danger in their being to-gether it was in the Soho portion of their trip— a gentleman and an unchaperoned, unmarried lady of good breeding out together, alone. But no one would recognise them in the bohemian neighbourhoods bordering the West End.

'Relax, Claire, what's the worst that can happen on a jaunt to a bookshop?' Jonathon teased her as Mayfair fell behind them.

'People would say you compromised me. We could end up married.' She voiced the fear that plagued her without thinking.

Jonathon laughed. 'You say that like it's a bad thing. Would that be so horrible? A fate worse than death?'

'It's not funny.' She tried to hold on to her chagrin, but it was useless. Jonathon's laughter was infectious. Claire felt herself smiling. 'Still, I wouldn't want a husband who was *forced* to marry me. I certainly wouldn't want a husband who was spineless enough to bow to a silly rule and let it decide the rest of his life.' Even if it was Jonathon. That might be worse, to know she'd ruined the life of someone she truly cared about.

Jonathon arched a dark eyebrow. 'Your suitor must be quite the paragon then. Those are high standards.'

'He's not a suitor, not in truth, you know that.

I told you from the start he hardly notices me.' Claire paused looking for the right words. 'He's more like a wish.'

Jonathon looked over at her, his smile making her stomach flutter. 'Don't worry, Claire. We'll make him notice you yet.'

She doubted it. 'The wish' in question had kissed her and hardly noticed. If he hadn't noticed her then with his mouth on hers, their bodies pressed to one another, she doubted he ever would. She'd merely been a convenient outlet for his desperation. 'Turn right here, the bookshop should be the next street over.' It was time to stop daydreaming and start thinking about the outing. 'We'll try to speak French the whole time. Don't worry, I'll be there if you need me. Just relax. You do very well when you don't think about it. Remember, we're looking for a copy of Diderot's *Le Neveu de Rameau.*' At yesterday's lesson they'd designed and practised a script about what today's interactions might include. He wouldn't always have the luxury of preparing a script, but for now it seemed like a good way to ease him into real-life interactions.

Jonathon found a place by the kerb to park the

curricle and came around to help her down. His hands lingered at her waist, an energetic grin taking his face. '*Allez. Que les jeux commencement.*' He was possessed, too, of the same eager brand of anxiousness she was. This would be a real test of what they'd accomplished in her garden and they both wanted him to pass.

She spoke French to him as they walked the short distance to the bookshop, warming up like actors before a show. She didn't want Jonathon to face the shopkeeper without some practice to ease himself into the situation. If she was right about him having performance anxiety, she didn't want him freezing up the moment he was under scrutiny. That was what today was about for her, a diagnostic of sorts. How far had he come? Where were his weak points?

The bell over the door jingled and they stepped inside. Jonathon greeted the bookshop owner with a flawless *bonjour* and asked for the Diderot book, which the shopkeeper found immediately. So far so good. They were off to a nice start, but this only proved he could memorise a script and execute it. Claire had no intention of settling for that. She wouldn't always be there to write and practise scripts with him.

Claire wandered down an aisle of poetry, engaging the shopkeeper in a discussion. They were off script now and she wanted to see how Jonathon responded, how quickly he could adapt. After a few minutes, the door jingled and the shopkeeper excused himself to help the new customer. Claire selected several slim volumes and headed towards a table in the back where customers could sit and read.

She opened a book to a random page and slid it towards him. 'Would you read? I think you will like Machaut. He's considered the last great French poet who was both poet and composer.'

'Le Remède de Fortune.' He looked up from the book with a sly grin, never breaking his use of French. 'Is there a personal message in this for me?' he teased, his French easy and fluent as he made the offhand remark. His eyes scanned the work and flipped through a few pages. 'Ah, perhaps your suitor should read this. The hero in our story needs to be taught how to be a good lover before he can succeed with his lady.' Jonathon wagged his dark eyebrows in play. 'Perhaps

I will take a few notes, too. A man can always improve.'

They laughed a little too loudly, earning a look of censure from the shopkeeper. How had this happened—that she should be sitting in a book-shop, laughing in French with Jonathon Lashley over love poetry? What a difference a few weeks and a few pretty dresses made.

Don't forget the enormous amount of courage and the urging of your friends. You were against this at the start. You were still protesting it as late as a few days ago, her conscience reminded her.

It hadn't been as simple as changing her appearance. The first lesson had been a disaster and she'd been nervous during the lessons that had followed, overly conscious of every time he touched her, every time he spoke. It had taken all of her concentration to focus. But now, if one overlooked the ill-fated kiss, there was a comfort between them. When had that sprung up?

'Est ce-que j'ai deux têtes?' Do I have two heads? Jonathon dropped his voice to an appropriate whisper. 'You're staring.'

'Pardon.' Claire smiled and shook her head.

'And you're stalling.' She didn't want him to break down now. He'd done extraordinarily well on this outing. Maybe she was pushing for too much too soon. She reached to take the book from him. 'Perhaps I should start.'

Jonathon watched Claire's mouth. It was rather convenient that their lessons required it of him. She had the most delicious lips, pink and the bottom lip carried just a hint of sensual full- ness to it, promising delight to those who might tempt to drink from that mouth, a promise that was born out in her kiss. Kissing her had been a misstep, though.

He could not bring himself to think of it as a mistake, merely a wonderful misstep. One did not kiss their teachers. Usually because those teachers were male. But also because it blended business with pleasure and it was easy to con- fuse gratitude over having learned something with other more passionate emotions.

One probably shouldn't dance with their tu- tors either for the same reasons. In the last few weeks he'd done both and enjoyed them far more than he should. Just as he was enjoying this outing, which wasn't really supposed to be an outing. He wasn't 'out' with her, he was on a field trip with his tutor and yet he couldn't quite convince himself this was the same thing as visiting the botanical gardens with his tutor, Mr Hadley, when he was a young boy. Probably because he wasn't a boy any more and probably because he hadn't kissed Mr Hadley or spent countless hours staring at Mr Hadley's mouth, which as he recalled, had a small wart on the left side. He spent most of the time trying *not* to look at it. He'd never wondered about Mr Hadley the way he wondered about Claire Welton.

She paused from her reading and he let his question tumble out, in French of course. 'Why so many languages, Claire?' He was gratified to see the question startled her, she was always so in control during their lessons, directing their conversations with an enviable coolness.

She stared at him, a little furrow forming between her brows. 'What does that have to do with Machaut's poetry?'

'Nothing.' Jonathon gave her a wide smile and didn't back down. He continued in French. 'It has to do with *you.*'

Lovely and intelligent, Claire Welton was becoming a potent temptation. It was hard to imagine the woman across from him was the same Claire Welton who had started the Season timid and dressed in what could only be described as 'adequate fashion'. 'Are you going to answer or do I have to stare at you all afternoon?'

She set down the book. 'You won't laugh?' His Claire had a vulnerable side. *His*? Hardly his, not in the usual way.

Jonathon shook his head. 'Of course not.'

'For the same reason I read. Words are escape, freedom. I can go places I've never been. Best of all, I can see the world differently. Languages all have unique words that English doesn't have equivalents for because the cultures they represent have different experiences than we do, different understandings.'

'*Donnez-moi une example.*' He was truly sucked into the conversation now, barely aware of how easily he responded in French to her French.

'*Votre ami,* Diderot.' She gestured to the book the shopkeeper had left on the table, 'He coined a phrase *l'esprit d'escalier*—the idea that one does not think of an appropriate response to a remark until one has left the party, or quite literally, reached the bottom of the stairs and it's too late to respond. I don't think we have an exact phrase for that concept in English.'

Fascinating. There was no other way to explain what it meant to sit there in the dusty bookshop and listen to her talk about escape, about freedom, about her desire to travel and see the world. To do so in French was only a small part of that fascination. She could have spoken in Turkish and it would have fascinated him. Admittedly, the French should have appealed much more given what he had at stake and what he'd struggled to overcome in the last seven years.

With Claire, he did feel he was on the road to recovery, but he wasn't quite there. One successful outing did not a victory make. He knew before she said, 'We should get back to our reading', that he still had a way to go. If he tried to read from the book of poetry, he would stumble. It wasn't exactly the note he wanted to end their day on. He prevaricated and Claire rose from the table, sensing his reluctance. Perhaps she, too, didn't want to risk the little successes of the afternoon.

'Maybe something different? Machaut can be difficult at first.' She went to an aisle, no doubt intending to find another text. When she didn't return immediately, he followed her, finding her engrossed in a slim volume, her back to him, her head bent just so, exposing the nape of her neck left bare from the upsweep of her hair. She made a pretty picture and an irresistible one. An urge to claim this moment, to claim *her*, swept him in a powerful wave. What would she do, if he kissed her here? Would she come alive as she had in the Rosedale garden? Would he?

He strode up behind her, his hands gripping her arms in gentle alert to his presence, his mouth close to her ear. 'What are you doing, Claire?' She jumped a little, startled out of her reading by his nearness, perhaps by his touch. It was a familiar touch, the kind a lover would use, but he didn't let go.

'Looking for something we can read.'

'Je ne veux pas lire, Claire.' His whisper sounded hoarse. Good, let it be a foreshadowing of what he did want, of what he meant to have

if she would allow it. Was any of the intrigue he felt returned on her part? *'Je veux te baiser.'* He kissed the bare space of her neck. Claire stiffened and he knew a moment's trepidation. He'd overstepped himself, once more swept away by the moment.

'You mean, *je veux t'embrasser...*' She whispered the correction, breaking from the French for the first time since they'd entered the store. 'You want to *kiss* me.'

'Oui.' Jonathon let a slow smile creep across his face. 'What did I say?' He had her backed to the wall now.

'That you wanted to f—' She blushed. 'It's a naughty word, Jonathon.' Well, maybe he wanted to do that too. Just because he had manners didn't mean he didn't have baser desires too. The two were not mutually exclusive. He was a man after all and she was a beautiful, intriguing woman.

He started to reframe his question, but she cut him off, a finger pressed to his lips. 'The answer is no. You may not kiss me.' Her eyes danced and she made no effort to move away.

'Why?' Jonathon drawled, flirting with his

eyes on her lips, not convinced he'd been rejected entirely.

'This time I'm going to kiss you.' Her arms were around his neck, pulling him close, her mouth finding his, full, open, and welcoming as it claimed his. Then his arms were about her, holding her against him, feeling the press of her, the curves of her, all warmth and willingness and eagerness, this was *her* kiss after all. She had initiated it, but the elation was all his. She wanted to kiss *him*! His bold Claire wanted to kiss him! It would be complicated later, but for now, it was pure, raw, joy and he let it shoot through him in lusty bolts.

The kiss was heady and hot, their mouths devouring each other by turn, his lips moving to her jaw, her throat, the pulse at the base of her neck. Only the last remnants of Claire's sanity kept him from attempting something more wicked. 'We have to stop.' She drew a ragged breath, her hands tangled in his hair, her mouth mere inches from his, her body giving no sign of agreeing with her mind. Jonathon pushed his advantage, reluctant to surrender the moment.

'Not yet,' he murmured, lowering his mouth

to hers, his hand sliding up the slim width of her rib cage, until the curve of his palms cupped the undersides of her breasts through the muslin of her gown. He ran a thumb over a nipple and felt a shudder ripple through her. This was a torturous game of have and have not he played. It was heavenly to touch her, to feel the firmness, the fullness of her breasts in his hand, but it was hellish to have to stop there, to not take them in his mouth and kiss them as he did her lips, to not see them bared, naked in his hands.

'Have you ever thought about not stopping, Claire?' This was madness. His words were evidence of it. He dare not take this any further and yet he dare not stop. 'Do you want to see what's on the other side of this passion?' Jonathon gave a groan, his hips grinding against hers as her sighs filled his mouth. 'I could show you pleasure finer than this.' His hand gripped the material of her skirts. It would be the work of a moment to have his hand behind them, the work of a few moments more to slide his fingers into her wet place and give her the pleasure her body was craving.

There was a cough behind him and Claire gave

a gasp, her gaze hurtling to a spot over his shoulder, her cheeks flaming in mortification while the shopkeeper launched into a torrent of French.

'*Mon Dieu! Est-ce pas un bordel! Sortir, prendre votre amour ailleurs.*'

Honestly, as they hurriedly gathered up Claire's hat and left money for their purchases, Jonathon couldn't tell if the man was genuinely offended or if he simply had to put up a pro forma protest because one really should not devour another's mouth or body in a public establishment. There was no getting around it. That was precisely what he and Claire had been doing. Together.

That kiss had been about as 'two way' as it got and he refused to feel ashamed over it. He ushered Claire out of the store as if they'd done nothing wrong and very properly bid the shopkeeper adieu. The shopkeeper glared at them, but Jonathon merely laughed as the door swung shut behind them. He'd not had nearly that much fun in ages. For the first time, in a long time, the smile he wore was there by choice instead of force.

Claire's face was blazing by the time he pulled the curricle away from the kerb. 'I'm sorry,' she began, but he silenced her with a shake of his head.

'What are you sorry about, Claire? Kissing me? Or getting caught?'

'Getting caught, of course.' Claire blushed even deeper, completely flustered once she realised what she'd said. The blush made her beautiful, a woman admitting to her passions. Would she look that way lying beneath him? Sated and replete from lovemaking? God, how he wanted to know. His body was rock hard from the wanting.

Jonathon laughed, steering the team into the traffic.

'Aren't *you* sorry?' Claire persisted.

'No, absolutely not.' He shot her a sideways look. 'However, having said that, you do understand there's no good way for a man to answer the question?' He lifted his eyebrows and pierced her with a direct look. 'This afternoon was a most pleasant revelation. I've discovered I *can* speak French and *you*, Claire Welton, are a wild soul indeed. Only one question remains: where shall we go tomorrow?' That was a lie. There were more questions that needed answering, like the one he'd asked her before the shop-keeper had interrupted them.

'I shall have to think about that,' Claire replied, her eyes dancing, her earlier mortification giving way to the hilarity and adventure of the situation. 'It's not every day a girl gets expelled from a bookshop for kissing Jonathon Lashley. I can't imagine what sort of encore would top today's excursion.'

'I can, if you'd let me show you.' It was a bold, wicked thing to say, but then again *she'd* kissed him. He was not the only interested party. 'Will you promise me something? Save me two dances tonight and we can discuss it then.'

Claire raised a cocky eyebrow, willing to play the game. 'Tomorrow's excursion or the pleasure of kissing you?'

'Both. I don't recall saying they were mutually exclusive.' He gave her a meaningful look. '*Two* dances, Claire. There will be no more running out on me.'

Chapter Thirteen

Two dances! He'd pledged the little bitch two dances. Cecilia fumed with angry tears smarting in her eyes from the sidelines. She'd caught sight of Claire's dance card quite by contrived accident earlier in the evening when they'd passed in the retiring room. Claire's card was fuller than usual, but that hadn't been the surprise. The surprise had been seeing Jonathon's name in bold letters printed on the card not once, but twice!

Twice! Twice was the maximum dances a gentleman could offer to a lady. It was the number Jonathon reserved for *her*. To offer that many dances to Claire somehow made Claire, an adequately dressed wallflower, equal to her, Cecilia Northam, a diamond of the first water, a woman destined to be the next Countess of Oakdale. Heaven forbid! It was not to be borne. Jonathon was hers and he needed reminding of it. Claire did, too.

Just look at them! She couldn't help but notice the pair of them flying by on the dance floor, Claire in a lovely lilac and a beatific smile on her face, Jonathon laughing down at her as if the little wallflower had said something witty. He looked as though he was enjoying himself. Immensely. There was an easiness, a tenderness when he looked at Claire. Maybe Anne was right and he had kissed her, after all. She'd prefer to believe Anne was just being spiteful with her news. But seeing them like this, it was hard to dismiss Anne's comment as complete heresy.

She twirled her champagne glass between her fingers. Signing up for two dances was one thing. Getting both of those dances was another. Lilac was a lovely colour, but it showed water stains. Badly.

'Have you decided?' Jonathon whispered, swinging her through a turn. 'Where shall our next adventure take place?'

'The French market tomorrow near Fitzrovia.' She'd decided that afternoon, not long after he'd dropped her off. He would have a chance to barter and argue. Haggling with the vendors would force him to think on his feet. There could be no script like today. Anticipating the conversations would only get him so far. His wits would have to do the rest.

'I like the challenge of that.' Jonathon smiled his approval and she nearly melted. She didn't tell him the rest—that there would be handwritten signs at the stalls, just a few words at the most at a time. She was hoping to trick him into reading without thinking in the hopes that the spontaneity and informality of the setting would break through what was left of his performance anxiety.

'Good.' She beamed up at him. 'I'll bring a shopping list and a basket.'

'And our other adventure, Claire? I would like to walk with you in the garden tonight.' His voice dropped, husky and private at her ear, his hand tightening on her back to draw her closer.

She didn't feign ignorance. She knew precisely what adventure he meant. She'd thought of noth-

ing else since he'd first uttered his rather provocative suggestion: that he could show her great
pleasure. 'You know that's the very sort of invitation our mothers counsel us to reject.'

'Only because they fear you will be ruined.'
He appealed to her intellect, her sense of logic.
'What if I told you I could give you the pleasure
and leave your honour intact? There would be
no risk to you.'

'Except discovery.' There was always a risk.

'I would never allow that to happen, Claire.'
He whispered his potent arguments with the skill
of Lucifer in the garden. It would be so easy to
believe him because she *wanted* to believe him,
wanted—how had he put it?—to see what lay
on the other side of this. Not just because she
was curious and untried, but because it was him
doing the asking. She wanted to see what was
on the other side of this *with him.*

She lowered her lashes and flirted. 'Why, Jonathon Lashley, I never imagined you as a rake.'
She felt alive with him, like she was once again
her true self—a woman who spoke her mind, a
woman who reached out for what she wanted.

'That makes two of us.' His voice was warm

at her ear. 'I never imagined you a wallflower. When you were younger, you were always too vibrant, too alive for that. I thought for certain you would take the *ton* by storm, too much for any man.' His lips brushed her ear. 'Will you come alive for me, again, Claire?'

The dance was ending. She had to make a decision. He had quite deliberately manoeuvred them to finish the dance near the French doors leading outside. 'We need only to slip outside, Claire. The night is warm, the stars are bright.' To walk, to talk, to kiss, to touch, to rekindle what had flared to life between them in the bookshop. What if this was her only chance? What if the urgency which had driven him to her side was also the urgency that sent him to Vienna too soon?

Claire seized her courage with a smile. 'I would very much like to go outside with you, Jonathon.'

It might have been magical, the stars might have been as bright as he suggested, the air as warm. She wouldn't know. A blonde vision in exquisite ice-pink silk stood before the doors, blocking the way like the sword-wielding angels at the gates of Eden. Her message was much the same. Access to the garden was being denied.

'Lashley, there you are!' Cecilia swept forward with a brilliant smile, champagne in one hand, her free hand going around Jonathon's other arm in a charming act of possession. 'It's so good of you to look after dear Miss Welton.'

Jonathon stiffened and Claire was assailed by myriad emotions competing for her attention. Old Claire wanted to give in to being cowed by this dazzling, confident young woman who could have any man in any room. Part of her felt guilty. She didn't want to steal another's beau. That had never been her intention. But the logic of guilt wouldn't hold, not quite. Jonathon wasn't Cecilia's just because Cecilia wished it to be true. But neither was that logic entirely intact. It was much like a dam threatened by flood waters, weakening in places. Jonathon had paid Cecilia *some* attention. Enough attention to set the gossips speculating. Just as he had her. The realisation broke the dam.

Claire cast a glance at Jonathon. Had he walked in the gardens with Cecilia? Had he promised her protected pleasures? Had that been the reason

Cecilia felt so confident in her claims? *I never imagined you the rake.* Perhaps she should have. Perhaps this wasn't the first time he'd played such a part. He'd already freely admitted the man he was in the ballrooms was a façade.

Behind that veneer was a man who had seen war, who had seen the world and the worldly things in it, and a man who had participated in those things as a man often does. He'd been ready to lead her down that worldly road and she'd been ready to go, thinking she knew Jonathon Lashley when nothing could be further from the truth.

She was so engrossed in the horrible train of thought she didn't see Cecilia move. 'Oh!' Cecilia gave a gasp of surprise, tripping forward over Jonathon's arm towards Claire, her full champagne glass tipping on to Claire's bodice as Cecilia lost her balance, clinging to Jonathon to steady her. Claire leapt back in shock, but too late to avoid the spilling champagne.

'Oh, my! How clumsy of me!' Cecilia gushed, looking entirely helpless and innocent, casting a beleaguered gaze at Jonathon as if she were the victim here. 'I don't know what happened.

Someone stepped on my hem, I think. It's such a crush in here.' They were starting to draw a crowd. 'Oh, dear, Miss Welton. Your dress! Just look at it. It's ruined. It was so lovely. Oh, where's a handkerchief when you need one? Perhaps if you get the dress off right away, your maid can salvage it. My maid is excellent with stains. I can have her send over her receipts. It's the least I can do, but I do think haste is critical, Miss Welton. You must go at once.'

Apparently the crowd about them concurred. A well-meaning lady stepped forward and took her arm, leading her away before Claire could protest. She was being dismissed! This was nothing more than one of Cecilia's strategies. How could she protest, even if she wanted to? What would she say? 'I'd like to stay and continue to dance in a ruined gown?' or 'She spilt it on purpose.' No one would believe that. Why would the beautiful Cecilia ever need to stoop so low? It would only serve to make her look like the foolish one and Cecilia the hero. But she wasn't wrong. One glance backwards confirmed it. Cecilia stood amid her admiring crowd with a smug look of satisfaction on her face and Jonathon by her side.

'Claire!' Beatrice rushed to her through the thinning crowd on the ballroom's perimeter. Everyone had surged forward at Cecilia's gasp. 'What has happened?'

'*She* did this on purpose!' Claire cried in frustration.

'Hush, wait until we're alone,' Beatrice said sternly, leading them out into the quiet hall. 'There, now we can talk.'

'She spilt her champagne! She wanted to separate me from Jonathon.' Just when things were going so very well. He'd invited her into the garden. To sin. Maybe she should be thanking Cecilia for saving her from a mistake.

Beatrice gave a rueful smile. 'Of course she did. Anyone who saw the pair of you dancing could see he was enchanted with you.' Bea looked down at the stain and put an arm around her shoulders. 'Your dress is soaked. I'll take you home.'

In the dark of the carriage, the doubts came. Had Jonathon been toying with her, taking advantage of her trust? Was he indeed a wolf in sheep's clothing? Had he seen her as an easy mark? Even now she couldn't quite believe it. Didn't want to believe it. Claire looked across at Beatrice. Is this what Bea felt for the erstwhile father of her child? Not wanting to quite believe the worst even when the evidence presented itself in stark clarity: Jonathon hadn't come after her.

'I should go after her and see if she's all right.' Minutes had passed and Claire had not returned. The crowd had slid away once the drama had ceased, leaving him with Cecilia.

'Hardly. She's probably left by now. This is for women to manage. What would you do?' Cecilia laughed at the notion. 'Do *you* have a secret receipt for instant stain removal?'

'I could make her feel better.' He wanted more than anything to take Claire in his arms, to console her. A wet dress was of no consequence, not to him. He'd wanted to shoo away the crowd that was determined to make a spectacle out of the minor event, determined to ruin the evening with their prying eyes and narrow minds.

Claire had been alive and charming in his arms just moments before the accident, but there'd been no mistaking the mortification in her eyes and he had *felt* her confidence leeching away. When she'd looked at him, he'd had the distinct impression some of that mortification was directed at him, as if she somehow blamed him for what had happened.

'Make her feel better? You are too good to be true.' Cecilia ran a soft hand along his arm, a quiet, private smile on her lips. 'But that's you, my dear Jonathon. You are always looking out for others less fortunate.'

Jonathon tensed. She'd never used his Christian name before and here she was doing it in public. She dropped her lashes. 'I worry for you, that people will take advantage of your kind nature.'

'I'm not that kind.' His voice was gruff, impatient. If he could leave, perhaps he could find Claire.

'Yes, you are. Miss Welton is proof of it. She is proof, too, that you are malleable. She's got you wrapped around her little finger and all because you showed her a bit of attention.' Cecilia looked up beneath her lashes. 'You've danced with her, you've shown interest in her and see how she's blossomed? She should let you go and move on to men of her calibre.'

'Men of her calibre? Who would that be?' Hearing Claire classified and discarded so readily made him bristle, yet this was Cecilia, who was touted as a paragon of womanly perfection, a woman he ought to prefer.

'Sir Rufus Sheriden for one. He offered for her once.' Cecilia smiled sweetly. 'She refused, but she's wiser now. She's seen what her level is, what she can hope to aspire to.'

'Sheriden? That blowhard?' Jonathon grimaced. 'Is that who Claire is trying to impress? She did mention she had a suitor.'

Cecilia drew a fingernail down his sleeve in a gesture that left him empty, her touch as uninspiring as Claire's had been inflaming in the bookshop. 'And you believed her, of course. She doesn't have a suitor, not an avid one anyway unless Rufus Sheriden is trying again. She probably just said as much to get your attention and talk you in to spending time with her. Really, Jonathon. You men need to pay more mind to ballroom politics.' She tossed him a smile. 'But that's why you have we women.' She slipped her arm through his. 'Walk with me?'

'My father told me he saw you at the club and the two of you spoke.' She gave a coquette's glance as they moved about the perimeter of the ballroom. 'Are there any plans you need to apprise me of?'

'No, nothing I can think of.' Jonathon's response was half-hearted. He was having trouble keeping his thoughts centred on Cecilia's prattling while the rest of him wondered just how awkward would it look if he called on Claire at eleven o'clock at night. He was busy trying to think of how he might spin a nocturnal visit that didn't require sneaking into her bedroom or climbing a trellis when Cecilia's words finally penetrated.

'A girl needs to plan. It might be nothing for you gentlemen to throw on a dark suit and show up at church, but a trousseau takes time.'

Jonathon stopped and stared blankly. 'Trousseau?'

Cecilia gave a haughty laugh. 'Why, yes, all the lovely dresses and linens a girl brings to her marriage.' She explained as if he were a clueless nodcock. He knew very well what a trousseau was. That was the part that had him worried. 'I have these exquisite Irish linens embroidered with…'

He did *not* want to hear what they were embroidered with for fear it might be his initials. Jonathon did not mince words. Mincing was how a man ended up married. 'Your high esteem flatters me, but let us be clear, I have *not* put forward a formal offer for you, nor have I *ever* spoken to you about such a thing. Any plans on your part would be premature, I assure you.'

The harshness of his words would have daunted most women, even most men. But Cecilia merely gave him a steely smile. 'I disagree. Marriage to me is the gateway to your future.' She feigned a look of confusion. 'Or are you having second thoughts about the posting to Vienna? You can't get there without me. You need my father's support. *I* assure *you.*'

Couples moved out on to the floor, taking up positions. Cecilia's smile changed into something sweeter as if she had not just demanded marriage from him. 'A waltz! Shall we, Jonathon? Everything has worked out as it should. I believe you're free for this dance, after all.'

Chapter Fourteen

Jonathon turned a dark Mayfair corner, his mind uninterested in what his feet were doing as it mulled over the sad reality: He wasn't free; not free to countermand Cecilia's high-handed manipulation or her haughty assumptions that he could be bought in marriage; not free to pursue a relationship with Claire, no matter what his feet thought to the contrary.

He didn't need to look up at the house towering in front of him to know where his unconscious wanderings had taken him: The very place he was not supposed to be: Claire's after midnight. He had no right to be here. He could promise her nothing beyond what he'd already promised and that was hardly enough. He could not offer her the only thing a well-bred lady could accept from a gentleman: marriage. Not because she didn't deserve it, but because *he* didn't. Assuming they suited one another for marriage.

Whoa. Marriage? Was that what his reeling mind was hiding in its recesses these days? Even if it was possible, the idea of marrying after a few French lessons and stolen kisses was a bit extreme, no matter how provocative those kisses had been. He was setting the cart miles ahead of the horse at this rate. Marriage assumed, too, that he deserved her. A man who left his brother behind in a foreign land didn't deserve her, or any chance at personal happiness after squandering that chance for his brother to experience the same. Yet he'd had the audacity to pretend he did. He'd cheated Thomas of his life! Every time he laughed, every time he felt the smallest inkling of joy, he was reminded of what his brother would never have.

Lately, when he was with Claire, the reminder was constant. Almost. To be honest, the joy, the peace, was so great he'd lose himself, he'd forget about the guilt. That was even more frightening. He knew how to live with the guilt. He wasn't sure he knew how to live without it.

Jonathon stared up at the house. That was the guilt talking. One could either argue the guilt kept him focused, or chained, depending on perspective. These days, the perspective was the latter. It was the guilt that kept him chained in his mental prison of regret. He should never have let Thomas ride down that road. But he had and had paid for that decision every day since his return from the Continent; he'd lost his ability to read French out loud, he'd lost the right to happiness. That was fine, he didn't deserve it. Why should he be happy? Why should his life go on when his brother's had not? Such penance hadn't bothered him too much until now. In its own way, that penance had given him direction upon his return. It had given him a sense of duty, an absolution to perform for failing to bring Thomas home safe and sound. He'd been content to let guilt rule his life. There'd been nothing he wanted that demanded he let the guilt go.

But now, he wanted the one thing he couldn't have and didn't deserve. The freedom to choose. He would still choose Vienna. Peace for Europe could be made there and he could make it.

But he would perhaps choose to go alone. Only he couldn't make that choice without jeopardising the appointment altogether. Without Cecilia, Lord Belvoir would block his appointment. Not in a vote—the House of Lords didn't confirm appointments, but in other subtle ways: funding, support, networks that would help and protect him abroad, all the tools he needed to be successful.

He wanted to be successful on his own merits. Just as he didn't want to be important only because of his father's birth, he didn't want to be chosen as a diplomat simply because of his wife's connections. He wanted to *earn* it. He'd not realised how much the position had come to hinge on Cecilia until she'd thrown it into stark relief tonight.

Jonathon picked up a handful of pebbles. He tossed one in his hand, testing its weight and trying to remember which window was Claire's. It was in back by the garden. He told himself he wanted to see her to assure himself she was all right, but it would be partially a lie. He wanted to see her for himself. He needed her. Whatever they could or could not be to one another, she could help him sort through the rather disappointing revelations of the evening simply by being with him. Or she could help him forget.

Jonathon slipped through the gate that gave into the garden. It had taken a waltz and an interminable supper hour before he'd been able to depart the ball. It was well past one o'clock. He should have gone home. But instead, he'd sent his carriage away and come here. Perhaps he'd be climbing trellises after all. He'd climb a mountain if that was what it took to reach her. The truth was, if there was peace to be had tonight, it would be in Claire's arms and the future could be damned.

Ah, there it was! The third window towards the back. He was sure that was the room. A little thrill of victory coursed through him. It had a small, semi-circular wrought-iron balcony, more decorative than useful. A person might just be able to stand there and catch the morning sun on her face. The little thrill of victory was replaced by a stronger surge of lust. To his body's chagrin, Jonathon could very well imagine Claire on that balcony, hair loose, face tilted upward to the dawn, dressed in a fine linen shift that caught the light.

Standing on the ground day dreaming offered no progress that direction. He tossed a pebble. It made a satisfying clink against the narrow French doors of the balcony. He counted to ten and waited. There was no response. He tossed a second pebble and then a third in rapid succession. She did not come. There was no sign of life.

Jonathon grimaced. If she would not come to him, he would have to go to her. There was nothing for it. He'd have to climb the rose trellis. He gave the trellis a speculative look, gauging the distance between it and the balcony. He'd use the trellis for height, then he'd have to use his muscle to overcome the gap where the trellis gave out and the balcony began. His arms would just be able to span it and he could lever himself up from there. Very plausible.

From the ground that was. Being suspended twenty-five feet above said ground tended to change a man's perspective. So did thorns. Ten sweaty minutes later, Jonathon had learned two things: first, summer roses only smelled sweet. They were in fact the devil's own flower, riddled with thorns just where a man might want to put his hands for a good grip. It had taken a few prickings in the dark to learn that. Second, evening clothes and dancing shoes were not at all ideal for climbing. The good news—his dark evening jacket was no longer too tight, now that it sported a relieving rip right down the centre seam in the back. At the moment, he didn't care. He felt like he'd summited the Alps. Jonathon reached for the doors and pushed them open. Claire was inside. Peace was inside.

Claire's mind knew someone was in the room before she awoke. Her body knew who it was. 'Jonathon!' Her eyes flew open to confirm. It was Jonathon, but not the Jonathon she was used to. This Jonathon, who stood framed in beams of moonlight, was a veritable King of Midnight. His hair fell forward into his face, rakish and rugged, his clothes dishevelled. But it was his eyes that drew her; twin blue flames of determination burned in his gaze as if coming here had cost him something and he had chosen to come any way.

Then it occurred to her that it had indeed cost

him something. 'How did you get in?' She sat up, her mind fully awake now. He couldn't possibly have come up the stairs. He gave a nod toward the open doors. 'The balcony?' Her response was tinged with disbelief. Dear heavens, that was dangerous! The roses with their thorns, the trellis that didn't reach all the way up. She could see it in her mind now, the space between the iron spindles of the balcony and the trellis where only muscle and strength could span the gap. 'Are you insane? You could have fallen! Why?' she scolded.

A wry smile quirked at his mouth. 'Because I promised you something and I never break my promises.'

He was here for pleasure. Claire stilled, the air around them charged with electric intent. He'd climbed the trellis for her, risked discovery for her. If someone should hear him, should come through the door of her room, they would both be compromised beyond amends. There was no denying the risk factor carried some excitement of its own. But it wasn't that simple. The problem with waking up was remembering and remembering two entirely different things. Her body remembered the afternoon, full of passion and adventure, while her mind remembered the evening full of dashed hopes, disappointments and doubts.

'Will you have me, Claire?' he prompted her, his voice hoarse, his body taut with emotion, desperation perhaps? Maybe that was too strong of a word. Uncertainty, then. He was uncertain. Of her. Handsome Jonathon Lashley, who was always sure, *wasn't* sure of her; wasn't sure that she, Claire Welton, who had no choices in any given ballroom, would want him who had every choice. And it was important to him that she did. He didn't want to be rejected, but he wasn't sure he wouldn't be. He understood her doubts as clearly as if they shared one mind. She saw now in stark clarity why he'd climbed that trellis. He wanted to know if she would accept him, if her feelings matched his in spite of the impossibilities that lay beyond these moments.

The Vienna post, the duty he must do to attain it, and whatever else he hid behind his smiles and blue gaze had existed before this and they would exist after this. She would not worry over what she couldn't change. Instead, she would be thankful she was walking into this with eyes wide open. She would not be ambushed by reality on the other side of midnight. If there could only be now, then so be it. She would take now over never any night.

Claire rose from the bed, the decision made before her bare feet touched the cool floor. She crossed the room to him, arms encircling his neck with wondrous ease, her lips feathering his mouth. 'Yes, Jonathon, I will have you.' The pleasure, the pain, she would have all of it, for as long as it lasted.

His mouth was on her then, hard and fierce in its claiming. He tasted of victory and exultant relief. A thrill ran through her. He had wanted this badly. She could feel the tension of his body uncoil beneath her hands, only to be replaced with a new sort of anticipation. The afternoon's passion surged back in force between them. It would be temptingly easy to rush this, to pick up where they'd left off before being expelled from the bookshop, instead of savouring the opportunity to start from the beginning once more. But Jonathon would not be rushed.

He slowed the tempo of their kiss, cradling the

nape of her neck in the cup of his hand, the press of his mouth lingering and languorous, their bodies moving into one another as the kiss deepened. He was all heat and hard planes against her. She revelled in the feel of him through the thin fabric of her night rail. This was so much better than feeling him through the limitations of gowns and undergarments. Perhaps she could make it even better for him.

She broke the kiss for a moment, her eyes meeting his as her hands worked the knot of his cravat until the cloth came loose. She gave him a coy smile. 'You are wearing too many clothes.'

He gave a sly grin in return. 'What else do you plan to divest me of?'

She smoothed the shoulders of his dark coat and pretended to contemplate the question. 'Definitely this. It must go at once. The waistcoat, too.' She pushed the coat back and he helped remove it but she didn't miss the ripped seam. 'Your tailor will shoot you for this.'

Jonathon's gaze landed on her, hot and intent. 'I'll tell him it was worth it.'

Claire swallowed, basking in the compliment, a lump forming in her throat, blocking words.

She let her fingers speak for her, slipping the buttons of his waistcoat through their holes. It was much easier to get the waistcoat off than the coat. But here she hesitated. Only trousers and shirt remained.

'What next? Perhaps my shirt?' came the wicked suggestion, Jonathon's voice soft at her ear.

'Absolutely,' Claire answered boldly, stepping away to resume her place on the bed. 'Why don't you take it off for me so I can watch?'

He made her a small bow. 'As you wish, my lady.' But it was as *he* wished and he wished to play with her a bit. She saw it in the tilt of his smile, the flare of mischief in his eyes. She settled against the pillows and turned up her lamp to give the room a modicum of light. She didn't want to miss a moment of this. He made a show of slowly removing the fasteners at his cuffs, the collar, pulling the tails of his shirt from his trousers until at last the shirt was loose.

She imagined sliding her hands beneath it and running them up the bare planes of his chest, imagined the feel of his skin against the palms of her hands. Then, he slipped the shirt off and she imagined no more. He stood before her, half-naked, his shirt tossed to a pile on the floor, hands on narrow hips, blue eyes challenging her. 'Do you like what you see?'

She nodded, not trusting herself to speak. He was gorgeous. Fully clothed, he'd merely been handsome. The adjective hardly did this man, with his firm abdomen and sculpted chest, justice. She patted the space on the bed beside her. It was her turn to tease. 'It's still a bit dark in here. I can't quite see. Come a little closer.'

He took the invitation, stretching out alongside her, his head propped in his hand. He couldn't get much closer than this. 'Do I please you, Claire?'

She gave a little laugh, her hand trailing across his chest in exploration and wonder. 'How could you not? You're beautiful.' She raised her gaze to his, her voice an honest, quiet whisper. 'You've always been beautiful to me.' Her hand traced a fine line along his shoulder and stilled. 'Scars and all,' she ventured softly, the importance of the moment hitting her full force. To be naked, even partially naked with another, was to expose oneself in intimate ways. 'Was this from the war?'

'From the war, from my stubborn foolishness.' She knew, as did most of London, that he'd come home wounded, dangerously so. There'd been a time when it had not been clear he would live. But knowing it was not the same as seeing it.

She retraced the line with her hand, this time noting how close the scar was to his chest. A scant few inches had separated life from death. He had healed well, but the scar would be with him always. 'It looks painful.'

'Terribly. Although I'm told under normal circumstances it would have been a fairly minor wound. The bullet didn't exit. Still, it could have been pulled out and I could have been stitched up. But the bullet I was shot with was rusty. That makes it poisonous all on its own. A horrible infection followed.' Jonathon tried to laugh, not wanting to inflict that horror on Claire. 'Fortunately, I don't remember it. I was delirious, out of my head with fever once the infection truly set in.'

'That was when they sent you home?' Her question was quiet.

'I don't remember much of that either. I am told there was some concern I wouldn't make it home. I raved in French the whole trip back.' He took her hand away from the scar and raised it to his lips. 'I don't want to talk about the war tonight, Claire.' Or any night, Claire thought with a flash of intuition. As a rule, people shied away from topics that were unpleasant and Jonathon took great pains to always be pleasant. There were secrets there, perhaps even nightmares. But he was right, tonight was for other things.

He reached for her and she went easily, letting him draw her flush against him so that their lengths matched. His mouth found hers perhaps as much to start the pleasure as to stop the words, the questions. His hand slid beneath her night rail, warm against her leg, the fabric rucking up as his hand progressed up her thigh. He murmured against the column of her neck, 'You are beautiful, too, Claire. Far too beautiful for the likes of me.'

She gave a throaty laugh. 'Such flattery, Jonathon.' But for the night she would believe it. He made her feel beautiful, wanted, with his words, with his touch. His fingers skimmed the place between her thighs and her body wept with delight and with knowledge. This was what he'd meant to do in the bookshop, to touch her like this, to conjure this sensation from her. She was glad now the shopkeeper had caught them. She wanted to savour the sensations, wanted to linger over the pleasure.

He touched her again. This time his stroke was insistent, no mere skimming graze, and her body seemed to leap to life. 'Mmm...' A slow moan escaped her lips, her legs parted, following the logic that surely more access meant more pleasure. She was not wrong. Jonathon cupped her mons, stroked her, building a slow, hot fire within and all the while she felt her core weeping, preparing for something more. Warmth pooled in her low and potent, waiting to be loosed. Her hips arched upwards, seeking the 'more'. Jonathon's fingers parted her, exposed her and she gasped at the intimate intrusion—shocking and exquisite in its boldness. His thumb teased the tiny bean hidden within and her body went wild with a thousand sensations, one word chorusing in her mind *again, again, again*!

With each pass, each stroke, she soared, she

wept until she could feel her own slickness against Jonathon's hand. The pleasure became too much. Her body pressed into Jonathon's hand, her body crying with contradictions, wanting more and yet wanting release. It was too much. It was not enough. Jonathon knew. Each stroke brought her closer to whatever she sought until she was *there* at last. Soaring, falling, shattering, with a scream muffled by Jonathon's mouth.

'Oh, sweet heavens,' she said at last when the power of the moment had settled. 'I hadn't known such a thing was possible.' Her voice sounded breathy to her. Jonathon was gazing at her with something akin to awe in those beautiful eyes.

'Now you know.' His own voice was husky and it occurred to her that while she'd found release he had not, not physically any way.

Her own audacity got the better of her. 'May I do that to you? *For* you?' Suddenly, she wanted more than anything to give him pleasure, to watch him find pleasure and know she'd been the one to give it.

His eyes glittered, dark with want as he spoke

a single word. 'Yes.' His hands moved to the fall of his trousers, but she pushed them away.

'Let me.' She wanted to do all of it, be responsible for all of it. Her hands trembled as they worked the flap. She could feel him hot and ready beneath the fabric, already in a state of arousal. Pleasuring her had already brought him pleasure it seemed. A smile took her. Her response had pleased him, had been, in fact, exactly what he'd hoped.

The realisation made her bold, confident. He lay on his back, his hands behind his head, his body open to her, exposed as she had been to him. He was hers for the taking, every inch of him magnificent. His phallus stirred under her gaze, starting to strain. It was all the invitation she needed. She closed her hand about him, hearing the sharp intake of breath at her touch and then an exhalation of pleasure. 'You feel so damn good, Claire.'

She slid her hand down his length, exploring, testing the power of her touch to rouse him, to pleasure him. And then up, to be welcomed by a bead of moisture at his tip. Up and back, her hand made the journey, his body arching into her stroke, until it gathered itself, giving her warning that he, too, was about to shatter. Only it wasn't a shattering, a breaking apart when it came, but a surging, potent and hot as she held him, feeling the strength of the shudders racing through him, watching the arch of his muscles and then the relaxation taking him as pleasure ran its course.

He reached for her, pulling her close against him with the last of his waking strength and she went, laying her head against his chest, fitting her body to his and for a while they slept, but she already knew, as exquisite as the pleasure had been, it hadn't been enough. Tonight had not satisfied as she'd hoped. It had only provoked, proving it was nothing more than an appetiser on passion's plate, and when she woke, he would most likely be gone, perhaps in more ways than merely the physical.

Chapter Fifteen

Lucifer's balls, *what* had he done? It wasn't the first time he'd asked himself that question since leaving Claire's in the wee hours of morning the same way he'd got in. By now he was quite familiar with what he'd done. Jonathon twirled the stem of his brandy snifter in idle frustration. Maybe the more important question was what was he *going* to do? He'd been sitting here since early morning. The sky had still been grey when he'd banged on the door of White's. Since then, he'd progressed from coffee to brandy. This was his second glass. That was saying something considering it was only one in the afternoon. He was no closer to an answer.

He'd starting drinking at eleven instead of going to French lessons. He could not go to

Claire until he had an answer. They'd both tacitly pretended last night had been a night out of time, a night that existed apart from the realities of their world. But he had not bargained on the pleasure being so exquisite, so meaningful. No, that was a lie. He would not have gone if he hadn't thought the possibility existed. He'd taken no small risk in climbing that trellis. He'd known very well what lay at the end of that journey. Last night, it had been enough to simply discover it, claim it. But today, he wanted more of it and today, he couldn't have it. Reality intruded.

He owed it to Claire to stay away now that they both understood what lay between them. He'd kept his promise. She'd had pleasure and she had not been ruined. But he could not dare anything more. It would not be fair to either of them. So, he'd sent a note informing her he wouldn't be there for his lesson. He'd played the gentleman in that choice, but he felt like a coward. As for the planned trip to Fitzrovia and the French market, he let the weather do the rest.

It had been pouring since ten o'clock, keeping everyone inside and ruining the possibility of another excursion even if it had been possible.

Jonathon had to settle for an afternoon spent at White's which offered plenty of time to read the foreign newspapers and reflect on the fact that doing so was nowhere near as exciting as reading in a French bookshop with Claire, or climbing into bedrooms with Claire, or Claire's hand on him bringing the most personal of pleasures.

'May I join you?'

Jonathon looked up from the French news to greet Preston Worth. He smiled at his old friend and motioned to the empty chair. 'Please. I could do with some company. The weather has driven everyone to ground.'

'Unless one fancies ladies' tea parties.' Preston took a seat and gestured for a waiter to bring him a drink. 'I hear you've been doing the pretty. My mother tells me you came to Lady Morrison's at-home the other day.'

'Not on purpose.' Jonathon laughed and held his hands up in mock defence. 'I was looking for someone.'

Preston gave him a sly look. 'Does it happen to be a brunette with chocolate eyes who's taken a newfound interest in clothes and speaks flawless French?' The allusion was unmistakable.

'Cognac, her eyes are the colour of cognac, not chocolate and dammit, Preston, this is why one's friends shouldn't go into intelligence. Do I have no privacy?'

Preston smiled smugly and overlooked the dig about intelligence. 'So you *were* looking for Claire Welton.'

'She *is* my French tutor, as you well know, apparently.' He was a bit chuffed Preston knew. For his sake and Claire's, Jonathon would rather have kept that bit of information under wraps.

Preston leaned forward, triumph leaving his expression, replaced by sincerity. 'Your secret is safe with me. Having friends in intelligence also means they know how to keep a secret. You can trust Owen and me. We are souls of discretion.'

Jonathon shifted in his seat. 'Owen doesn't know.'

Preston chuckled. 'Doesn't know or you *think* he doesn't know? Owen knows the colour of the king's underwear on any given day. The man knows everything.' Preston paused. 'Speaking of "everything", how's the French going? Is it coming back?'

Jonathon rapped the small drink table between

them with his knuckles. 'For luck,' he explained. 'I would hate to jinx things now. I think so, better than I hoped. Claire is a fine instructor.' It had been on the tip of his tongue to mention the outing to the bookshop, but he thought better of it. He preferred the idea that he had some secrets at least.

'Claire? First names and all? I would say that is progress indeed.' Preston drained his brandy. 'She's a fine dancer, too, and *don't* cut up at me for noticing. You've danced with her every night lately. It's not a secret. Anyone who cared to notice could. Is that part of your tutoring as well?' There was a veiled edge to his tone.

'What is that supposed to mean?' Jonathon answered with an edge of his own.

Preston twirled the stem of his snifter with an idle nonchalance. 'I don't know what it means, Jonathon. That's why I'm asking you. Does it mean *anything* at all?'

Jonathon was glad the club was nearly empty. Preston's voice suddenly seemed louder than necessary, but he couldn't ask his friend to lower his tone without implying that perhaps something was indeed afoot. Implication was all the bone Preston would need to dog him about it until he confessed.

I took your sister's friend out yesterday without a chaperon and ravaged her in a French bookshop until the shopkeeper threw us out. Then we finished what we had started in her bedroom last night. Just with hands, though, no damage done.

He didn't need an especially creative imagination to know how *that* would go over. Preston had always been protective of his sister's friends even when they were nine-year-old nuisances.

'Ah, your silence condemns you, Jonathon.' Preston gave the devil's own grin.

'I am helping her attract the attention of a beau she's interested in. It's a fair exchange for her tutelage,' Jonathon replied, sounding far too defensive. His answer sounded like a denial. He hated himself for the words. They might have been the truth a few weeks ago, but it was only a slim part of the truth now. He wasn't dancing with her to help her, but because he wanted to. He loved the feel of her in his arms, the caress of her eyes on him as they swept the dance floor. After yesterday, he wasn't willing to share that caress. He certainly wasn't willing to turn her over to a suitor. He was starting to feel jealous of this suitor she so desperately wanted to impress.

Preston lifted a brow. 'Really? I was unaware she had a suitor. May hasn't said anything. Who is he?'

'I don't know. She won't say.' Jonathon shrugged as if it was of no consequence. He refused to believe Cecilia's assertion that Sir Rufus Sheriden had a longstanding interest that might be reciprocated. Claire had kissed *him*, he reminded himself, unable to help the smile that spread across his face at the memory, of Claire wrapping her arms about him and pulling him close in the bookshop, her mouth covering his. There were other memories, too, that mocked the idea her attentions were engaged elsewhere. How could she be when her hand… He had to stop right there. He shifted in his seat. If he didn't stop, he'd be giving too much away to a man who was already canny.

'What are you hiding? A man only smiles like that when he's thinking of a woman.' Preston's eyes narrowed in speculation. 'The question is, what woman? Claire or Cecilia?' His voice dropped to a hush, his face registering the truth Jonathon couldn't speak. 'By Jove, you're falling for Claire Welton.'

'Yes.' There. He'd said it; the *new* truth that he was just beginning to recognise. He was falling for Claire.

Preston nodded thoughtfully. 'How far do you plan to fall?'

'I don't know.' He might have already fallen, the descent complete before he'd even realised the danger. 'Does one plan these things?' He certainly hadn't. He'd had a plan, a very detailed one until he'd sat across from Claire at the Worths' dinner. That plan had slowly eroded ever since. The irony was that he'd only approached Claire in order to help that original plan, not derail it.

'And Cecilia Northam? Where does she figure into all of this?' Preston leaned forward, dropping his voice further.

'I don't know.' Hadn't he just said that?

'What *do* you know? Perhaps we should start with that. In fact, let me start.' Preston held up a finger for every item. 'First, you need a wife to go with you to Vienna. Nothing buys respectability like having a wife at your side. That means the clock is ticking, old boy. You need to marry by summer's end, sooner if you want to wedge in a honeymoon that doesn't involve travelling to your post. Second, Cecilia Northam has been groomed to be a diplomat's wife. Lord Belvoir wants a title and political position for his daughter. He wants a future prime minister for her if he can get it, this is a fairly open secret in the *ton*. Third, Belvoir and Cecilia want that husband to be you, also a fairly open secret. They are angling for an offer before June is out.' Preston raised another finger and added to the list. 'Fourth, Belvoir has the power to force your hand. If you don't come up to scratch, it may not matter how good your French is or that you have personal connections to Owen Danvers. Belvoir can ruin your chances and see that the post goes to Elliot Wisefield. The man is vindictive enough to do it.'

Preston sat back in his chair. 'It's time for some risk analysis, old boy. Cecilia secures the post for you. Without her, it's dicey. Maybe you have enough influence without her, maybe you can survive whatever firestorm her father sends your way. It's a big maybe, though. Are you willing to lose the Vienna post for Claire?'

'Put that way, choosing Claire seems the height of idiocy.' Jonathon expelled a tired breath. He'd known this already. It was an equation he'd been through countless times in the last several years as he'd battled back from the wound, from the grief of losing Thomas not just once, but over and over again when false leads didn't play out. It was more than the post he was risking. The post merely symbolised the things he desired: a legacy of peace, a chance to go back and find out the truth about Thomas, a chance for closure on the past and the beginning of a future at last.

Preston shook his head, a dark shadow crossing his face. He leaned forward and placed one hand on Jonathon's leg in encouragement. 'Not if you love her, not if you plan to fall all the way.' It made Jonathon wonder what Preston knew about such falls. Love was not something Preston ever spoke about. Jonathon was not even aware Preston had experienced it. His friend was a closed book when it came to his personal relationships. 'And Jonathon,' Preston added, 'with a girl like Claire, I think there's only one way to fall.'

Jonathon nodded, hearing the warning and the endorsement. Preston would support him no matter what he chose, even if that choice was Claire, but he was not to ruin Claire, not to toy with her. If he pursued her, it had to be in earnest. So be it. Perhaps it was best Preston didn't know about last night. Or the bookshop. Or what he intended to do next. Jonathon called for ink and paper, a renewed sense of purpose coursing through him.

Preston shot him a quizzical look as he began to pen a note. 'What are you doing?'

Jonathon gave him a wily grin. 'Falling.' And the ground was coming up fast. He prayed the landing wouldn't kill him. But that was a question for which he had no answer.

Jonathon had become something of an unanswered question these last weeks. Cecilia plucked at the blossoms of Jonathon's bouquet where it sat on her writing desk. She was losing him when she'd been so certain of her victory. She looked out over the garden. True, there was no formal agreement between them. Nothing bound Jonathon to her beyond her own personal expectations. But she'd thought Jonathon had informally agreed with her on those expectations. He danced with her, he sent her flowers, he stood at her side, escorted her to events on occasion. They were invited to the same places.

Now, all those safe assumptions had become uncertain and uncertainty made Cecilia nervous. She'd admit it privately to herself, but she'd never say it out loud to her friends. No one could know the great Cecilia Northam, reigning beauty of the *ton*, was unsure of herself or of Jonathon Lashley.

But this was uncharted territory to be sure. She wasn't used to being nervous. She was always very sure of herself and even more sure of others. She was good at creating a desired response. At least she used to be. The ice-pink gown had not gone over as well as hoped. Jonathon had told her the gown looked lovely, but it hadn't stopped him from dancing with Claire Welton, again. And again. And again.

The phenomena had happened often enough that everyone had taken note. People were starting to talk. She'd heard the whispers about how pretty Claire looked, how the girl had blossomed this Season. The gossips were starting to nod and smile sagely to themselves and say insipid things like 'third time's a charm it seems'.

The gossips said it was amazing what a nice dress could do for a girl, but Cecilia knew better. While it was true that Claire *was* dressing better, and her eyes sparked with a certain lively light, it wasn't a dress that put the sparkle there. It was Lashley that made Claire pretty. Without him, Claire would still be Claire, wallflower extraordinaire, three Seasons since her debut and still alone.

It was proof of just how exquisite Jonathon was if he could get a girl like Claire to bloom. There was no man more attractive, no man better mannered, no man who danced as well, fenced or rode as well, spoke as well. A man like that deserved a woman like herself, his equal in perfection. It was an obvious conclusion to her. But even spilled champagne had not been enough to make the conclusion obvious to Jonathon.

Last night had proven to her it was no longer enough to simply remind Jonathon of what she offered. She had to show him what Claire lacked. The best way to do that was to show him her and Claire together and she knew just how to do it. Her parents were hosting a small, intimate and exclusive musicale featuring a renowned Italian soprano. She would invite Claire and Jonathon could see the two of them side by side. He would come to the logical conclusion. Claire couldn't possibly complete with her face to face.

Cecilia began to pen the invitation, a horrible thought forming. If Claire was nothing without Jonathon, what would *she*, herself, be if she lost him? The answer haunted her: A girl three Seasons out with no prospect. A girl like Claire. Her hand shook. A blob of ink blotted the clean invitation and she had to start again. In those moments, Claire was not just the competition, she became the enemy and enemies needed to be conquered.

Chapter Sixteen

The invitations arrived simultaneously, delivered to her room by no one less than her mother, who handed them over with an enquiring smile. 'Two notes, for you personally, Claire.' Her mother stepped inside her room. Claire couldn't remember the last time her mother had been there. Usually, they met in the rooms downstairs for meals, for receiving, or in the carriage as they made calls or shopped.

Claire scanned the notes, both still sealed. Her heart beat a little faster at the sight of one of them. Jonathon. The second one from him today. Would it be more bad news? He'd not come to his lesson and the weather had ruined the chance to go to the French market even if he had intended to go. Last night had raised more questions than answers as to what lay between them. She could tell herself all she wanted that last night was for fantasy only, that nothing could come of it. But that didn't stop her from wishing otherwise. The other was a woman's hand, but she didn't recognise it. An awkward silence full of expectation began to grow when she made no move to open the notes. Perhaps her mother would take the silence as a hint she wished to open her notes in privacy and leave?

The hint conspired against her. Instead of leaving, her mother entrenched, a most unusual strategy for a woman who traditionally favoured a *laissez-faire* approach to life. Her mother was a calm woman, not easily flustered or bothered by the goings on of the world. 'Is that one from Mr Lashley?' Her mother took a seat on the edge of her bed, clearly signalling she was not going to be dismissed until the missives were read.

Claire did not want to open that note particularly, not when there was a good chance it was either a request to sneak away to one of their French locations or to apologise for any untoward behaviour or worse! Dear lord, she hoped Jonathon wouldn't be so brash as to put any reference to last night or the bookshop into a note that would compromise him. If her mother knew he'd been here, and what they had done, there would be no explaining it. Claire thought quickly, her mind racing through her options. If she opened the note, her mother would want to see it. Given the events of the last two days, it was unlikely the note contained innocuous information. Giving her mother the note was out of the question, but she could give her the truth, although she would rather give her mother neither. The less her mother knew about Jonathon the better. Her mother had been the most disappointed when things had soured with Sheriden.

Claire slid the unopened note under a jar on her vanity, establishing that she was saving the exact details for a private moment. 'Yes, I believe it is.' She offered the truth as casually as possible.

'French lessons seem to be going well,' her mother said vaguely.

'Yes.' Claire decided to keep her answers short and terse.

'Your Season seems to be going decidedly better than usual now that you've taken an interest in it.' Her mother smiled. 'I told you it just needed a little management on your end. Mr Lashley has been dancing with you quite a lot. I don't suppose dancing is part of the French lessons?'

'Yes, Jonathon seems to have made a habit of it, although I've assured him it's not necessary.' In her attempt to treat the remark lightly, she made her mistake.

Her mother pounced. 'Jonathon, is it? Have you two become as close as all that? First names, is, well...' She fluttered a hand.

'It's nothing, Mother.' Claire leaned back against her vanity, her hands gripping the edge against the blatant lie. He'd kissed her in the Rosedale garden. She'd kissed him in a French bookshop. She could still feel his hands on her, the strength of his body as he'd come up behind her, his mouth at her ear whispering decadent words. *'Claire, I don't want to read.'* He'd put his hand on her breast. He'd climbed a trellis for her at midnight, she'd had her hand on his manly core in the very bed her mother now sat on. What they'd done, what they'd become wasn't exactly *nothing* even if what existed between them lay undefined.

Her mother was not satisfied. 'Are the flowers downstairs that arrive like clockwork nothing either?'

'He is appreciative. He wants this position in Vienna badly.' She *hoped* that was a lie, too. She wanted to believe last night was more than a show of appreciation.

'Flowers, dancing, he even called at Lady Morrison's to enquire as to your whereabouts.' Her mother built her case, her soft, doe eyes growing shrewd. Lady Morrison's would have been the day he'd come to Evie's and waited for a half-hour downstairs, but Claire kept that to herself—voicing it wouldn't help her argument. Her mother wasn't done. 'It seems like a lot of unnecessary trouble for French lessons, no matter how badly he wants the post.' Her mother paused. 'He's not the only one going to a lot of trouble these days. I see other things, too, Claire. I see you, looking beautiful in altered gowns. I see you taking an interest in your appearance and in society. You haven't complained at all this Season about going out. Usually by now I have to pry you out of the house. And I see why. If a handsome man like Mr Lashley was waiting to dance with me, I'd not want to stay home either.'

'We enjoy one another's company,' Claire prevaricated. 'I wouldn't make too much of it.'

'And slipping off to destinations unknown in the middle of the afternoon without a chaperon?' There was a quiet steel in her mother's voice now as she dropped the most damning piece of evidence. The irony was that the adventure had been for learning purposes, it had simply turned in to something more. Her mother rose and paced to the window overlooking the garden. 'Do you think I'm an idiot, Claire?'

'No, of course not.' She did, however, think her mother wouldn't pay enough attention to notice. Apparently, her mother had noticed quite a lot, not only this year but the other years as well. Claire had misjudged her there. They had been polite but distant family members since the debacle with Sheriden.

Her mother let the lace panel drop over the window and turned to face her. 'Your father and I have let you be these last two years, after Sheriden. We did not understand, at the time, how much you didn't want to marry. If you want a quiet life of books and solitude, you shall have it. We won't force you to marry for the sake of marrying, but if that has changed, we should be informed, Claire.'

Claire was silent, absorbing the words. It was the most personal conversation her mother had had with her since the refusal. 'Claire?' her mother prompted. 'I am asking you point blank—is Jonathon Lashley courting you under the pretence of French lessons?'

'I don't know,' Claire replied softly, lifting her gaze to meet her mother's. She could see her mother's frustration in the knit of her brow. Her mother thought she was being purposely evasive. But this was the sad truth. She had so little experience with courtship games between men and women. 'Sometimes I think perhaps he is.' Last night had certainly seemed like it. It was the first time she'd ever said the words out loud. 'But always, there are the lessons between us, a reminder that without them, he wouldn't be with me.' Would he?

Her mother resumed her seat on the edge of the bed. 'Do you wish he was? Do you want him?'

She had to be careful here. *Did* she want him? It made him sound like an object to be purchased, a sweet to enjoy. 'I hardly know him.' Now she was truly evading.

Her mother brushed the objection away. 'We know his family. Viscount Oakdale is eminently respectable and we know his prospects, which are very good. He has money, his family has money and he'll likely go abroad as a diplomat. Ultimately, Lashley will inherit the title, although not soon. His father married young and will live another twenty years. Lashley won't see the title until he's fifty if he's lucky.' Her genteel mother surprised her with a rather practical dissection of Jonathon's prospects. When put that way, it was no wonder Jonathon was so eager for the Vienna post. He wasn't about to while away his life waiting to inherit well into middle age. He wanted to do something useful.

But the bigger surprise were her mother's next words. 'We are people of some consequence, Claire. We may be quiet and keep a retiring profile by choice, but your father has connections. If you want Lashley, we can get him for you.'

'No!' Claire's response was vehement and instant. 'I don't want him that way, trussed up and delivered like a Christmas goose.' It would make her no better than Cecilia, who had picked Jonathon out and begged her father for him. 'Should anything evolve between us, I want it to be natural. I want him to choose me on my own merits, not my father's persuasion.'

Her mother's eyes pointedly went to the note peeking out from under the jar. 'He wants to meet with you again, secretly.' She smiled. 'You see, I don't need you to open the envelope. I was young once, too. I remember quite well what young men in love are like.' Her smile faded. 'Go to him then, you will anyway, so I might as well know about it. But do not let him trifle with you. If you are caught, there will be no more talk of choosing. He'll be yours then, personal merits being amenable or not.' She stood and crossed the short distance to her and placed a kiss on her brow. 'Be careful, Claire.'

Claire sat at her vanity, reaching for the two notes, her mind reeling and full. Her mother *knew*. Had known. Her mother was endorsing a secret rendezvous. She was starting to understand where she got a thirst for adventure from.

It existed in her mother, too, buried deep down, just like her, coming out in surprising ways that weren't always obvious.

She opened Jonathon's note first, staring at the bold, straight script. He wanted to meet at an eating house in Soho for dinner, tonight. He wanted to see her again. For now that was enough. Never mind that the venue was a chance to practise French and on the surface had nothing to do with last night. She would see him again and that would be a start. The rest would sort itself out.

Claire glanced at her clock. It was just now five. She had plenty of time. Her mother might endorse it, but her mother would still expect her to be discreet. She'd have to put on a show of going to Evie's or May's and make her way from there. Alone. Jonathon had written he was sorry he couldn't come and escort her since a meeting would delay him. It was probably best her mother didn't know that part or she might rethink her endorsement.

Claire reached for the second note and opened it, her eyes dropping to the signature at the bottom. Lord and Lady Belvoir. She frowned and began to read. The message was simple enough.

It was invitation more than it was a note. She was invited to a musical evening featuring Italian soprano Signora Katerina Pariso.

It was an exclusive invitation to an exclusive event. She didn't miss the fact that this invitation was for *her*, not for Lord and Lady Stanhope. That alone made it seem odd. Odder still was that she was invited at all. She had no doubt Cecilia was behind this in some way, although she wasn't sure what inviting her proved. If she hadn't been so certain Cecilia had spilled the champagne on purpose, she'd think it was an effort at apology. But Claire knew better.

She put the invitation down and stared at her reflection in the mirror. She wasn't egotistical enough to believe this overture signalled she'd arrived, that she'd made such an impression this Season that she was now welcome in these lofty echelons, that Cecilia wanted to recruit her friendship. If that was what the invitation was supposed to lead her to believe, then it failed miserably. But something was afoot.

She'd never know if she didn't go. There was no other option but *to* go. On the surface, there was no reason to refuse. This was a coveted event. Only the *crème* of the *ton* went. To refuse would be insulting. To refuse would afford her no answers and to refuse would make her appear cowardly. All she could do was show up, hold her head high and hope for the best. The event was a week away and it seemed a long way off compared to meeting Jonathon in two hours. She had just enough time to change, call for the carriage and get to May's.

For the evening, Claire chose a dress of powder-blue muslin trimmed in tiny cream lace. Evie had added a matching cream fichu to tuck into the lowered neckline. The gown was plain, but one of Claire's favourites for its touch of femininity and it was perfect for this dinner out. An eating house wasn't a silk-and-satin venue. Any evening gown she owned would look out of place. An eating house was attended by merchants, craftsmen, and clerks, not by a viscount's heir. She chose a matching shawl of soft pastel colours and walking boots and was off, excitement streaking through her at the prospect of another adventure.

She'd never been anywhere by herself before, if one didn't count walking to Evie's and even then her maid was usually with her. She took the carriage as far as Evie's, then sent it back for her parents' use that night. She took a hired hack from there and then got out to walk the remaining streets to the eating house, the address safely tucked into her reticule if she needed it.

The first few streets were thrilling. She was surrounded by the sights and smells of the working class high and low mingling with the diverse population of emigrants in this part of London as the day ended, everyone getting off their shifts. The streets were full of people hurrying home to their dinners, people finishing their daily errands and all around her, there was the sound of different languages. Soho was known for its international flavour and it was evident here. She could pick out the French, the Italian, and a little German. How vibrant this was from the staid paces of Mayfair with its mansions and stolid English.

But as she neared the eating house, it became apparent she was being followed. A group of lads—young men really, they were all at least twenty—had picked up behind her and now they were whistling and calling out lewd invitations.

She ignored them, keeping her eyes forward, her step quick but not too quick. She was conscious of not showing any fear, nothing that would inspire them to escalate their efforts.

Her strategy worked well until one of them grabbed her arm and yanked her to a halt in sight of the eating house. She could see it just across the next street.

'She thinks she's too high and mighty to pass the time with us, gents.' The leader had greasy black hair and cold eyes. When she fought to free her arm, his grip tightened painfully and he backed her to the rough brick wall of a building. 'She's got a little fire in her, too, for all that she gives herself airs. Thinks she's a lady.' Claire felt his eyes move down her body and her skin crawled while her mind raced. Bravado would make him dangerous. He might not have intended any real harm with his catcalls and whistles, but he'd *do* real harm to save face if it came to proving himself in front of his boys.

'I don't know, Jonesy, she might be a real lady at that.' Another one, a beefy, heavy-set young man spat on the pavement. 'That dress is good quality. My sister would like a dress like that.

Think she might give it to us and walk home in her shift?' Claire struggled, trying to get a few good kicks in, but he was too fast for her, too strong.

'I'd rather have a kiss and a little feel, wouldn't you, boys?' The leader holding her to the wall leered, laughing at her struggling efforts. 'A kiss for each of us, laddies, and a bit of touching. It's not every day we poor boys get to cop a lady's breasts. Then we'll be done with our business here. Sound fair?'

'I think your business is done *now.*' Low dangerous tones parted the gang, the men falling away as Jonathon stepped towards the leader, his eyes two blue avenging flames, the flash of a knife blade catching the twilight in his hand. There were five of them to his one, but he was unbothered by the odds.

'Let her go, or taste my steel.' His voice was calm, controlled, as if he dealt with street thugs daily. 'She is not for the likes of you.'

The men backed away until it was just he and the leader. This was the part Claire feared, the part where the leader would put his pride ahead of practicality. He was unarmed. He should walk away, but that would entail a loss of face. His gang would tease him about it.. Claire felt his grip on her arm loosen and she breathed easier, stepping quickly towards Jonathon. He moved in front of her, shielding her from the gang. There would be no kissing, no touching.

But the leader wasn't ready to admit defeat. He held his hands out to his sides. 'There's no contest, you with your weapon, and me with nothing to defend myself. No chit is worth getting cut over. But she's a pretty one, she's worth a little something and you've stolen our fun, guv'nor. I think you owe us a little sport in exchange. Fight me for her, fists only. First one down loses. You lose, I get to kiss her. You win, the two of you can go on with your evening. Either way, you get to go on with your night, only if you lose you might always wonder whose kiss she prefers.' He waggled his eyebrows. 'Who knows, maybe the lady likes a bit of rough.'

Jonathon sheathed his knife and began to remove his coat. 'Hold this for me, Claire.' It took a moment for her to realise what he meant to do.

'No, there will be no blood shed over me,' she protested.

One kiss was certainly better than kissing all five and who knew what else. 'I'll give him a kiss. It's just a kiss.'

'The hell you will, Claire,' Jonathon growled, his eyes on Greasy Hair. 'Now, stay back out of the way and let me deal with this cur.' He took out the gold links from his cuffs and rolled up his sleeves while one of the men drew a chalk circle around the two combatants.

'First one down loses. There is no stepping out of the fight circle. Stepping out results in a forfeit.' The beefy one who coveted her dress called out the rules. 'No weapons, only fists. Blood doesn't count as down. As long as two men are standing, the fight goes on.'

The circle looked impossibly small to Claire. How could Jonathon possibly win? He wasn't a street fighter. She was starting to see what a disadvantage he was at; it was their rules, their street. She thought that for all of five seconds until the beefy man called out 'Go!' and Jonathon swung hard for the man's jaw with a lightning-quick punch and kept striking, first with his left, then with his right, and once more before Greasy Hair landed a punch to his gut that

sent Jonathon staggering backwards, dangerously close to the chalk line.

'Watch out! Jonathon, get him!' The words
flew out of her mouth as she got caught up in the
fight, adrenaline sweeping her away as Jonathon
regained his balance and swung out, his fists fast
and lethal. He caught Greasy Hair in the nose.
Blood spurted and Jonathon didn't stop. He came
at Greasy Hair again. His shirt and waistcoat
stretched across his shoulders, his body exerting
its determination to end it. There was something
glorious and primal about watching his body, all
fluid, violent grace and athleticism as he pum-
melled Greasy Hair—there was no other way
to describe it. It was definitely a pummelling.

Jonathon took a final swing and Greasy Hair
went down. The fight was over. Jonathon didn't
wait for a declaration of victory. He shot a hard
look at the gang of men, issuing a silent invitation for any and all to try him. Then he strode
to her side, wrapped his arm about her and led
her away.

He didn't stop until they stepped inside the eating house. Even safe inside, his face still wore
a fighter's grim expression. His hands gripped

her arms as he studied her, looking for any sign of hurt. 'Claire, are you all right?'

'I'm fine,' she managed. 'He was just rough, that's all.' If she said anything else, she was quite certain Jonathon would stalk out of the eating house and finish the bounder.

Jonathon pushed a hand through his dark hair, his uncooperative lock falling forward as he blew out a breath. 'I am so sorry. This was all my fault. I never should have let you come alone. I don't know what I was thinking. Can you forgive me?'

'There's nothing to forgive,' she assured him, holding his gaze with her own to convince him of her sincerity. But her shock over all that had happened would not be held at bay much longer. It was running riot in her mind. Any moment, it would tear loose. She stared at him hard, trying to digest the transformation. Her princely gentleman, her divine waltzer, had transformed right before her eyes into a street fighter, a man of blatant power and strength and physical prowess. Why was it so hard to believe? Hadn't she had an inkling of this last night when he'd stormed her room?

'Sweet heavens, Jonathon, you broke his nose for me.' She was starting to tremble. She'd never been that close, that *intimate,* with violence before. But he had. That much was clear.

'He had his hands on you. I would break more than his nose for that alone.' He growled, his voice a rasp, his face close to hers in the cramped quarters of the eating house's tiny hall. 'You, Claire, are worth fighting for.' His voice cracked with a groan. 'God, Claire, I wanted to kill him with my bare hands.'

'I wanted that, too,' she confessed fiercely, just before his mouth descended on hers, rough and ravaging, the power of the moment overwhelming them both.

Chapter Seventeen

Her fingers gripped the lapels of his waistcoat with a talon-like ferocity, refusing to let him go, her body wanting him against her, wanting him closer than even that if it were possible. Claire revelled in the rough play of it; the devouring press of his mouth, the harshness of the wall's uneven surface at her back, the hardness of him rising against her, all muscle and male.

'Claire,' he gasped her name, a hungry, needy sound that made her reckless. His hands were in her hair, tugging her head back, exposing her throat to his mouth, a most delicious, decadent exposure. She'd never been kissed liked this, not even their hungry kisses in the bookshop rivalled these. She had never imagined kisses could be so primal, so wild, and that she'd want more, so much more than that wildness could offer on its own.

She tugged at his cravat, wanting his throat for herself, too, wanting any piece of him she could get. 'Jonathon, I don't want to eat dinner.' Her voice sounded hoarse, as needy as his.

His carriage, the full-sized town coach, not the open-air curricle, was outside. She had no recollection of exactly how they made the short walk. Her mouth was too busy, her hands too busy to pay attention to such mundane details. Jonathon managed to give the command to drive and they were off. She didn't care where. She only cared that she was on Jonathon's lap, straddling him in a most unladylike but convenient manner for what she wanted. For what *he* wanted. In her current position there could be no doubt of that. The fight had left them restless and roused, every nerve, every sensitivity exposed.

She finished with the cravat and dragged it from his neck, her fingers moving on to his quickly discarded collar, his neck exposed to her at last. She pressed a kiss to the hollow of his throat, feeling his pulse beat hard and confident beneath her lips. It still wasn't enough.

Sweet heavens, how she ached! Her body had no trouble recalling what it now knew existed. There could be so much more than this!

Instinctively, her hips ground hard against his, asking for more. He gripped her waist. 'You will be the death of me, Claire, if you keep that up,' he warned, or was that encouragement she heard in his rough voice? Gone were the cultured, easy tones she was used to. 'I know what you want, love.'

His hand slipped beneath the tangle of her skirt, his warm touch sliding up her thigh, unerringly coming to the core of her and the source of her ache. Perhaps later she'd be embarrassed, or feel some shame over the thought of his fingers teasing apart her folds, of them sliding inside her to find her wet and wanting yet again and in a coach no less, not even surrounded by the trappings of a bedroom. But now, in the moment, it was the most glorious sensation she'd ever felt. His thumb grazed the tiny nub, sending a familiar shiver through her. Only now, she knew it was merely the beginning.

'Like that, did you?' He kissed her long and slow, his teeth drawing out her lower lip as his thumb made another pass and she gasped, helpless against the twin pleasures he'd coaxed from her.

'Move against my hand, Claire. Yes, like that. Do it again, and again.' She did, her breathing turning to pants, the exquisite sensation growing with movement, with each of his passes, caresses. Their kisses turned savage, matching the tempo set by his hand and his wicked thumb—oh, sweet heavens, that thumb!

'I think I shall burst,' Claire confessed in ragged breaths, the pressure and the pleasure building in her without release, proof that last night had not been an anomaly; proof that he could be the source of endless pleasure for her.

Jonathon laughed against her throat, a seductive sound all its own. 'You most certainly will. Let it happen. It's what you're looking for.'

She was beyond words when release came, her ability to express herself reduced to husky moans and gasps and a final, rather loud cry as the ultimate pleasure crashed over her and she clung to Jonathon as it claimed her and passed, one thought occurring to her: She hadn't known it was possible to feel this sensation not only once but twice, this sensation for which she had no name, no adjectives in spite of having four languages at her disposal. And she certainly hadn't known *him*. This evening's events confirmed it. He was so much more than she'd ever imagined.

His arms were about her, her head resting against his shoulder, her legs on either side of his thighs. She was close enough to smell the faint remnants of his soap at day's end mixed with his sweat, and the scents of the street. How perfectly those smells represented the mystery of him: the boxer, the fighter, mixed with the gentleman. She was close enough to know that while she'd had her need assuaged once more, his was not. She slipped her hand between them to where his erection strained unsatisfied in the darkness of the carriage. She put her hand over him, tracing the length of him through his trousers until she felt the tip of him and heard him groan.

'Claire, you don't need to—' he began but she silenced him with a kiss and whisper. If he was part-street, part-gentleman, perhaps the same could be said of her. Did she smell not only of the lady but the wanton, too? The bold woman who wasn't afraid to cry out in his arms and give herself over to the passions he roused?

'I want to.' Her other hand hunted in the dark for the fall of his trousers. Already, the cloth was too limiting. She wanted to touch him the way he'd touched her, no clothes, no barriers between them.

She freed him, wishing for more light. She wanted to see him and yet the darkness gave her a sense of liberty she might not have felt otherwise. There was no reason to be shy in the dark. Claire ran her hand up the length of him again, her hand encircling him, her thumb exploring the rough under-ridge of him, feeling the wet bead at the very apex of him. 'I wonder if my thumb is as wicked as yours...' she purred, skimming over the tender tip.

The answer was a croaked and validating, 'Yes.'

She stroked him harder, faster, then slower, listening to the sharp inhalations of his breathing to guide her.

'Please, Claire, faster.' He arched against her hand. 'Bring me off, now.' His voice was no more than a groan of agony and ecstasy. His body was gathering itself, she could feel it in the tensing of his muscles. She stroked faster, once, twice and then the release took him in pulsing spasms while she held him, jerking and twitching with life. As intimate as the moment was, it left her much as it had last night. This was not enough, nor was it an answer to the questions that remained unsettled between them.

Perhaps Jonathon felt it, too. He was silent in the aftermath. The quiet of the carriage was broken only by the sound of their breathing and the rustle of garments. He handed her a handkerchief and she took her reluctant cue to take her own seat across from him. 'I'll see if I can scare up some dinner.' Jonathon rapped on the roof and leaned out the window, the carriage coming to a halt not long afterwards. He jumped out. 'I'll be right back. When you're ready, have my driver light the lanterns.'

Dinner was produced in rapid order: cold meat, cheese, bread and a bottle of wine from a nearby tavern. Jonathon winked as he pulled the cork from the bottle. 'I bet you've never had a carriage picnic before.' He poured her a small glass of the wine. 'Careful, it sloshes easily.' To prove his point, the carriage chose that moment to lurch into action. Claire was ready for it.

She wished she was as ready for the man who sat across from her, coatless, sleeves still rolled up from fisticuffs, slicing bread and cheese. He handed her the food, a tower of meat and cheese built on a piece of bread, and gave her a devilish smile that flipped her stomach. 'You're quite a revelation, Claire.'

'As are you.' She met his gaze steadily, knowing there were things that needed to be said and questions that need to be asked. 'It seems we've come quite a way from French lessons in the garden, yet I know nothing about you.' She took a sip of wine and waited for his response. How would he play this? Confession or denial?

'You've known me for years, Claire,' he replied with a certain nonchalance. But Claire was not fooled. The answer was too casual. The statement discomfited him. She pushed her advantage.

'*Au contraire.* You, Jonathon Lashley, are not the man I thought you were.'

'For better or for worse?' His eyes glittered

dangerously, calling to mind the consummate seducer instead of the ballroom prince.

'For better, I think.' Perhaps Beatrice was right after all. One never truly knew the measure of a man. And yet, she found this new side of Jonathon...exciting. It would be an adventure to discover this man who had fought for her, who had drawn blood for her, this man with flashing eyes and a sharp knife, who'd pleasured her thoroughly and intimately twice now and who'd allowed her to do the same for him.

He arched an eyebrow. 'But you're not sure?'

That was the understatement of the evening. Claire put down her bread and fixed him with a hard stare. 'Of course I'm not sure. How could I be? We've ventured far from the beaten path, you and I. Nothing between us is defined. There are no rules about what will happen next, what *can* happen next.' In all her daydreams of being courted by Jonathon, none of them had taken this eventuality into account. Those daydreams looked naïve and shallow when compared to this consuming passion and the complexities surrounding it. Perhaps it was true, that one should be careful what one wished for.

'What am I to make of this? The only thing I am sure of is that you've engaged my services as your French tutor. Beyond that? Nothing. You won't tell me why we have to accelerate the lessons, yet you send me flowers I never asked for. You've danced with me more than necessary.'

You've kissed me, pleasured me, shown me what passions the body is capable of.

'As far as mixed messages go, there are plenty to choose from.'

A flicker of laughter flared in his eyes. 'You have secrets, too, Claire. You can hardly condemn me for mine when you hold yours so very close. Who is the suitor? Is it Sheriden come around again now that he's realised what he gave up the first time?' He continued when she said nothing. 'See, it's not that easy, is it?'

He took a final bite of his bread and wiped the crumbs away on his trousers. 'It does make me wonder, Claire, what kind of suitor this man is if you're pleasuring *me* in a carriage instead of him. I dare say after the last two nights you could capture his attentions if you wanted them.'

That stung. 'You started it!' She sounded like a four-year-old. She could think of nothing else to say that was a worthy response. *L'esprit d'escalier* indeed. 'If anyone has made this complicated, it's you. You have Cecilia Northam expecting a commitment and yet...' She didn't dare voice the rest.

And you were kissing me up against a wall in Soho, and climbing into my bedroom as if there was no tomorrow. You put your hand on me, you gave yourself to me and you made me believe every word you said.

Who was to blame? Him for uttering the words, or her for believing them? They'd both known better. Even if the words were true. He had obligations beyond her, *dreams* beyond her that she knew very little about.

'You're right. And yet. That pretty much sums it up.' He let out a breath, the unfinished words hanging between them. The anger went out of him. He pushed a hand through his hair. 'I don't think we really want to fight or blame. We've exposed ourselves tonight and now we're just trying to protect ourselves from hurt.'

'I don't know that we can do that—protect ourselves. It's too late.' Perhaps he was right. Outside, the landscape gave way to Mayfair mansions. They were nearly home. The tumultuous evening was over although it was still early by *ton* standards. Balls would just be getting underway. If she wanted, she could join her parents at the Selfridge rout, but she was in no mood for dancing tonight. It was hard to believe so much had happened and it was only ten o'clock.

The carriage came to a stop outside Stanhope House. She reached for the door handle but Jonathon was faster. 'Wait, Claire.' His hand closed over hers on the handle. 'What if there were no secrets, no Cecilia?'

She gave a sad laugh. 'But there are, Jonathon.' Who knew what his were, but did it matter? Secrets were secrets for a reason. They were pieces of potentially damaging information if put into the wrong hands. She thought about telling him there was no suitor and the reasons why she *hadn't* told him, probably would never tell him. What would he think of her then? Would he think she'd manipulated him to get his attention? 'If we shared them they would change everything.'

'Everything has already changed, Claire,' he admonished. 'A French tutor and a pupil don't need details. But friends do. I thought we'd established we were that at least.' Jonathon laced his fingers through hers. 'I think it's fair to say we've moved beyond tutor and pupil.' His voice pitched low, trying to reclaim the intimacy of earlier, wanting his wicked angel back on his lap.

But he understood, too, that he'd overstepped his boundaries tonight by claiming liberties he had no right to access. They were not affianced, there were no promises between them. He'd had her twice in an intimate manner when he should not have had her even once. He could not have her again without committing to her. The thought of never experiencing passion with her made his stomach tighten and his mind marvel. How had this happened? How had she become so beautiful and dear to him without him realising it? He had wanted to kill for her tonight, an urge he thought he'd left behind in the war. He'd watched the hours slip by too slowly until he could expect her. He'd drunk away the afternoon, regretting not going to his lesson. Now, he had to know. Were those feelings he had to get used to? 'Do you think there's no chance for us, Claire?'

She did look at him then, her eyes sharp as her head snapped up to face him. 'A chance for what, Jonathon?'

'If I wanted to court you, would I be welcome or would I be too late?' Doubt stole over him. He'd never asked a woman such a thing. Interest had always been implied. 'Tell me the truth, Claire—have I been nothing more than a distraction while you ponder your suitor's offer?' He didn't think he could withstand being used in that manner, not by her, and yet he wasn't convinced he deserved more.

He had stunned her. She would have pulled her hand away if he hadn't held on. Perhaps it was what he deserved; to reach out for happiness and be denied. It was his penance for Thomas. Why should he claim happiness when Thomas could not?

In the next moment, she was stunning him. 'You are determined to have my secret, are you not?' Her brown eyes held sadness, regret. 'I should have told you from the start and now you will despise me, but it seems I have no choice if you're to understand why this can't go any further.' She drew a deep breath. 'There is no suitor.

There never was.' The rest came out in a rush he barely had time to process. 'The only suitor I ever wanted was you.'

'And now? Have I failed in some way?'

'No! You've exceeded my expectations at every turn.' She paused and glanced down at her hands, gathering courage. 'You are much more than I knew and that man is better than any of my imaginings. I did not mean to toy with you, but I can't help but feel that I have. I have led you on in order to keep your attentions, I made you believe there was a man of interest.' She shook her head. 'Now, I'm embarrassed about how I acted. The girls dressed me up, did my hair, May found a way for us to be thrown together and I allowed it.'

'Because you liked me, nothing more,' Jonathon said softly. The kaleidoscope of little shards were falling into focus now, the bits and pieces aligning themselves in formation. He'd been right. The dresses were for a man. But he'd not guessed they were for him. He remembered the sky-blue gown with the chocolate piping and how he'd stared when she'd entered the Worths' drawing room. He remembered, too, how she'd quite fortuitously sat across from him and May Worth had sat beside him. It had been May who'd dropped that little titbit about Claire's French. Without that information, he might never have sought her out.

Full stop.

He'd only been partially joking with Preston the other day about having no secrets when one's friends were in intelligence. The Worths were the leak. Preston would have known he was in need of a tutor and May had always been an inveterate eavesdropper even when they were young. He reached for her hand, claiming it again from her lap. 'You went to a lot of work, for me. I'm flattered. Did you think I wouldn't be?'

She hesitated. She'd been expecting his anger. She'd not been ready for this. 'I thought you would feel used, manipulated.'

He shook his head. 'You merely created an opportunity for us to be together. As you pointed out so succinctly earlier, I was the one who started *it*.' He paused here, running his thumb over her knuckles. 'I started it, but am I right in assuming we *both* want more?'

Despite her confession, they were back where they started, but perhaps they were closer to an answer. 'The way I see it, is that it's easier than we thought, Claire. There is no suitor to stand between us and your secret is out in the open, no longer a barrier to us.'

'But it is not the only barrier,' she chided. 'There is your appointment to Vienna to consider. You will risk that post if you openly pursue me. I can't let you do that, Jonathon. You've worked too hard. I cannot possibly stand in the way of your dream. I hope it is evident that I care too much for you to do that.' He watched her throat work, noting the effort this recent disclosure cost her. Her free hand fumbled unsuccessfully with the door. 'Please, let me out before we say things we can't mean and make promises we can't keep.'

He released her hand and carefully swung open the door. He helped her out, performing his role with numb perfection until she was safely inside. Only when he was alone in the carriage did he let the full import of the words take him. They were a blow as stunning as any punch Greasy Hair could have landed. He understood her meaning. She wanted out of more than the carriage. She wanted out of their association. No more French lessons. No more long walks in the garden. No more sneaking off to Soho.

What a mess he'd made of things. He pinched the bridge of his nose and tried to fight back the overwhelming wave of disappointment. He'd lost Claire just when he'd decided he wanted her, needed her.

Chapter Eighteen

Needed her? To need her seemed an understatement. In a practical sense, he *didn't* need her. The lessons were about done. Any day now, Owen would hear from his contact in France about the latest leads on Thomas and Jonathon would be ready. He'd comported himself excellently at the bookshop. His flawless spoken French had returned nearly full force of what it had once been.

As long as she's with you. You've never done it without her. What if you can't? You still can't read French out loud.

Did that really matter? He'd probably never be asked to read French out loud. There was consolation in knowing how much he'd achieved in the last four weeks, but it was a meagre prize compared to what he was giving up: Claire Welton.

No, it wasn't the need that bothered him. It was the wanting. The rational mind argued that all dreams had a cost. She was merely his price. Just as committing himself in a politically advantageous marriage was part of that price; a price he had not originally minded paying, had indeed felt it was his due to pay; more penance for Thomas. He *still* felt it was his due to pay. He'd not realised how keenly he'd feel the toll, however. When he'd made his bargain, he'd not had anything to lose, anything to give up.

Jonathon climbed the front steps to his rooms at the Albany on the Piccadilly border—bastion of wealthy, young, unmarried gentlemen during the Season. The halls were quiet, everyone out for the evening. Good. He needed time to think, time to figure out what he was going to do. How would he convince Claire he'd fight for both her and Vienna?

She didn't think victory on both fronts was possible. She'd made that clear tonight and she knew the price of achieving Vienna. He knew Claire's consolation. She cared for him enough to pay. She would sacrifice her dream in order to save his. Just as Thomas had. In the end, they'd both left him.

Those two ideas chased themselves around his mind. Claire cared for him.

Claire had left him.

The problem with receiving good news mixed with bad was that one's brain couldn't quite decide which emotion to embrace: the elation of the high or the depression of the low. It was even more confusing when the two were inextricably linked: she'd left him *because* she cared. Thomas had gone down that road *because* Thomas had loved him, enough to risk dying for him, in place of him.

He fitted his key into the door of his rooms and stepped inside. The room was dark. He'd given his man the night off, but Jonathon could sense immediately he wasn't alone. He bent down and withdrew his knife from his boot. That weapon was seeing quite a lot of use tonight. He'd didn't think he'd drawn it in five years, maybe more. Tonight, he'd drawn it twice.

'Who's there?' he called out. 'I know you're here. Show yourself. You should know I am armed and in a mood to fight.'

A rich, rolling chuckle filled the room. A form rose from the chair. 'It's me, Jonathon. If you'd leave a lamp on, you'd know who was in the room.'

Jonathon expelled a breath and sheathed his knife. 'Owen, what are you doing here? More importantly, how did you get in?'

Owen stretched. 'I am here because I have news. How I got in is irrelevant. Come, have a seat. You're earlier than I expected you.'

Jonathon sat down, instantly alert. 'Your man has been in contact?'

Owen nodded. 'Yes, and the man in question, the one living on the Lys, is indeed English. The informant refuses to say more without meeting you.' Jonathon felt his body tense, his hands clench around the arms of the chair. He forced himself to wait, to hide his impatience. He wanted to walk out the door right this minute and head for France. He didn't want to plan, to talk. After seven years of wondering, alternately hoping and grieving, he wanted action.

'Now, before you go haring off, there are things you must know and consider.'

'Beyond which boat to take?' Jonathon offered drily.

Owen scolded him with an arched eyebrow. 'You don't need a boat. He's coming to Dover.' Here Owen hesitated. 'You have to reconcile yourself to the fact that the man he knows of might not be Thomas. Second, if it is Thomas, he might not wish to be found. He might not welcome your discovery.'

'He might be held against his will,' Jonathon retorted. 'Perhaps he is working the farm under duress.' He'd heard accounts of such things happening, of men being held captive, even drugged against their will and forced to live another life.

Owen shook his head. 'It's been seven years. If he was being held for ransom, his captors are the dumbest kidnappers alive. They're making no money on him by keeping him hidden away.' Owen leaned forward. 'There are other possibilities, too, Jonathon. If it is Thomas, he might not remember his former life. Combat can do terrible things to a mind that a man will block out no matter what the cost. Have you thought of that?'

'That he has lost his mind? His memories?'

The idea was ludicrous. How could Thomas forget who he was? 'Amnesia is temporary. Even if he'd been affected by it, his memory would have come back by now,' Jonathon argued, but he was no doctor, what did he really know about such a condition? Why had he lost his ability to speak French? But that ability had come back, coaxed to life again with Claire's help. 'Surely my brother's condition would have improved.'

Owen shook his head. 'Look at you, Jonathon. You've already assumed Thomas has been found. Did you hear a word I said? There are no guarantees. This is nothing more than an anomaly one of my men noticed passing through the village—an Englishman working as a farmer who bears a general resemblance to your brother.'

'An anomaly that was significantly different to report,' Jonathon said staunchly. He would not let go of the hope something had been found at last that explained the lack of a body. 'I combed the roads, the meadows, the battlefield, the hospitals,' he began, his voice rising uncontrollably. 'Thomas wasn't there. I would know. If he wasn't with the dead, then he is somewhere among the living.' His voice broke over the last words. He'd been shot for those efforts, lingered on a deathly threshold with fever for those facts. They had to be worth something.

Owen gave a near-imperceptible nod of his head. 'How's your French these days?'

'Good. Excellent, in fact.' As long as he didn't have to read anything out loud or discuss kissing. Owen didn't need to know that. Either scenario seemed unlikely to occur in the near future.

'You'll need it. The informant doesn't speak English. He'll be in Dover in two days.' Owen rose and stuck out his hand.

Jonathon shook it, victory coursing through him. 'I wouldn't have it any other way.' Finally, action, a chance to go back and atone for what he should never have done in the first place: he should not have let Thomas go. He should never have left the Continent without answers. Two days was not long. He'd have to leave immediately.

'Do you think I am crazy, Owen?'

Owen gripped his arm. 'I think you are hopeful.' Then added with a wink, 'Now, what Miss Northam thinks might be entirely different, if you indeed care any longer. I hear that perhaps your attentions may have been redirected. Would you like to verify?'

'Not particularly. Tonight's been rather rough, Owen, if you don't mind I'd like to be alone.'

He knew there was no chance of that actually occurring. As soon as he lay down, his thoughts crowded in. He dreamed of Thomas. Nothing as vividly coherent as the usual dream; this was a kaleidoscope of images, snatches of memories, snatches of fears over what he'd learn from the informant. He dreamed of Claire, too, hot dreams where her body pressed to his, where he made her climax again and again, her head thrown back, her dark hair falling down, her eyes filled with passion and desire for him. It was all for him and he'd let her go. Or was it the other way around? Oh, yes, he remembered it correctly now. *She'd* let *him* go.

He woke sweaty and aching, his head throbbing with that one truth at dawn. She harboured deep feelings for him—feelings that she'd been willing to forego in order to save his dreams. Maybe that sacrifice would be worth it, if he could in turn save Thomas. He found a valise in his wardrobe and began to pack for Dover, starting with his pistols. He'd been down this road before. It could be dangerous.

It was positively perilous to keep looking at the clock, watching the big hand snake towards the six in proof that Jonathon wasn't coming. In fact, he wasn't ever coming again. Lessons were over, her opportunity to attract his attention, over. Claire paced the small sun room, fighting the attraction to the clock, to the hope that perhaps she was wrong. It wasn't too late yet. It was still possible that he might come. Even now Jonathon could be on his way, stuck in the traffic of London. But soon, she'd have to give up that little fantasy. Once the clock reached eleven-thirty, it would be a ridiculous pretence.

Claire stopped in front of the big window that let in the light, although there wasn't much light to let in today. The weather was still grey and rain threatened like it had the day before. She leaned her head against the cool panes of the glass. Had it really been only yesterday she'd received his note? That she'd gone to Soho? No matter how old she got, she would never forget the sight of Jonathon fighting in the street. For her. And what had she done? She'd let him go.

No regrets. She told herself. She'd done what was right. He was destined for greatness and she was destined for nothing. She'd set herself on that course years ago just as assuredly as he'd set himself on his. She would only hold him back and he would come to resent her for it.

If she'd known pursuing Jonathon would be this complicated, she would never have embarked on Beatrice's mission to see each of them launched into happiness. She should have been more careful of what she wished for, but she hadn't really believed she would succeed. The girls would be scolding her if they knew her thoughts. She could almost hear Beatrice now. 'Well, you've got Jonathon Lashley, what are you going to do with him?'

She desperately wanted to go to her friends and lay this latest burden at their feet, but she couldn't. This was her relationship and only she could manage it. This new, adventurous Claire who'd come to life had to take responsibility for herself. She smiled a little to herself. She had changed. She'd taken back her life. Not because she had a man, she still never wanted to be a woman who defined herself through the man on her arm, but because she'd found herself again.

It had been a relief to find her alive and well, buried beneath layers of a quiet woman who'd chosen withdrawal to engagement, a woman who was withering away in the dust of obscurity. Jonathon had not made that discovery happen, any more than her friends had made it happen. Ultimately, the choice to re-engage was hers alone, but Jonathon *had* given her the opportunity to make the discovery and she'd taken it. Jonathon wasn't afraid of her intelligence. He admired it, respected it and, in return, he'd given her a safe place in which to be herself and try her wings. It was perhaps the greatest true gift any person could give another. That he had chosen to give that gift to her was worthy of examination.

No one gave such a gift haphazardly. One would have to care for someone deeply to invest in that kind of offering. A little cry rose in her throat. *Jonathon loved her.* Oh, dear sweet heavens, what had she done? In her mind, she saw the taut outlines of his face the night he'd climbed into her room, waiting for her acceptance, the pain on his face last night, when she'd broken off with him. She saw other images, too, like his beautiful head thrown back in ecstasy as she pleasured him, the way he looked before he kissed her, as if she were his feast. She'd hurt him. He had been willing to fight for her, not just in the streets, but in the drawing rooms and ballrooms of the *ton. Claire, you are worth fighting for.*

He had been willing to take the risk, but she had not. She'd led him to believe *he* wasn't worth fighting for when nothing could be further from the truth. She'd always believed that right and best were synonymous. Now, she wasn't so sure. Was it possible that the right decision was not necessarily the best? She'd made a terrible mistake. She had to find Jonathon and tell him.

Everything seemed to happen in slow motion while she had speeded up. Nothing could happen fast enough to suit her; not the bringing of the carriage, not the journey through London through all the midday traffic. Three streets from the Albany, Claire gave up the last of her patience and hopped out. She could walk the remaining distance faster than her coachman could drive. At last, she stood in front of Jonathon's door, breathless from excitement, from nerves, from the haste she'd made, and knocked.

She heard footsteps behind the door and she drew a breath, ready to make her speech. The door opened.

'Jonathon, I've made a mistake, I am sorry.' The words rushed out before she realised. This wasn't Jonathon. This was… 'Preston! What are you doing here?' Nothing made sense. This was Jonathon's door. She'd come to see Jonathon. He should be here, not May's brother.

Preston gave her a considering look, arms folded across his chest. 'What are *you* doing here?' He grabbed her arm and pulled her inside, shutting the door behind them. 'Good heavens, Claire, this is a boarding house for bachelor gentlemen. Did anyone see you?' He looked genuinely concerned.

'I don't think so.' But she wasn't entirely sure. Most gentlemen were either still in bed at this hour or out with errands. The halls had seemed empty, but in truth, her mind had been too occupied with other things to give much thought to the consequences of her actions. The only consequence she was interested in was finding Jonathon.

'We have to get you out of here.' Preston was striding through the room, looking for something.

She peered around his moving form to the door leading into the other room. 'I came to see Jonathon. Is he here?' She fully expected to see him emerge any moment. Surely he would have heard her voice and the commotion by now.

Preston stopped his searching. 'No, he's not here. He's gone to Dover on business for Sir Owen Danvers.'

'What?' Claire felt her stomach sink, the whirling of her mind come to an abrupt halt. Jonathon wasn't simply 'not' here, he was gone. She'd come to tell him she loved him and he was gone. It seemed the height of injustice. 'Why? What kind of business? How long? When did this come up? He said nothing about it.'

'I'm sorry, Claire. I can't say anything more than that on the subject. His business is his own. It's not for me to say.'

Preston offered her a kind, brotherly smile. 'If

it's any consolation, I think the business came up rather suddenly. I don't think he had much advance warning.' He touched her arm. 'Let me take you home, Claire.'

'No.' Claire met Preston's gaze with a determined stare, daring him to deny her. 'I need to talk to Jonathon. Take me to Dover.'

Chapter Nineteen

The Antwerp Hotel was as upscale of an inn as one would find in Dover and Jonathon was heartily ready to embrace its luxuries. It had taken a little over two days to reach the port city, thanks to a side errand Owen had asked him to run and the mud-churned roads from the recent rains. To say the least, travel had been a bear and he'd been anxious, perceiving every delay as adding hours to his arrival.

'You are in room seven.' The clerk at the desk gave him a warm, friendly smile, a glint of something akin to bonhomie in his eye. Jonathon couldn't fathom it. The clerk didn't know him well enough for such an assumption. 'Dinner will be up shortly.' Again, the mischievous glint. Jonathon gave a nod. He didn't remember the service being quite so good. He hoisted his valise and headed for the stairs. A hot meal would restore his spirits. He'd had far too much time alone with his thoughts. Not trusting the weather, he'd taken the coach to Dover instead of riding. Alone with his thoughts for hours on end had not done him any good. His thoughts had bounced from the prospect of finding Thomas to the prospect of having lost Claire and the ideas had chased themselves about in his head until he was weary. At the door marked with a seven, he fitted his key and pushed it open. He took a step inside, his attentions fixed on putting his key away.

'Jonathon, you're here at last.' By Jove, he'd finally gone round the bend. He'd thought of Claire for so long he was imagining her voice with lifelike accuracy. He looked up and froze. He wasn't dreaming. It was definitely her. Claire rose from the chair, her amber eyes soft with the firelight, her mouth curving in a generous smile as if she were welcoming him home. He liked the sensation such an image engendered. He wanted to go to her, to wrap her in his arms, but she'd given him up two days ago. What did it mean that she was here, miles from London? 'Claire, what are you doing? How did you get here?'

He studied her, taking in every detail of her person. She was dressed for travel in a seasonal carriage dress of blue India muslin. A cloak he recognised as his own lay across the arm of the chair, a valise sat on the floor, still fastened, still packed. She had not arrived much in advance of him. He was starting to understand the desk clerk's mischief now. She'd not been secretive about her purpose.

'Preston helped me.' He'd probably have to have some words with Preston, but that could wait. Claire's story spilled out in semi-chrono-logical order. 'Preston was good enough to hire a post chaise for me. I arrived here half an hour ago. I went to your rooms in London, but you were gone.' She moved towards him then, catching his hands and holding tight. 'I've made a horrible mistake and I had to tell you, to talk to you right away.'

'A mistake?' There was so much to take in he couldn't quite fathom it all at once. What mistake would this be?

'When you realise you love someone, Jonathon, and they love you, enough to fight for you, you want to tell them at once. You don't want to wait until they're back from Dover.' Jonathon felt every nerve in his body go on alert. She was talking about him. She drew a deep breath and careened on with her mesmerising words. Her amber eyes shone. 'I love you, Jonathon Lashley, and I love who I am when I'm with you. I love what you've let me become.'

Claire loved him. Stunned was the only way to describe what he felt; stunned that someone would carry that depth of emotion for him; stunned that Claire would travel this far to tell him. It couldn't have been easy. It was more than he could have hoped for. He'd spent his day thinking of ways to get her back, to convince her, and here she was, having come to that conclusion on her own. It was the best sort of victory.

He brought her hands to his lips and kissed them each in turn. 'You have left me speechless, Claire. I don't know what to say, so I hope this will suffice.' He kissed her then, long and tender, letting his body convey what his mind could not until the maids brought up dinner.

He shot Claire a look as they laid the little table in the front of the fire. 'Only a half an hour ahead of me? You were incredibly industrious.'

A saucy maid with brown curls peered up from her work. 'Your wife is an amazing woman. Your dinner was her first priority. She ordered it the moment she had her room.'

'My wife,' Jonathon drawled, watching Claire blush under his gaze, 'is amazing indeed.' As was the supper. His mouth started to water as the maids departed, the table ready. Covers were removed from a platter of braised rabbit, fresh spring greens and baby carrots steamed in their bowls, a new loaf of bread and pale country butter in a small crock lay on a cutting board and a bottle of red wine stood sentinel in the centre of the table. 'My wife has done well.' Jonathon tossed her a sly smile.

'I had to tell them something.' Claire sat and fussed with her napkin, avoiding his gaze. 'The clerk wouldn't let me in to your room otherwise.'

'It's fine. It's flattering.' Jonathon sat down across from her and began to fill their plates.

Unbuttoning the Innocent Miss

'I'm glad you're here.' He slid a slice of rabbit on to her plate. Did he broach the awkward subject between them or did he merely enjoy the meal and her company? He opted for the latter. It was safer ground. He would let her decide if they talked of anything more and when.

They spoke of their journeys and the roads. They finished the wine and the candles burned down. The meal had been enjoyable and yet Jonathon felt a familiar tension begin to simmer as supper came to an inevitable end. Despite their proclamations, much lay unsettled between them, not the least being what would happen tonight.

Claire rose from the table, her voice betraying a nervous edge, her eyes not quite meeting his. 'If you would excuse me for a few moments?'

Jonathon took his hint. 'I'll be downstairs. I need to check on a few things with the innkeeper.'

He would give her twenty minutes, he decided in the taproom. Twenty minutes for whatever she needed her privacy to do. But deuce take it, they were the longest twenty minutes of his life. It took only three of those minutes to confer with the innkeeper and decide his contact had not yet checked in. Perhaps tomorrow.

He checked his watch again. Twenty minutes. Finally. Surely that was enough time?

The innkeeper slapped him on the back. 'Newlyweds? I can tell, you are eager to get back to your bride.' He was a heavily built man with a hearty chuckle. 'Enjoy it, man, because it won't last, but it's good while it does. I've been married nearly thirty years, those days have been gone for a while now, but I still remember them.'

His wife chose that moment to come out of the kitchen, a woman as big as he, armed with a rolling pin. 'What are you doing out here, gabbing away? I've got dinner to see to and there are customers to serve. I can't do it all, lazy man.'

'See?' The man held up his hands in surrender, letting her drag him away to the bar. 'Enjoy them!'

Jonathon laughed and headed upstairs. Maybe his steps were quick on the treads. Maybe he was eager. Maybe he was just curious to see how far Claire was willing to take the impersonation of his wife. Was that so wrong? Despite the circumstances and his anxiety over the informant's news, he hadn't been this happy in a long time. He meant to hang on to it not just for 'as long as he could', but for ever. Claire had come for him.

He knocked at the door to give her fair warning and stepped inside. Claire stood before the fire much as she had when he'd arrived. Only this time she had traded her carriage gown for a robe of white silk that belted at the waist, her dark hair falling in loose waves over one shoulder. There was no mistaking her intentions. This was an offering, a seduction all rolled into one. They had reached a new point of no return. 'Claire, are you sure?'

She stepped towards him, her hand at the belt of her robe, tugging at the sash in answer. 'I've never been more certain of anything in my life.' The robe fell loose, the sleek fabric parting to offer a tantalising glimpse of skin, of breast, of a dark shadow of hair below.

'You've had dinner, Jonathon. Are you ready for dessert?' She gave a shrug of one shoulder, letting the robe fall to her feet, revealing herself fully. Jonathon's mouth went dry. By the saints, Claire Welton knew how to tempt a man.

'I believe I am,' Jonathon managed. He wanted to look at her, to enjoy her in a way he had not in their previous encounters. There had been too many clothes, or too little time. Tonight, there was neither. He let his eyes linger on the fullness of her breasts, the trimness of her torso, the slimness of her waist, the flaring width of her hips and length of her legs. Her height had not occurred to him one way or the other before, but perhaps it explained why they had waltzed so effortlessly together, walked so easily together. Then again, those activities might come easy because she was simply Claire and had a way of putting him at ease with himself. He didn't need his masks when he was with her.

She backed away towards the chair and sat, legs crossed, the very image of Godiva in her nakedness. 'Now it's your turn. Take off your clothes, Jonathon.'

'Don't you want to take them off?' he queried.

She gave him a coy smile. 'No, tonight I want to watch. A lady likes to look, too.' Ah, so she'd noticed. Jonathon grinned and complied, pulling off his boots and discarding his coats. He could get used to this confident, dominant Claire who was in charge of her passion. He loved the openness of her imagination to such bold exploration. Why would a man ever want to change *this*? Why would a man want a blank slate when a man could have a woman of intelligence, of confidence instead of someone cowering under the blankets out of duty?

Jonathon worked the fastenings of his trousers and pushed them over his hips, his back turned to her, deliberately making a show of it. He liked the feel of her cognac gaze running over his bare skin, liked knowing that what she saw pleased her. 'Keep watching, Claire.'

'Yes,' Claire whispered. What had started as her seduction of him had rapidly become his seduction of her. She was helpless to look away. The long, smooth muscles of his back, the muscled curve of his buttocks, the masculine concavities at his hips entranced her.

Then he turned, facing her with the firelight behind him, hands on those narrow hips, thumbs angled to draw the eye downward toward his groin and the jutting peninsula of his phallus rising from the bristling dark thatch of him, hard and rugged to match the muscled power of his body. Who would have thought such strength lay beneath the dark evening clothes and bright smile? He had them all fooled for years, she realised. Did anyone guess at what lay beneath the clothes? She could easily believe this man who stood before her was a soldier hardened by battle, a fighter who wouldn't shirk from fisticuffs in an alley. And he was hers. For however long it lasted.

Her pulse raced as he approached the chair. He held out his hand and uttered the most provocative invitation she'd ever heard. 'Come to bed, Claire.' She rose and took his hand.

There was no turning back now. There'd been no turning back for a long time, not since the day she'd mopped tea off his trousers and chased him into the hall to accept his offer. Claiming Jonathon was claiming herself. For the first time she was taking what she wanted. Even if she had to reconcile herself to the reality that she could love Jonathon Lashley for ever, but she couldn't keep him that long.

He followed her down, the bed taking their weight. He kissed her long and thoroughly, his tongue tracing its tip over her lips. This was a loitering kiss, a languorous drinking of each other which there was no need to rush. They had all night. What a luxury that seemed! They were free to drink of one another, to taste, to touch, to look their fill as slowly or as rapidly as they chose, as often as they chose.

His fingers skimmed over the base of her throat where her pulse beat, trailing slowly to the valley between her breasts, his hands cupping and caressing, his thumb-pads dragging over their suddenly sensitive peaks.

'You are beautiful, every inch of you.' Jonathon's eyes feasted on her, his adulation inspiring her confidence in turn. This was decadent indeed, to lay naked in front of a man, a lover.

Her hand skimmed the muscle of him, travelling lower along his chest, along the ridges of abdomen and hip until she had the hot, hard length of him in her hand. She would never tire of the feel of him. This time, she knew what to expect and it only served to enhance the wonder of it. 'I think the old wives have the wrong of it,' she murmured, her hand moving down his length. 'They say familiarity breeds contempt, but I disagree. I think it breeds anticipation.' She laughed, revelling in the newfound power of passion awakened in her. Had this wanton been inside her all along? Had it just taken her courage to release this brave, bold woman who took the pleasure, asked for the pleasure she deserved? 'I know what you can provide and that makes me all the more eager for it, Jonathon.'

'You'll be having that pleasure sooner rather than later, if you keep this up, minx,' Jonathon warned hoarsely. 'There's only so much exploration a man can take.' She placed a soft kiss on his mouth and ran her thumb over his tip. 'You're weeping for me.' Her fingers spread the liquid bead down his length, priming him for what came next.

'Like you.' Jonathon moved a hand between her legs, mirroring her actions. He cupped her at her core, his hand moving against her mons. Jonathon braced himself on his arms and looked down at her. 'You are my coffee-haired witch, my cognac-eyed Delilah.'

'Coffee? Cognac? You make me sound like a drink.' She laughed up at him.

'I'd like to drink you, perhaps I shall.' Wickedness glinted in the blue depths of his eyes. Jonathon grinned and slid down her body, leaving kisses at her breasts, at her navel, at the dark juncture between her thighs, each kiss serving to ratchet up the intensity of his touch. Only then, with her body primed for pleasure and his breath warm against the dampness of her curls did she understand what he meant to do. Her legs tightened about him out of reflex. Surely he couldn't mean to do *that*?

'Easy, Claire, you will like it. I will make it good for you,' he coaxed. 'Open for me. It's all right.' He held her thighs apart, his grip steadying her. She relaxed beneath his touch, her muscles easing. At the first pass of his tongue, her mind eased as well. This was indeed a most delightfully wicked pleasure. His tongue found her nub and licked, sucked, licked again while she arched beneath him, finding the rhythm of her own pleasure in answer to him.

She heard him give a sharp moan, an indication that this intimacy pleased him to give it as much as it pleased her to receive it. Together, they drove one another to recklessness. She bucked, her moans an aphrodisiac nonpareil as she began to crest against him, reaching out for the pleasure, the fulfilment, and he gave it to her, his own breathing coming in rasps now.

She gasped incoherently and Jonathon levered himself over her. His words came in a broken torrent. He was close to losing himself as well. 'I promised I could wait for you to recover. I promised myself I'd be gentle.'

'Then don't. Don't wait. Don't be gentle.' Her legs were wide and ready for him, her body racked with pleasure. 'Bury yourself in me, Jonathon.'

He pulled her arms high above her head, holding them in his grip, her breasts pushed hard into him as her body arched in affirmation. He'd driven them both wild, made both of them reckless with wanting. Jonathon lowered himself into the cradle of her legs, his body positioning itself, fitting itself to her with an ease that spoke of homecoming. They were primed for one another, wet and slick with their intimacy. He slid into her, the tightness of her channel stretching around him, surrounding him. She gave a sharp gasp, a reminder that while her body was running hot with desire, it was still her first time and he was a full-sheathed male inside an untried passage.

Jonathon stilled, the muscles of his arms taut with the effort, the discipline of his will overcoming their rampant need. She arched against him, in signal to continue, and he began to move, slowly at first—the tantalising glide inward, then the teasing slide outward, their hips meeting and breaking and meeting again like waves along the shore, gently, and then with the ferocity of the pounding surf. She writhed against him, madness driving them to the edge of pleasure and then over it with a final spilling thrust. For the first time, they'd found that pleasure together.

He sank against her, exhausted, his heart pounding, the sweat of sex on him, that elusive scent of salt and musk. He found the strength to roll to his side, and pulled her to him, her head resting on his good shoulder. Had she ever been so entirely undone? Nothing could have prepared her for this feeling of bonelessness.

'Claire, are you all right?' he asked softly, 'Lie still and I'll get you a cloth.' He began to push up from the bed, but she placed a hand on his chest in gentle restraint.

'No, it will keep. I don't want to give you up just yet. Lie here with me.' She walked her fingers in an idle path across his chest. 'Is it always like that? Like I think I will die from it and yet I can't stop myself from embracing it?'

'Running towards disaster?' Jonathon chuckled. 'That's not very flattering.' Then he sobered, his hand closing over hers where it lay on his chest. 'It's not a disaster at any rate. The French have a word for it, *le petit mort*. The little death.'

'Ah, something in French you know that I don't.' She sighed and settled into quiet contemplation as she gathered her thoughts, now that passion was receding and other issues were starting to encroach. 'Jonathon, I know what I am doing in Dover,' she began tentatively, fearing the answer. 'I came to tell you I love you… that pushing you away was a mistake. But what I don't know is what are you doing in Dover?'

Chapter Twenty

Jonathon shifted, uncomfortable with the question. What would she think? Would she think he was crazy or that it was a foolish hope?

'What?' She raised herself up on one arm, cajoling him with a sleepy smile. 'You can climb into my bedroom and wring my secrets out of me, but I can't do the same for you?' She was teasing him, but in the dim light of the room, he could see the uneasiness in her eyes. Her question had inadvertently become a test of trust.

'Jonathon?' Her body tensed when he hesitated, the light in her eyes diminished. 'I see.' She had come to him, declared herself to him and trusted him to protect her. Now, it was his turn to reciprocate. This had become a defining moment for them. She had made the leap of faith. She was waiting for him to follow.

Jonathon swallowed. 'You will think I am crazy.' He couldn't bear it if that were true. He understood why his parents had stopped looking, stopped hoping. He didn't speak about it in society in general because they didn't care. He'd grown tired of the patronising pity in people's eyes whenever he brought Thomas up.

'What could be crazier than allowing you to believe I had a suitor? Your secret can hardly be more embarrassing than mine.' She squeezed his hand. 'Try me, Jonathon.'

'It's my brother, Thomas. There's been word that he might be found. There's an informant who is coming to meet me, who says he has information.' He could hear the hope in his voice as he said the words out loud.

He watched her brow knit, watched her expression change into contemplation. 'Your brother? Isn't he dead?'

'Maybe. His body was never found.'

'*Has* he been found, then?' she asked gently. He could see her doing the maths in her head, her mind debating the doubt and probability of such a thing. Seven years was a long time. Any moment she'd ask the question: *If he was alive, why hadn't he returned home by now under his own power?* It was what everyone asked.

She settled back down, resting her head against his shoulder. 'It seems you have quite the tale to tell, Jonathon. Perhaps you should get started. We only have all night.' Just like that, an enormous weight, one he hadn't fully realised he was carrying, was lifted from him.

It felt good to talk, or maybe it was that it felt good to talk to her. There in the dark, with her body against his, he told her about Thomas, how his brother had ridden off with the dispatch in his place, how his brother had not made the meeting place, how he had wandered the battlefield and roads looking for Thomas until he'd been shot down, unable to search any further. 'The trouble is, I don't know if I want to find him. In some ways, I think I am afraid to find him, afraid to know what happened to him.'

Those last words were out before he could take them back. He'd not meant to say that much. He'd never spoken those words out loud, not to anyone, not even Owen. He needed to find Thomas, alive or dead, to assuage his own guilt at having left his brother behind. But *want*? No, he didn't *want* to find Thomas. Didn't *want* to learn why Thomas chose not to come home. There was more guilt down that road of not wanting. It was a dark question he did not examine often. He waited for Claire's response, waited for her condemnation. What kind of person didn't want to find his brother alive? But what he got in return was a single word, a single question.

'Why?' she whispered, her hand covering his, her eyes soft. There was no judgement in her gaze, only concern for him. It unlocked the dam that had held back his thoughts for so many years. Words flooded from his mouth.

'Because war changes a person. If he's been found, why hasn't he come home sooner? Did he choose not to? Or has he lost his memory? Maybe he's not Thomas any more.' Memories defined who a person was, gave them a history. If they were gone, Thomas would have built new ones without him. 'Who am I to disrupt whatever new life he's found?' That would compound selfishness with the guilt he already knew. Dragging Thomas home was for him, for his parents.

It had occurred to him that Thomas might not thank him for it.

'I think you put too many horses before the cart, Jonathon.' Claire smiled gently. 'Go and see what this man knows and then decide what you should do. Your heart will know what is right.'

Jonathon shook his head. Her faith in him overwhelmed him. 'How do you know that when I don't?'

He felt her laughter warm against his chest. 'Do you remember that summer at the Worths when the four of us wanted to go fishing with you and Preston?' Her eyes sparkled with little amber lights. 'Preston was adamant we not go. But you simply went into the shed and pulled out four more rods and handed them to us. You spent the day helping us bait our hooks and reeling in a few fish. You even showed us how to gut them.' She wrinkled up her nose.

He did remember that day. He'd never dreamed four girls could keep him that busy. 'By the end of the day, none of us wanted to fish again. But we discovered that by ourselves. You knew fishing wasn't for us, but you also knew we'd never accept being *told*. You never had to worry about us going fishing with you and Preston again. You invested one day and won a lifelong reprieve. Preston, on the other hand, was willing to beg for one day. We would have just kept nagging him every time the two of you went out.' She kissed his cheek. 'That's how I know. You've always known the right thing to do and the right way to do it, even if your brain doesn't recognise it. Call it instinct.'

He was certain now. Claire was too good for him, a man who'd left his brother behind. She saw the real good, not the manufactured social good based on what he looked like and how he acted. 'You humble me, Claire.' She enlightened him, too. Being with her gave him a glimpse of what marriage ought to be, could be; this being able to see into another's soul and understanding them for who they were. Claire proved it was possible marriage could be something more than two people forming an alliance to exchange goods and services. It would bring him a different kind of peace than the one he sought in Vienna, a more valuable, personal peace. Would she come to hate him for it? To claim her and all she offered meant to put her in the eye of scandal. But surely she'd understood that when she'd come to Dover. Surely, this consummation that had taken place tonight was a prelude to other consummations to come. Tonight was just the beginning.

'I'm glad you came,' he whispered into her hair. The words were inadequate. He was glad she had come, that she was with him in this next step in his search for Thomas, glad that he was no longer alone.

Claire kissed the flat rise of his nipple, nipping it with her teeth. Where the hell had she learned such a thing? She slanted him a decadent gaze, her eyes a dark shade of melted chocolate, hot and rich, and he knew. She'd learned it from him. His body tightened with anticipation as her kisses trailed down his torso. What else had she learned from him? What else would she dare?

'What are you doing, Claire?'

She gave his cock a considering look before she slid down his body. 'I wonder, does my mouth work for you, too?'

He felt himself grow hard as if he hadn't spent the last hour slaking his needs. 'It works,' he growled, but his reluctance was only feigned.

Her hand slipped beneath his phallus and cupped his ball sac. 'And this?' Her eyes glittered as she gave the tender bag a squeeze, watching him the whole while.

'Yes, that works, too. Why don't you see for yourself?'

She licked her lips, pulling her hair to one side in a move worthy of any Venetian courtesan. 'Oh, I mean to.' She put her mouth to his tip and he shuddered, letting the delicious pleasure ripple through his body. He intended to fully enjoy this, and he did, until he couldn't, until it ran it away with him, and he was a bucking, thrashing mess begging her to bring him off. He cried out at the end, a wordless yelp.

'Veni, vidi, vici,' she whispered, crawling up his body and taking her place against his shoulder.

'Conquered me, have you?' Jonathon chuckled. 'Well, perhaps you have.' He was beyond exhausted now, beyond replete.

'Not conquered. Crossed.' She drew an idle design on his chest. 'You, Jonathon, are my Rubicon.'

'And you are mine,' he murmured, feeling

sleep come to claim him. There would be no going back. Tonight changed everything. What came next wouldn't be easy but he wouldn't have it any other way.

'Come with me.' His words were soft in the darkness as he shook her awake. Claire burrowed under the cocoon of blankets in sleepy resistance.

'Where?' The night which had seemed so luxuriously long was fleeing by the moment, pushed away by the encroaching cold light of dawn. If she opened her eyes, she could see it through the crack in the curtains. If she listened carefully enough, she could hear it in the faint cries of the milkmaids in the streets. She didn't want to do either. She wanted to hold on to the night, hold on to him and the idea that last night changed everything, made everything possible when in reality it changed nothing. She would remember that once she woke up.

'To meet the informant. He's downstairs.' His fingers plucked at the blankets, urging her out of bed, urging haste.

Her sleepy brain was starting to wake up and

register certain facts. Jonathon was already dressed. He'd already been downstairs. He had come back for her, waited, even though she could see tension in the tightness of his mouth, of his smile as he mustered the patience for her to dress. This was important to him and, because he'd asked her to share in it, it was important to her as well. Today, he was relying on her strength. She offered him a confident smile as she stepped from behind the dressing screen and took his hand. 'Whatever happens downstairs, we'll see it through together.'

The private parlour was set up for breakfast with a platter of eggs and sausages and basket of rolls along with a pot of coffee. Delicious though it smelled, Claire doubted anyone would be eating. Jonathon went through the motions of filling a plate he wouldn't likely touch. 'Best not to let the man think we're nervous.' He nodded towards the platters, indicating she should make a plate, too.

'I don't know why I'm anxious. We've had our hopes up before. This isn't the first claim.' Jonathon buttered his toast and she recognised his need to talk, his need to keep busy.

She brought her plate to the table and sat. 'Tell me about it.'

'Well, the first time was four months after Waterloo. We received a ransom note. I was too weak to travel to France and check the validity of the claim. Owen Danvers checked for us and it turned out to be a fraud. The second time, however—' He broke off, his eyes moving over her shoulder to a point by the door. He rose hastily, brushing the toast crumbs from his hands. 'He's here, Claire.'

The man in question was wiry in build, with dark hair and strong Gallic features in his sallow face. *'Je regrette, monsieur,'* he began in heavy French, clasping Jonathon's hand as he explained how the tide had not allowed the ship to dock, how they'd had to be rowed in from quite a distance. 'I would have been here before dawn, otherwise.'

The man had no English. Claire glanced at Jonathon. His features were tight with concentration as he made his response.

'Il n'y a rien.' He gestured to a chair at the table, continuing in French. 'Please, come and sit. Eat. There are fresh rolls. You must be tired.'

The man shuffled forward, eyes darting towards her. He was as suspicious, perhaps as anxious, as Jonathon was.

'This is my wife, Claire.' Jonathon hadn't even hesitated over the declaration. Claire felt herself flush. The man seemed to relax. Perhaps it was a good sign that he, too, was nervous.

The man sat and buttered a roll. 'I have travelled a long way,' he began, his dark eyes narrow and assessing as they watched Jonathon.

Jonathon nodded, his own features hard. 'Owen Danvers tells me you have news that is worth the journey.' This was the diplomat, the negotiator coming out—the man who could create polite, veiled messages. Even more impressive was watching him do it in French. This was one more side of Jonathon she'd yet to see in action.

Jonathon reached inside his coat pocket and pulled out a money clip. He slid the money on to the table between them, an indication of what the journey was worth. A reminder, too, that the man was being paid well. No favours were being done here, this was business.

The man eyed the money clip. 'Danvers promised me more than that.'

'He did,' Jonathon agreed easily. 'There will be more when we hear what you have to say. Neither Danvers nor I am paying for lies.' Claire's gaze slid between the two men.

The man held up his hands in assent. 'I deal only in truths. I will tell you what I know,' he said in affronted French, accompanied by a sneer at the insult. 'There was a wounded man who was taken in and nursed at one of the farms on the Lys River. He was there for some time, I'm told—'

'Attendez!' Jonathon interrupted, the sharpness of his tone taking Claire by surprise. 'You were told? Your information is not first-hand?'

'Non, monsieur. I am the messenger only.'

'Why should I believe you?'

The man's gaze held Jonathon's. 'Because I have this, *monsieur.'* He took a small object from his coat pocket and pushed it across the table. Claire strained to see the item.

'Thomas's ring.' Jonathon reached for it, visibly paling as he held up the thick gold circle set with an emerald. 'It was from our grandfather,' he explained, his eyes touching hers. But his shock was fleeting. He was terse when he turned his attentions back to the informant. 'Rings fall off, are lost in the mud, sometimes for years. Rings are also stolen, perhaps pried off the hands of unconscious soldiers. This is proof that someone, somewhere, encountered Thomas, nothing more.'

The informant was undeterred. He reached inside his pocket. 'There is also this.' He placed a polished seashell on the table, a trinket of no value and yet Claire would have sworn she heard a moan escape Jonathon. He took the shell in gentle fingers, treating it like the most delicate of objects.

'No one would bother to steal a seashell,' the Frenchman said softly. *'Vous comprenez?'*

Claire swallowed hard against the lump in her throat. The shell meant Jonathon could no longer argue the items were stolen and merely passed along. A seashell had no value except to the person who possessed it.

'Our family went to the seashore one summer,' he said softly to her in French, perhaps for the informant's benefit. 'We stayed with an old friend of my father's. Thomas and I played on the beach every day. We were only eight or nine and he cried the day we had to leave. He loved the ocean so much.' Jonathon paused, his throat working fiercely against the emotion of memory. She wanted to go to him and wrap him in her arms, but he would not want to be made vulnerable in front of this stranger who held so much power in these moments.

'My father threatened to thrash him if he didn't stop his crying. I slipped him this seashell when Father wasn't looking. I'd found it on the beach our last morning there and I'd polished it up. I told him it was lucky. He carried it everywhere with him.' Even to war. Even to death. Claire knew what he was thinking and it broke her heart. She would spare him this pain if she could.

The informant smiled kindly, the first friendly expression Claire had seen him give. 'It is a good story, *monsieur*. You and your brother were close.'

Jonathon gathered his self-control. 'How did you or your master come by these things?'

'My master owned the farm where this man was nursed. They became friends during his convalescence. The man...'

'Not the man,' Jonathon corrected. 'Thomas. The man has a name.'

'*Très bien.* Thomas recovered from his wounds, which was no small accomplishment. He'd been shot several times. He was suffering from fever when his horse wandered on to our farm. To this day, we don't know exactly how they came in our direction, we are a bit off the beaten path. It was clear though that they'd wandered for days. He'd probably got lost and then disoriented. We thought he'd die. But he didn't. He lived.' Here, the man paused, his eyes full of sympathy. 'My master says he was never quite himself. He didn't always know who he was. He thought his name was Matthew.'

'That was his second name,' Jonathon supplied.

'Some days though, he knew he was Thomas, but not much else,' the man offered in consolation. 'But the wounds, the war, had done something to his memories. He'd scream in the night like soldiers do.' Jonathon nodded and Claire wondered what nightmares came to him.

'You said he recovered?' Jonathon pressed.

'To a point. He helped out around the farm. He

liked working with the animals. On good days he rode his horse like the devil. He was something to watch. I've never seen a rider like that. But there weren't that many good days. We knew he didn't belong with us, but my master had no way to contact anyone, didn't know who to contact. Then, last year, Thomas took sick. His wounds had damaged his health and the winter was harsh.' The man shook his head as if he still didn't believe what had happened. 'One day he told my master, "My name is Thomas Lashley." He gave my master this ring and that shell and went out riding. He wasn't well enough and the lord knows his horse wasn't either. The winter had ruined both of them. That horse was twenty if it was a day. He didn't come back. That evening his horse limped in to the barnyard, coated with mud. It had been ridden hard. We fed it, cleaned it, made it warm, but the horse laid down and was dead in the morning.'

Claire covered her mouth, stifling a sob. Jonathon reached out for her hand and she let him take it, knowing that touching her was not only for her comfort but his. 'Oh, Jonathon.'

Jonathon was bravery itself. He nodded his

head, acknowledging the story. 'Thank you for telling me. May I ask? Did you find a body?'

The man shook his head and Claire thought she saw a spark light Jonathon's eyes. 'We went out the next day to look for him. We did not find him, although we found the place he must have fallen.'

'Thomas does not fall,' Jonathon said staunchly, automatically. Claire shot him a worried look. He was being stubborn, but surely he had to admit the search was over.

'Monsieur,' the informant offered patiently, 'the ground was churned up. There had been an event of some sort. The horse came back and he did not. He loved that horse. He would never have deserted it. There are wolves in the forests.' He caught Claire's eye. 'My apologies, *madame*, but I must speak plainly or *monsieur* will harbour false hope. There are plenty of reasons a body wasn't found. Perhaps wild animals, or perhaps simply a man went off into the forest to die alone the way animals do when they can no longer be of use to their pack. Animals know when it's their time. I think your brother did, too. He knew he was failing. He knew death was coming.' He paused to let Jonathon mull it over. 'We had only the one piece of information to go on, just his name. I am sorry it took us the better part of the year to reach you.' It was the informant's way of saying the conversation was over. There was nothing more he could tell Jonathon.

'We are grateful, thank you,' Claire offered in French when Jonathon remained silent. She nudged Jonathon. He drew out the second money clip and numbly placed it on the table. Whatever strength, whatever power of will he'd possessed to make it this far, to conduct this interview in French, to have fought for this moment all these years when others had given up, was gone now. The rest was up to her. He needed her to step into the breach.

Claire rose and walked the man to the door. 'Thank you for coming. You will find there's enough there to pay for your travels and a reward for your information as well.'

'Is he gone?' Jonathon's voice asked dully behind her.

'Yes.' She crossed the room and knelt beside him, gripping his hands. 'It was worth it to come. Now you know.'

That was when Jonathon broke. He slipped from the chair into her arms, sobs racking his body as she held him against her. 'He was alive, Claire. Good God, for six years, he was alive. I should have tried harder.'

Chapter Twenty-One

The guilt and grief of seven years took him in its relentless grip. All she could do was hold him and let him sob even though her helplessness to do more tore at her heart. In this regard, hope had not been his friend, it had prevented him from truly grieving. Only now, when the hope was gone, could he let go and move on. But that was a choice only Jonathon could make for himself.

Moving on meant acknowledging the search was over, that there was nothing more he could do. Defeat was not a circumstance Jonathon embraced well. He'd not given up on his French, he'd not given up on her. It was natural he didn't want to give up on his brother. She'd heard it in his voice when he'd challenged the informant about the lack of a body.

'I should have done more.' That was the guilt talking.

'What more could you have done?' Her voice was intentionally sharp, slicing through the haze of pain. She wasn't offering the words as a trite consolation. She was asking, as if the answer mattered. Because it did. Jonathon had to move on and he couldn't if he wouldn't let go of the past.

Jonathon pulled back, meeting her eyes with a tear-clouded gaze. 'I could never have left. I should have stayed, I should have found him before the trail grew cold. Then none of this would have happened.'

'You were shot, dying yourself,' Claire reminded him. 'There was little you could do.' It seemed to Claire that if he couldn't let go of the past today when all had been revealed, then he never would. What happened here on the wood floor of the Antwerp Hotel suddenly mattered in the extreme. It was an odd place to do battle for a man's soul, but that's what this was.

Now that she'd seen the very core of him exposed, she understood the darkest secret he carried. It wasn't that he'd been to war and seen people killed, nor was it that the war haunted him, or even that the war and the guilt over his brother had stolen his French, messed with his head in a way that prevented him from retrieving that skill until now. No, the darkest secret Jonathon Lashley carried in his depths was that he believed he didn't deserve to be happy. His guilt demanded his life be lived in sacrifice.

Hadn't he lost enough already?

Wait.

A thought came to her. What had he said that night in her bedroom? He came home feverish, raving mad in French. She'd not thought anything of it. At the time. She'd been rather focused on other things and understandably so. A man had just climbed into her room. But today, the mention was important. That trip home had been the last time he'd spoken French without extreme conscious effort. She'd heard of cases where guilt was so traumatic it blocked certain things out of one's mind. There'd been a widow in Little Westbury whose grief over her husband's death was so severe she couldn't actually remember he had died. She would keep asking where he was.

'Why didn't you tell me the real reason you couldn't speak or read French any more?' She laced her fingers through his.

The question seemed to settle him, his control was coming back. That was a good sign. Jonathon pushed his free hand through his hair. 'I didn't want you to give up on me. I didn't want to hear that my problem wasn't teachable. I had to get my French back if I was to get to Vienna, I had to try. There was too much at stake not to.'

'I wouldn't have given up on you.' A hint of a smile crossed her lips as she remembered the disaster of that first lesson. She knit her brow, seeing the flaw in her reasoning. 'If it's the guilt holding your memory of French back, why have we succeeded in getting you this far?'

A tic jumped in his jaw. 'What I needed was you. You made me forget, you helped my mind free itself. When we walked in the garden and laughed and talked, I could forget for a while.' He gave a ghost of his usual smile. 'I think you might have been the saving of me, Claire.' It was a lovely thing to hear, to cherish.

She moved into him, stroking his jaw with her

hand. 'How ironic. All this time, I thought you were redeeming me.'

He kissed her then, long and slow and full of feeling. 'I was unaware you needed redeeming. You seemed to be doing a pretty good job of that all on your own. You had told Rufus Sheriden to go to hell and the rest of society, too. Such courage makes a man jealous.'

'Not everyone understands that.' He made her feel like a queen. The hunger was building between them, a spark of celebration beginning to stir. Out of the ashes something affirming rose.

'I do,' Jonathon murmured against her neck.

And she understood him. Enough to give him up, but not yet. She reached for him, her hand closing over his length through the fabric of his trousers, signalling her own need.

'You'll be sore, Claire,' he cautioned.

There was challenge in her eyes. 'I have the rest of my life to be sore.' She tugged him to her, pushing his trousers down past his hips until he was free. Jonathon rose above her, the muscles of his arms taut beneath his coat as he took her, hard and fast. He was a primordial god in those moments, primitive and fierce in his desire, and she answered him, a goddess of desire in her own right. Her hips rose to his, joining him in the rhythm without hesitation, her body arching into him. Pleasure would come fast, pushing him to the brink. Her legs wrapped tight around him, urging him to the cliff. He gave a hard, final thrust and they flew. Together. Her cries mingled with his, their bodies tangled, his soul, if not fully retrieved, at least safe from the abyss.

She held him to her as long as she could, holding him close, her body loath to part with his until they had reconciled themselves to the earth once again, where all good things had to come to an end.

'What do we do now?' Jonathon whispered at her ear.

'We go home.'

And I give you up one more time.

She murmured, turning in to him, glad he couldn't see her face, glad he didn't guess the direction of her thoughts. He wouldn't like them. He'd want to argue. But she knew what was right *and* best. She had promised herself she would take whatever pleasure the moments with Jonathon offered her and not wish for more the first time she'd crossed this bridge back when he'd climbed into her bedroom.

In coming to Dover, she'd crossed another bridge, giving herself permission to love him and permission to keep him for as long as possible, knowing from the start loving him was not synonymous with keeping him, that 'for as long as possible' was a finite amount of time. Of course, she'd hoped that time would have lasted longer than one night in Dover. It hadn't. Sometimes the people a person loved the most were the ones that couldn't be kept, the ones that had to be set free. She could love Jonathon, but she had to let him go.

Vienna was more important than ever now. If he could help a region find peace, her sacrifice would be worth it for a world with no more war, or perhaps more selfishly her sacrifice would be worth it for a Jonathon who felt he'd done his penance and could live guilt free.

The little bitch was going to pay. Cecilia threw the pale-pink roses to the drawing-room floor and stomped on them with a vicious twist of her heel. The two of them were together! She knew it. His roses showed up on schedule, but Jonathon hadn't been seen for three days at any of the fashionable events. Or the unfashionable. Once his absence had become noted, she'd checked. He wasn't at his clubs either. Worse, Claire Welton was gone as well and no one seemed to know where.

She might not know where Claire had gone, but she knew with whom. Claire and Jonathon were together. Secretly. Doing who knew what. No. Stop. She feared she knew that, too. That conniving little slut.

An evil smile crept across her lips. She had to give Claire some credit. The girl hadn't backed down. She'd gone after Jonathon with everything she had. But now, 'everything' was spent. Claire had nothing left to give Jonathon. But she did. As long as Jonathon hadn't married Claire Welton, he was still fair game. Cecilia tapped a finger to her chin. A simple speculation from her would do it; a few words whispered in the right ears. Rumours spread like wildlife this time of year whether they were true or not. She would divide and conquer whenever they returned. She would ruin Claire and Jonathon would be desperate to distance himself from such a scandal, desperate to align himself with the right sort of woman and she would be waiting. With open arms.

Chapter Twenty-Two

Viscount Stanhope waited for them upon their return. Lights burned bright in the Welton town house like beacons calling their errant daughter home, when Jonathon's coach rolled up to the kerb well past dark. But Jonathon was ready. He had been ready for this the moment he'd climbed the rose trellis. A man who broke into a woman's bedroom had to be prepared for consequences or he had no business climbing that trellis in the first place.

He jumped out and offered Claire his hand. 'Shall we?' He'd had the carriage ride to align himself with the new reality of his world—a world without Thomas, a world in which the question 'what next' was answered by the future, not the past.

Despite the emotional outcome of his journey to Dover, he was in good spirits. He wished he could say the same for Claire. The closer to London they came, the more closed she'd become. Did she doubt him? Surely, she didn't worry he would desert her? She knew he would stand beside her. It wasn't even an issue of doing the 'right thing.' He wanted to marry her. He'd told her as much before Dover.

Jonathon took her hand. 'You are not ruined, Claire, you are loved. By me.'

She smiled at him then, her voice soft in the evening air. 'It's not that, Jonathon.'

Inside, Claire's father was indeed waiting for them, as was her mother, both wearing forced smiles, relieved to see their daughter home safe and yet knowing a safe return wasn't enough. Stanhope was a tall slender man with amber eyes like his daughter. He greeted Jonathon cordially and offered him a drink while Claire's mother hugged her tightly. Jonathon would take it as a good sign.

'I trust your mission in Dover was successful?' Lord Stanhope began, retaking his seat. 'Danvers and Preston Worth came by to explain how important my daughter's French skills were for the trip.'

So that would be the official story put about whenever there was a question. Jonathon wondered if anyone would buy it. 'Yes, the mission was successful even if the information wasn't what I'd hoped.' He shot a warm glance in Claire's direction where she sat next to her mother, pale and drawn. 'Claire was indispensable. I could not have got through it without her.' She'd comforted him when he'd broken in the inn. She'd started him back on the road of reason and healing where Thomas was concerned, not only with her words, but with her body. She'd shown him how to start letting go of his guilt and start living for himself. Every time she touched him, he was reminded of the new lesson: he was deserving of happiness. She was the physical embodiment of that. Claire had brought him back into the light. In the carriage, he'd spoken of Thomas, told her stories of their childhood, and it had been cleansing in its own way to remember his brother.

'We are glad, of course, that Claire could be of use,' Lord Stanhope began. 'However, the circumstances are somewhat unusual and there's been talk.' He picked up newssheets from the small table beside his chair. 'Your absence has been noted and remarked upon. You might want to read these. I've circled pertinent information so you needn't read the whole rag.'

Jonathon scanned them.

Miss W., who has been surprisingly prominent this Season, has now become quite obviously absent after attaching herself regularly to Mr L....

Another read:

It has been several days since Miss W. last graced the ballrooms of London, one can only speculate on the reason...

And, perhaps the most damning.

Based on their regular habit of dancing together, one must do the social mathematics

and assume that if one could find Miss W.
one would also find Mr L. quite close by...

Jonathon grimaced. He could stand the scandal. He'd expected something of this nature might arise. But he grimaced on Claire's behalf and the idea that she should have to endure it.

'Well, I believe a marriage proposal will put a stop to such speculations.' Jonathon smiled to dispel Lord Stanhope's agitation. Lord Stanhope was a quiet man who did not thrive in the midst of gossip. The past few days must have been hell for him. 'An announcement in *The Times* and the story from Danvers will have Claire painted as a national heroine once news gets out.'

Lord Stanhope's tight mouth began to ease into a smile, but Claire's voice stopped it halfway. 'No, there will be no marriage proposal. Jonathon, you don't need to do this.'

'I have every need to do this,' Jonathon said as delicately as he could. He had to protect Claire, even from her parents. If he blurted out half of what they'd been up to, Claire would have no choice but to accept him. He wanted her, but he didn't want her forced. He thought she'd wanted him, too, not just for a night, but for ever. This, he realised, was what had been eating at her on the way home. Dear Lord, when had she known she was going to refuse him? In the parlour when she'd held him? In the room when they'd made love? Before that even? Had it always been just one night for her? She'd tried to leave him once. Was she trying to do so again?

'Claire, is this about the Vienna post?' Again. He thought her coming to Dover had resolved that, that she'd understood and accepted that he was willing to give Vienna up for her if need be. He couldn't very well say any of those things out loud and imply there was a rather intimate history between them. One didn't go giving up plum positions on a whim. Sweat started to bead on his brow. Sweet heavens, the room was getting hot. Even with his diplomatic skill, it was deuced awkward discussing such a thing in front of one's lover's parents.

'It's about you,' Claire answered. 'You need that position in order to be happy. If I've helped you secure it that is enough for me.'

'*You* make me happy, Claire,' Jonathon argued.

'For now. What happens when the post is denied you? You will come to resent me. I could not live every day with your hate. I would come to hate myself.' Claire rose. 'If you will all excuse me, it's been a long set of days. I want to wash and go to bed.'

It was an old trick; winning an argument by leaving the room. Jonathon grimaced. If they were alone, he'd grab her and press her against the wall and kiss some sense in to her but that would hardly do here. 'Claire, this is not over,' he called after her. She didn't bother to answer. She just kept walking.

Lady Stanhope tossed him a nervous glance. 'Let her sleep on it. Perhaps she'll come around.' Jonathon didn't put much stock in that. When Claire took something into her mind, she was immovable.

'Perhaps you can talk sense into her?' Jonathon appealed to Lord Stanhope.

Lord Stanhope looked cynical. 'We will not force her. We tried that with Sheriden a few years back and look where that got us.' There would be no help from that quarter either, it seemed. It was time to take his leave and regroup. When he'd told Claire she was worth fighting for, he'd never thought he'd have to fight *her* in order to prove it.

The girls came as soon as she sent word the next day. If ever there was a reason for an emergency meeting of the Left-Behind Girls Club, this was it.

'What has happened?' Beatrice was the last to arrive. She bustled into Claire's bedroom, stripping off her gloves. She hadn't paused long enough to leave her things at the door.

May looked up from Claire's side. 'She's refused Jonathon.'

'For good this time,' Evie added for emphasis. Claire winced. Hearing someone else say it out loud was so much more final than thinking it in one's head. But she wasn't going to cry. She'd promised herself she wouldn't. She needed her friends, but she didn't need them to worry for her or to feel they had to do something to fix her situation. This was her problem. Her decision. Never mind that it had been tearing her apart since she'd left Dover. The closer London came, the deeper the knife had dug. She'd barely made her room last night before she'd needed the chamber pot. That's what happened when one threw away happiness, one retched and then one cried.

Beatrice settled into the overstuffed chair near the bed. 'Tell us. What happened in Dover?'

She told them everything. Evie wiped away a tear when she told them about Jonathon's brother. May sighed over the romance. Beatrice looked down at her hands. Claire supposed it was a romantic tale, perhaps fit for a Gothic, but not for real life. There was no happy ending here. Or rather, she'd had her happy ending. But afterwards life went on and even her ending had an ending because life was not contained between book covers.

'I can't have him, because having him will ruin him. It will make him less than what he is and it will be my fault,' she declared quietly, determined they not see how this was tearing her apart. She loved him so entirely, so completely. Perhaps, if she loved him less?

'You are so brave, Claire.' Evie gave her a wan smile of support and encouragement. Her friend meant well, but Claire fought the urge to argue with Evie, to shout that she wasn't brave. She was *breaking*. She might manage to glue the pieces of herself back together again at some point, but it wouldn't be the same. She'd never be whole, not without him.

Her stomach started to roil again. She fought back a wave of nausea. Just the thought of Jonathon lost to her was enough to make her physically ill. She was too cognisant of all she'd lost when she'd given him up.

'There's only one thing to do. You need to go away until this blows over. The Season will be done in a month. Perhaps you could come to the country with me. We could arrange to go early and say we're visiting my aunt,' May offered.

'Or you could come with me. I have to leave soon anyway.' Beatrice put a hand over her stomach. In a few weeks, even Evie's careful designs wouldn't be able to hide the early telltale signs of an advancing pregnancy.

Claire shook her head at her friends' generous offers. It would be so easy to take those offers. She could retreat and wallow in self-pity and perhaps self-righteousness in private. But she'd done that once already and it hadn't been to her benefit in the end. Retreating had only hurt herself. 'I am grateful. I can't run away. Everyone will know something is up if I hide. If I am to face down the gossips, I have to go out. Tonight. To the Belvoirs' musicale evening—'

'I don't think that's a good idea,' Beatrice interrupted immediately, horrified at the suggestion. 'None of us was invited. You'll be alone and in Cecilia's house. Even if she didn't start the gossip about your absence, she'll be mad if she believes half of what the gossip sheets have implied.'

'Then perhaps it's better to get it over with,' Claire said staunchly, although the idea of facing Cecilia turned her stomach sour. But the Claire she'd become needed to face this down. If she didn't face Cecilia and the gossip, it would only prove she hadn't changed.

'Well, if you are set on going, you must have something to wear.' Beatrice began organising the troops. 'Evie, look through her wardrobe. May, give Evie some help. I need to talk to Claire.'

It was clear Bea wanted privacy. Claire let Bea draw her to the long French doors leading out to her little balcony. Would she ever be able to look at those doors without thinking of Jonathon?

'What is it, Bea?' Claire asked in a low voice. 'Are you well?'

'I am fine, but I think *you* might have gone round the bend,' Beatrice scolded. 'Claire, you can't refuse him, no matter what your principles dictate.'

'I will not trap him. This is about doing the right thing,' Claire argued hotly. 'Don't think for a moment this is easy for me.'

Bea arched a dark brow, her tone dry. 'No one looking at you would think that. We'll need rouge to make you presentable no matter what Evie pulls out of your closet. We'll have Jonathon back by your side in no time.'

Claire looked quizzically at her friend. 'Haven't you heard a word I've said? I've let him go.' Oh, dear, the sick sensation came again and she squeezed her eyes shut and took a deep breath to quell her stomach. 'Can't you see how hard this is for me? Please, don't try to convince me otherwise, Bea, because it would be an easy argument to win. I'm holding on to the right choice by a thread. It would take very little for that thread to break.'

'It's not about trapping and it's definitely not about principles, Claire, not at this point,' Beatrice answered, undaunted. 'You have to march over to him and tell him you've reconsidered. Tell him you were tired and not thinking straight last night. I don't care what you tell him, just tell him you'll marry him.' Beatrice was full of urgency. 'Don't you understand, Claire? You had sex with him, multiple times.'

'Only three times,' Claire corrected.

'Once, twice, forty times, it doesn't matter. I bet he never once used any kind of protection. You could be carrying his child.'

Her initial reaction was one of betrayal. She was dying inside. She wanted empathy at the least. 'I didn't expect this from you, Bea. Of all people, I thought you would respect my decision. You, who won't marry the father of your child unless he truly loves you. You are hardly in a position to argue that principles be thrown out the window.'

Beatrice's eyes narrowed. 'My man isn't here offering for me. It's far easier for me to cling to those principles when that's all I have. But they are cold comfort, Claire. Trust me.' She sighed, her eyes sparkling suspiciously as her tone softened. She squeezed Claire's hand. 'I am so sorry. I wouldn't hurt you for the world. This is all my fault. I should not have started this. You didn't want to do it and I pushed you towards it. I meddled where I ought not.'

Her anger at Bea evaporated, replaced by a fierce, protective love of her friend. She couldn't have Bea believing she'd failed. 'Don't say that. Whatever happens, it was worth it. I fell in love and I found myself. Bea, you were right all along. It took Jonathon to make me see it. I'd become lost. But now I know I'm worth fighting for, even if the warrior who does the fighting is me.' She leaned over and kissed Bea on the cheek. 'I will never forget what you've done for me. You gave me the push I needed.'

Bea offered a tremulous smile. 'I just hope it isn't a push over a cliff.'

'It's not. Now, let's go see what Evie has pulled out of my wardrobe.'

She and Bea walked over to join the others. There was no time like the present to start facing her future. Claire smiled as Evie pulled out a few dresses. She would have to get used to this: smiling on the outside, convincing others she was coping, even recovering, while on the inside she was empty.

According to Evie, the future wore chocolate silk. If the future couldn't be decadent, it could at least look delicious, but deep in her heart, Claire knew it would always be dark. Dark and empty.

No, maybe not empty, not yet. Maybe emptiness would come later. For now, she *hurt*. Pain wasn't emptiness. Pain was *something*. Some day the pain would leave her, but she was in no hurry for it to go. When she stopped remembering, *then* Jonathon would truly be gone. Until that happened, the pain was a way to hold on to him for a little while longer. Ah, fabulous. She'd become a masochist.

Chapter Twenty-Three

Jonathon climbed the steps to the Belvoir town house with heavy feet. It was time to start facing his future. Thomas was dead. Claire was lost to him. She'd not answered any of the notes he'd sent that morning and her parents had not received him when he'd called that afternoon, desperate for the sight of her. A warm summer night had fallen over London. The sounds of merrymaking drifted out from the town house. It was to be a grand evening with excellent food and champagne, and an excellent soprano imported from Milan.

Normally, it was the sort of evening he enjoyed. He wished he could muster a modicum of enthusiasm for the entertainment. He suspected it might be a long while before he had enthusiasm for much of anything that didn't involve Claire and right now that was everything. She had made it clear she wanted to separate herself from him. For his sake, of course. But the sacrifice didn't make it any better. It made it worse. They loved one another, they belonged together. Why couldn't she see that? Why could she only see the price of it?

Jonathon handed his hat to the doorman and stepped inside. He shouldn't have come, but it was the one place he was assured he would not see Claire. As a rule, the lofty Earl of Belvoir did not invite the retiring Viscount Stanhope. He stepped into the drawing room where the elite of the *ton* and the political world were gathered. Cecilia was beside him immediately, beautifully turned out in pale-pink silk that was at once designed to be enticing and demure. With any other man, the goal would have been met. Jonathon had never felt so suffocated in his life.

She slipped an arm through his in a proprietary manner. 'Jonathon, you've come back and just in time. The gossip was growing positively lurid.' She smiled. 'But never mind it, you and I can put the rumours to rest tonight.' Already, they were drawing stares. Elite or not, it seemed everyone had a penchant for gossip.

She dragged him over to meet her father and greet her mother. Lord Belvoir gave him a smug grin of approval. The young pup had been brought to heel and was back where he belonged. Lady Belvoir fussed over him with a keen glance at her daughter. He didn't want this, any of it. It was something of mystery to him how he had once thought he could tolerate it. But he was a different man now than he'd been last year, or even last month. He'd been willing to pay the price for his dream even if it meant selling himself in a marriage of convenience. That was before Claire.

Claire had changed him, shown him that one can stand up for himself. He didn't have to put up with this. He just had to be brave enough. There was a piece of Claire's irony for him: it was the wallflower who was brave, who had eschewed society in an attempt to preserve herself, not he who had seen battle and handled sensitive negotiations.

There was a rustling by the door. Heads nearest the entrance started to turn, conversations stalled. A brief wave of silence covered the room as everyone took in the newcomer. Cecilia's grip on his arm tightened, a cold smile taking her mouth. 'Oh, good, the little tramp has come after all.'

Jonathon turned towards the door. Good God, Claire was here, alone and stunning in a gown of chocolate summer silk. The colour was divine on her, bringing out the coffee of her hair, the cognac ambers of her eyes. Cognac and chocolate were quite the aphrodisiacs on their own. Knowing what those lips tasted like completed the metaphor and uncomfortably so. She was a visual feast and she knew it. Jonathon stifled a smile. She'd come a long way from the girl who had tugged self-consciously at her bodice at the Worth dinner. She'd chosen this dress on purpose. She meant to make a statement, meant to draw the eye. She wasn't going to shy away from the gossip. She was going to meet it head on.

Her eyes met his and she froze for a moment. Perhaps she had not expected to see him. Or perhaps she had not expected to see him with Cecilia. Cecilia's chin raised a fraction higher and he recognised how this would look to Claire;

he'd written her notes, proposed marriage to her, sworn undying devotion and here he was with Cecilia on his arm as if nothing had changed from that very first night at the Worths. Her gaze moved on as a woman near the door engaged her in conversation. He fought the urge to go to her. If he crossed the room, it would only stir more scandal. He could not spoil this for her. But he would wait and watch, and stand at the ready to go to her side should she indicate she wanted his support. Cecilia's eyes narrowed dangerously, having followed his gaze.

'She wants you, Jonathon. Can't you see it? All those dances you gave her must have convinced her you had feelings for her. This is why you can't feed stray dogs. They end up following you home.'

She looked up at him under lowered lashes. 'But we both know her efforts are in vain. She can't have you. How could she when you're mine?' She trailed a finger down the length of his arm. Jonathon closed a steely grip around her wrist.

'Ouch!' She tugged, but he held on.

'I'm afraid you are mistaken. I am not yours

and we are done here.' Cecilia had gone too far. He had not gone nearly far enough.

'I can't believe you are choosing her over me!' Cecilia hissed.

Jonathon smiled. He had his answer. He knew how to win Claire and he could do it right now, perhaps *only* right now. 'I'm not choosing her over you. She would never want that.'

Claire didn't want to be a trade. She didn't want him to choose her *or* Vienna. Cecilia couldn't understand. Her whole life was a competition, winning and losing the measuring stick by which she judged her own success. 'I'm choosing me.'

Her parents surged around them, Lady Belvoir swept past with a cold look. 'Come, Cecilia, we have an unwanted guest to take care of. This is an exclusive event. She has some gall showing her face after this past week.'

Lord Belvoir's hand closed on Jonathon's arm, his voice a cautioning growl. 'If you take one more step, you will never see Vienna.'

Jonathon raised his voice, his decision made. He was indeed done here. 'Are you threatening me?' Heads swivelled.

'Be careful, boy. I can make sure you never

see a diplomatic post,' Belvoir warned, but Jonathon was past the point of caution. Let Claire see that he would give up Vienna because he wanted to, not because she compelled him to. Let her see that he was free to come to her if she should change her mind. She had no arguments left now. He could never come to resent her. This was his choice alone.

'I was unaware that marriage to your daughter was a qualification for diplomacy,' Jonathon shot back. 'The last time I checked, Britain preferred to send the best man into the field, a man who cannot be bought. I am that man. Let everyone here be aware of it and be aware of how you choose to wield your power.' People began to back away from them, murmuring among themselves. Belvoir had been exposed. He was a powerful man; would it matter? It didn't matter to Jonathon. He stalked towards the door but Cecilia's words halted him.

'This is all her fault!' Cecilia's voice rang shrill through the room. 'Claire Welton is a whore. She's turned your head, Jonathon Lashley, with seduction and now you're willing to throw everything away for her.'

Guests fell into stunned silence. There hadn't been such a cut direct in ages. He had to act now. For Claire. For himself. This could not go unaddressed. But Claire was faster, closer. Jonathon watched it all happen in slow motion. Claire's face was a portrait of icy disdain as she raised her gloved hand, slapping Cecilia across the face, before she turned and stalked out of the room. He was two steps behind her. She was not leaving without him. Not ever again.

So this was how the world ended, with a slap across the face. Claire pressed a hand to her stomach. She could barely breathe and her pulse was racing. She couldn't believe she'd done it. But words had seemed an inadequate response to being called a whore in front of London's finest. Really, her ship was sunk before the slap. She might as well go down with it, too.

'You slapped her!' Jonathon materialised by her side, his hand at her elbow helping her navigate the stairs.

'She had her hands on you. I thought that was the rule?' Claire started to tremble, the shock of it all threatening to overwhelm her. It would be the talk of the *ton* tomorrow. Probably by mid-night. She would be truly exiled, she supposed. She didn't think she minded. Not yet anyway. For now, it was enough to have Jonathon beside her.

'You slapped Belvoir, metaphorically speaking.' She was still stunned by what he'd done. His voice had carried loud and strong across the drawing room, making a public proclamation of his refusal to be bullied. Her heart had swelled for him in those moments. 'You've given up Vienna. Your dream.'

'Maybe. Perhaps I will still get the post on merit, not marriage.' Jonathon beamed at her. 'Although, I do plan to marry very soon.'

Claire's breath caught. 'Jonathon—'

He interrupted her protest. 'You can't say I gave Vienna up for you now, Claire. I gave it up for me, at least getting it that way. I want that post on merit and you have no more excuses.' He dropped to his knee and gripped her hand tight, laughter and longing dancing in his eyes. '*Veux-tu m'epouser*, Claire?'

Marriage? The words stunned her. She was starting to tremble again. Happy-ever-after was being offered, kneeling right before her and she had no more excuses. A bubble of joy welled up in her throat. She was tempted to tease him with a saucy retort, but this was too serious, no teasing matter. This was about her and Jonathon.

'Claire, you're shaking.'

'Now I'm crying, too.' She tugged at her hands, wanting to wipe away her tears as they spilled down her cheeks.

'Why?'

'Because this is about happiness, about dreams coming true. This is about for ever.'

'Damn right it is, Claire.' Jonathon rose and wiped away a tear with his thumb. 'Is that a yes?'

'Oui.' Quite possibly the best word in the French language ever.

He kissed her hard and long and then they were running, down the street, laughing up at the sky, filled with the thrill of living and loving.

'Jonathon, where are we going?' Claire gasped between the laughter, not that it mattered. She'd go anywhere with him.

'Into the future, together.' He grabbed her about the waist and swung her around in the middle of the street. 'Whatever it brings, Claire, wherever it brings!'

Claire laughed up at him, letting the joy of the moment take her soul. 'I wouldn't have it any other way.'

Epilogue

Welton ballroom—two weeks later

It would be her last party for a while. Maybe her last party ever on this grand scale. Who knew how things would end for her? Beatrice surreptitiously put a hand over her stomach as she surveyed the glittering ballroom. Tonight was a farewell on several accounts. Most obviously, everyone was gathered to send off Jonathon and Claire. Only three of the people gathered this evening were here to send *her* off. Jonathon and Claire would leave tomorrow for Vienna, his appointment had come through on his wedding day, a week ago. Sir Owen Danvers had presented it to him at the wedding breakfast. They would leave tomorrow for the next great adventure in their lives.

So would she. She would leave for the country, for exile.

It was the end of July, the end of her allotted time in the city for the Season, all her family could afford without being disgraced. She'd promised her family she'd leave for the country before anyone suspected her condition. She didn't dare wait any longer. The flat of her stomach was starting to give way day by day to a gently rising mound. She didn't regret it. She wished society didn't either.

She was ready to go. She watched Claire and Jonathon dance past, Claire radiant with happiness. The wedding had been public and extraordinary, held at St George's with flowers galore. The church had been packed with standing room only to see the man who had faced down Lord Belvoir in the man's own drawing room wed the sensation of the Season in an ivory creation embroidered elaborately at the hem with lavender and yellow flowers and forget me nots.

Some would say Claire had changed in the past months, but Beatrice knew better. Claire was the same as she'd always been, she'd just stopped hiding it and that choice had led to her happy ever after with the man she loved, the man she deserved.

The thought brought a wash of tears to Beatrice's eyes and she blinked them back as Evie and May approached. There was no time for tears, no time for regrets. 'You're not crying on us, are you?' May looped an arm through hers and hugged her. 'Evie and I will be back in the country soon enough. You only have to survive two weeks without us.'

Beatrice forced a smile. 'If I am crying, it's tears of happiness. I declare our first mission a success.' She gave Evie a mischievous look. 'Get ready. You're next.'

* * * * *

MILLS & BOON®

Why shop at millsandboon.co.uk?

Each year, thousands of romance readers find their perfect read at millsandboon.co.uk. That's because we're passionate about bringing you the very best romantic fiction. Here are some of the advantages of shopping at www.millsandboon.co.uk:

* **Get new books first**—you'll be able to buy your favourite books one month before they hit the shops

* **Get exclusive discounts**—you'll also be able to buy our specially created monthly collections, with up to 50% off the RRP

* **Find your favourite authors**—latest news, interviews and new releases for all your favourite authors and series on our website, plus ideas for what to try next

* **Join in**—once you've bought your favourite books, don't forget to register with us to rate, review and join in the discussions

Visit **www.millsandboon.co.uk**
for all this and more today!